THE PERILOUS PASSAGE

OF PRINCESS PETUNIA PEASANT

A Tale for All Ages

Victor Edward Apps

Teen activist Pet Peasant has no time for administrative red tape. All she wants is an audience with the high regent. Without changes in the law, her village will suffer. With her best friends, Pet sets off on a journey to the centre of power. But events spiral out of control quickly. Terrifying monsters hunt her. Why? Is there something special about her?

Pet's quest takes her across the realm, through a murky swamp tyrannized by an outlandish master and eerie woods twisted by dark magic. As the stakes rise, her friends fall, and the drums of war sound louder, an incredible and inescapable truth dawns on Pet.

The Perilous Passage of Princess Petunia Peasant was a finalist for the 2013 international Proverse Prize.

VICTOR EDWARD APPS was born in Canada and moved out to Hong Kong at the age of eight. A budding writer in his youth, he won the junior section of the 1996 *South China Morning Post* Short Story Competition and interned at *HK Magazine*. Between returning to Canada to study at McGill University, working as a high school teacher and subsequently switching careers into accounting, he was too busy to fit in any writing. Then the 2008 economic crisis happened and Victor found himself with time on his hands. He decided to sketch out some preliminary ideas for a glimmer of a story at the back of his mind, and then kept writing and writing. Months later, the first draft of "The Perilous Passage of Princess Petunia Peasant" was complete. Victor has since returned to Hong Kong and currently splits his time between a banking career and wondering what Petunia's next adventure will be.

THE PERILOUS PASSAGE

OF PRINCESS PETUNIA PEASANT

A Tale for All Ages

Victor Edward Apps

Proverse Hong Kong

The Perilous Passage of Princess Petunia Peasant.
by Victor Edward Apps.
2nd edition published in Hong Kong by Proverse Hong Kong,
November 2015.
Copyright Proverse Hong Kong, November 2015.
ISBN: 978-988-8228-10-2.
Printed by CreateSpace.

1st published in Hong Kong by Proverse Hong Kong, 20 November 2014.
Copyright © Proverse Hong Kong, 20 November 2014.
ISBN 978-988-8227-56-3.

1st edition distribution (Hong Kong and worldwide):
Chinese University Press of Hong Kong, Chinese University of Hong Kong,
Shatin, New Territories, Hong Kong SAR.
E-mail: cup-bus@cuhk.edu.hk; Web: www.chineseupress.com
Tel: [INT+852] 3943-9800; Fax: [INT+852] 2603-7355
1st edition distribution (United Kingdom):
Christine Penney, Stratford-upon-Avon, Warwickshire CV37 6DN, England.
Email: <chrisp@proversepublishing.com>
Distribution and other enquiries to:
Proverse Hong Kong, P.O. Box 259, Tung Chung Post Office, Tung Chung,
Lantau Island, NT, Hong Kong SAR, China.
E-mail: proverse@netvigator.com; Web: www.proversepublishing.com

Cover image by Leona Apps.

British Library Cataloguing in Publication Data.
A catalogue record for this book is available
from the British Library.

THE PRINCESS GOES *WHOOSH*

Princesses are beautiful. This is a long-established truth. Even this princess, with her pink face, deathly wailing and regular emission of objectionable smells; but then again, she was just six months old. These things were to be expected.

Despite her occasional messiness, the princess still brought a bright sparkle to her father's eyes. Unfortunately, the eyes of King Piotr the Just were also filled with great sadness. Queen Polly had passed away during the princess's difficult birth. Though this was a crushing blow, the king never let that sadness diminish the love he felt for his daughter.

Nurse Olganna supposed there was another reason King Piotr loved his daughter so much. The king never had to change her diapers! That duty fell to her. Olganna not only had been King Piotr's nurse, but had also nursed King Piotr's father before him. There were rumours that Olganna was the oldest living thing in the palace, but she was always quick to point out that the great oak tree in the Sculpture Garden had been there first.

Shaking her head, Olganna began the long, spiraling climb to the top of the spire. She was too old for this nonsense. All the other royal infants had had their nurseries in the central keep, but only yesterday, King Piotr had abruptly moved the princess's nursery to the top of the spire without explanation. The idea of climbing up that narrow, treacherous staircase several times a day was unappealing, to say the least. After all, Olganna was not a young nursemaid anymore.

Just as Olganna was reaching the fourth stair of many more to come, a voice rang out. "Nurse, have you seen His Majesty? I urgently need to discuss tomorrow's agenda with him."

Grand Vizier Lier was his usual flustered self. Cradling a massive pile of parchments, he craned his neck around the stack to make eye contact with Olganna.

"No, I haven't. If I see him, I'll let him know you are looking for him." Olganna turned back to her ascent. "Now if you'll excuse me, I have two hundred and twenty-seven stairs to attend to."

It was an intrepid journey, but eventually Olganna made it to the top. There, guardsmen Isabob and Stan glared at her with their steely eyes. Olganna did not mind. She knew it was all an act. Stan was probably hung over, as usual, while Isabob was actually one of the most sensitive people she had ever met. "How's the weather doing up here, boys?" she asked.

"Fine, Nurse," Isabob retorted as Stan opened the heavy oaken door for her, revealing that the princess already had some distinguished company. King Piotr and Evella, the court sorceress, were leaning over her crib and speaking in hushed tones. Their conversation ended abruptly upon the entrance of Olganna.

They stopped? thought Olganna, *On account of me?*

In the past, Olganna was regarded as an old, albeit roving piece of furniture. Nobody ever stopped talking just because she entered a room. In her time, she had overheard talk of war, declarations of forbidden love and whispered prayers. Not that she ever paid much atten   tion, for Olganna took great pride in her absolute discretion. Therefore, being the seasoned professional she was, Olganna's face betrayed none of the offense she felt. "There you are, Your Majesty. Lier was looking for you."

"I'll attend to Lier." Evella started towards the door. "Whatever he wants shouldn't interrupt this time with your daughter."

It did not take a wise and experienced nurse to know that such a meeting would end poorly. Lier would almost certainly reject any suggestion made by Evella. Their rivalry was well known in the palace. More often the king would consult Evella for advice over the head of Lier, who was the official grand vizier.

A shiver ran down Olganna's spine as Evella passed. There was just something about that woman which did not sit right with Olganna. It had to do with the…

Wait! Was that an open window?

"Who opened this?" demanded Olganna, as she quickly

strode over to correct the situation. "Cold winds do not help a child thrive."

At this, King Piotr stirred from his trance. "Leave it, Olganna."

The kindly nurse obeyed, but her eyes did not mask her puzzlement. Did he not have the best interest of his daughter at heart? Perhaps he was not feeling well.

Under ordinary circumstances, Olganna would have rushed over and felt the king's head. Within moments, she would have diagnosed the problem and prescribed an herbal remedy. However, this was not an ordinary evening. Something about the king was tense. Olganna said nothing, and despite all the wisdom in her body telling her otherwise, let the window remain open.

Olganna turned her attention to the sleeping infant. She was just now beginning to grow hair. A single dark curl of hair decorated her forehead. "I could wake her if you want. Her meal time is approaching."

"Let her rest," replied the king in a distant tone. "There is something I would like to discuss with you outside."

"If we whisper, we won't disturb the princess." Olganna hastily adjusted the princess's monogrammed blanket with its proud and swooping 'P.'

"Nonetheless, would you please step outside with me?"

Olganna followed King Piotr outside as he closed the door to the nursery. The heavy door shuddered into place. Isabob and Stan appeared as vigilant as ever.

"I was hoping to discuss the princess's diet with you…" the king began.

"The princess's diet is perfectly fine, as it has always been," Olganna snapped. "The kitchen prepares every meal to my exact specifications. I test everything before it is fed to the princess, just as I did with you and your father before you."

King Piotr's jaw tightened, but Olganna was not done yet. "What's going on here? Why the sudden move to the spire? What about that secret liaison between you and Evella over the princess's crib?"

Isabob's eyes nearly popped out of their sockets. He had never seen anyone address the king in such a manner. On the other side of the door, Stan struggled not to chuckle at Olganna's audacity.

A long pause hung in the air before the king replied, "Nurse Olganna, I appreciate how you might think that our long familiarity entitles you to certain liberties, but let me assure you that in my capacity as king of the realm, I have the ultimate authority and I need not explain my actions to anyone. It would serve you well to remember that."

That was not the response Olganna was hoping for, but a quick glance at the king's resolute face convinced her that any further inquiry would be futile. Just as she was about to mumble an apology…

CRASH!

It had come from the nursery. "The princess!" Olganna cried as she ran towards the door. Isabob and Stan got there first, but try as they might they could not push it open. Despite their strong and muscled bodies, they could only open it a crack.

Olganna negotiated her small frame around the struggling guardsmen and peered through the small gap. All she could see was flickering shadows and an odd orange glow. What was going on in there? Then a wisp of grey smoke flittered past.

"Fire!" howled Olganna. Her mind plunged into a frenzy of panic and dread. She could not process everything she was feeling, but she knew one thing with cold, dead certainty: the princess was not going to die this day and certainly not on her watch.

Olganna promptly joined Isabob and Stan in pushing the cumbersome door. With each frenzied shove, she realized how little she was actually helping. Olganna was an eighty-year-old woman whose muscles had drooped with time. But no, this was no time for doubt! She had to get into that nursery. It was as simple as that. So Olganna gritted her teeth and pushed with all the strength she had left.

The door swung open, more likely from the efforts of the burly guardsmen, but one should not necessarily discount the concentrated efforts of a single-minded Olganna. The three of them tumbled into the room. Fortunately, Olganna fell on top of Stan and Isabob rather than the other way around.

As Olganna looked up, she was greeted by a very disturbing sight. The princess's crib had been knocked over. So had the lamp and, as a result, fire was creeping across the rug. Flames licked at the overturned crib. Through the open window, mighty winds poured into the room, feeding the fire and gusting giant wafts of smoke about.

Olganna sprang over to the crib and thrust her hands into the mess of blankets to find the princess. There was no baby. Her eyes darted around the room. She saw Isabob tearing the tapestry off the wall to beat the flames. She saw Stan struggling to shut that window. What she did not see was the princess.

Where could she be? Under the chest of drawers, perhaps? On all fours, Olganna scrambled across the floor, but the precious child was not there. Maybe inside the cupboard? Olganna flung open its doors.   Again, no princess.

At this time, King Piotr entered the room and Olganna found she could not meet his eyes. Later, the king's tardiness in entering the nursery would puzzle Olganna, but she was not thinking about that now. Through trembling lips and with a wisp of a voice, Olganna informed King Piotr, "The princess is gone."

A heavy silence loomed. No-one moved. No-one dared breathe. The hush was eventually broken by the slightest whisper. It came from King Piotr.

"Forgive me."

CHAPTER ONE

People in Seacrest lived for a sunny day like this. They would wake early, take a deep breath of the clean air, and set off upon the ocean's gently rolling waves. Pet Peasant, however, was not like most people.

Generally, Ma had to bang pans three times before Pet even stirred from her sleep and then it took another five good crashes before she rolled out of bed.

After a hearty breakfast, which Pet despised because she was in a despising sort of mood, she bundled herself up and made her way out into the intolerable elements. Most Seacrest Folk always seemed comfortable in a single jumper. Pet would wear three at a time. She always suspected that her body was designed for a warmer climate.

As usual, Pet jumped into the cart next to Ma and cuddled up for extra warmth. Ma gently stroked Pet's black locks for the ride to town. At seventeen, some might think Pet was getting a little old for such childishness, but Ma was indulgent. After all, it would not be long before Pet found someone else to cuddle up to. With any luck, that someone would be the Duncanson boy. He was kind-hearted and could do heavy lifting. Unfortunately, every time Ma dropped subtle hints like, "That Duncanson boy sure is nice," Pet would moan for hours about how she did not want her mother sticking her nose into her 'private affairs.'

The trip down to Seacrest was conducted in its customary silence. The only noise came from their horses, Mucker and Tucker, as they clopped down the hill. Upon arriving in the town square, Pet reached into her pocket and retrieved her clothespin, which she promptly clasped over the bridge of her nose, clamping both nostrils shut. With her safeguard in place, Pet scrambled out of the cart and removed the tarpaulin covering the back. Beneath the tarp lay the objects of her disgust, basket after basket of vile fish.

It seemed a particularly cruel twist of fate that a girl who despised every aspect of fish would end up being adopted by a fisherman and his wife. Pet despised the stuff and Ma quickly learnt that if she did not prepare a separate seafood-free dish for Pet at mealtimes, Pet's disgust could very well starve her.

After Pet had unpacked the cart, Ma gave her a quick peck on the cheek and drove off to man the family's weekend stall, over in the neighboring village of Thinsteps. Pet herself remained behind to sell fish here in Seacrest.

"Petunia!"

There was only one person in town who insisted on calling Pet by her full name. Candice Butler found the short form demeaning and not at all befitting a lady. Pet, on the other hand, appreciated the irony. Candice appreciated other things, like flowers.

Before Pet could respond with a greeting of her own, Candice launched into her story: "I was out collecting flowers yesterday afternoon when I ran into Hugh. You know Hugh, don't you? He has green eyes. Well, he was off to meet some of his pals to practice swordplay. Hugh then told me that he had been asked by one of his friends to ask me about whether you would be interested in perhaps going with this somebody to the upcoming Mariners' Day Dance at Old Foggy's Barn. Do you know who that somebody was?"

Despite the confusing use of pronouns, Pet knew exactly where this conversation was going. "You can tell Hugh to tell Judd Duncanson that if he wants to ask me out to the Mariners' Day Dance, he should just ask me himself, but the response will be exactly the same as last time. A big fat *No!*"

Candice's gleeful response startled Pet. "That's just the point! It wasn't Judd who was asking. It was Lance North."

Wow! That was a totally different story! Lance North was the son of the town magistrate, the closest Seacrest had to royalty. He was tall, dark, and not grotesque (which, for this place, was saying a lot).

"Petunia, I do believe you're blushing," teased Candice, but suddenly her smile dropped. Someone who might not take the news so well was quickly approaching.

"Hey," Judd Duncanson came up to them, carrying a big bucket of dead fish. "They're really biting out there, so your pa asked me to bring this bunch to you. He thought you might get a real fine price for them, being pulled out less than two hours ago and all."

Pet began pulling the fish from the bucket with a perfunctory, "Thanks."

When Pet removed a particularly large snapper from the confines of the bucket, Judd chimed in, "I caught that beaut myself. Quite a wriggler, let me tell you, leapt clear free of the net, but I managed to keep a hold."

"And put ten big dents in her with your clumsy fingers." Pet tossed the fish to the half-price barrel. "No-one likes damaged goods."

The smile on Judd's face wavered but he continued, "So will I be seeing you two at swordplay tomorrow?"

In many ways, the question was a silly one. Candice never engaged in swordplay. She claimed she was on strict medical orders not to. Obviously, what Judd really wanted to know was whether Pet was going.

"Perhaps, if I get through my taxes tonight," Pet answered.

"That's gotta be the lamest excuse I've ever heard. Will this be before or after you wash your hair?"

"It's the fiscal year-end, if you didn't know; and the tax auditor is in town. He's visiting all the merchants in Seacrest, making sure they've correctly declared revenue. He's supposedly very tough. Yesterday, he visited the Timmens' stall and gave them a hefty penalty for forgetting to note one day's takings. It will take them three months to pay it off. I can't have the same thing happen to my parents' business. So while you're playing with your swords, I'll be figuring out whatever pension deductions and seafarers' benefits we're entitled to."

"Oh." Judd's smile vanished completely. Pet could not help but feel a small bit of dark satisfaction. In a barely audible voice, Judd murmured, "Sorry," and departed.

Right away, Pet felt Candice's hot gaze on her back. Reminding herself that she was not one to shirk from danger, no matter how sweetly packaged, Pet turned to face her accuser like a woman.

Candice's glare was equal parts daggers and disappointment. "That was needlessly cruel, Petunia Peasant. Judd was nothing but kind and you shot him down like a pheasant in Harling's Field."

Before Pet could grumble her customary apology, Candice continued, "I don't think I will be talking to you till you make amends with Judd."

"I'm sorry. He's just so earnest. I think he does it on purpose."

Pet hoped for a response, but soon realized none would come. Candice had made up her mind and if there was any part of Pet that had rubbed off on Candice, it was Pet's stubbornness. "I'll apologize to him this evening."

Candice nodded. Her message was clear: Candice would only speak to Pet again once the apology was complete. Realizing that no amount of trying would alter Candice's resolve, Pet began stringing the fish together as she had done so many times before. As her hands worked, she found herself wondering why she was so mean to Judd. Sure, he likely had a crush on her, but that alone could not be the reason for her short temper. After all, he was not oppressive with his feelings for her.

The only solid evidence Pet had of Judd's supposed crush was from a year ago. The two were walking on the beach together after a long, hard day on the sea. He had asked her to be his date to the public lashing of some captured pirate. Suspecting the proposal was motivated by the sentimental colour of the sunset, she turned him down. It was a moot point anyway; the lashing had been cancelled when the high regent outlawed corporal punishment. Punisher Frank had not taken the news well, though rumour had it that he had reportedly found a new job since, one that included travel benefits.

Slowly but surely, the market day came to a close. Pet was happy to hear the familiar clip-clopping of Mucker and Tucker. Soon, Ma was helping Pet load the remaining goods back onto the cart.

"How was your day?" Ma inquired.

"Good enough," Pet replied as she and Ma climbed into the front of the cart. Finally, Pet removed the clothespin, a symbolic gesture that her day of work had ended.

As the cart lurched forward, Candice waved and shouted, "Bye, Ma Peasant. Give my regards to Pa Peasant." Then looking straight at Pet, she arched her eyebrows and went back to packing up her own stall.

"Bye, dear," Ma called back and then inquired of Pet, "Are you two fighting again? What did you do this time?"

"Nothing, Ma."

Recognizing Pet's mood, Ma Peasant did not press the issue and instead focused on the drive home. The entire trip, Pet looked into the distance and tried to figure out how exactly she would apologize to Judd.

CHAPTER TWO

P̶en scratched ferociously on paper.
~~Dearest Judd,~~
~~Dear Judd,~~
Judd,

I am very sorry if I hurt your feelings this afternoon. Though it is true that I had to work on my family's taxes tonight, I had no right to be mean to you.

I don't know why I get so upset with you. It's not that you do anything wrong. Maybe you're a bit too cheery sometimes, but that's nothing to hold a grudge about. I wish I could explain it.

I hope that you will accept my sincerest apology.

Pet reviewed what she had written. Then she promptly crumpled the paper into a ball and tossed it on the floor to join a growing pile.

"What got you upset this time?" asked a voice from the doorway.

Pet had a reputation in town for her letters to the editor of the *Seacrest Chronicle*, primarily taking issue with its poor coverage of provincial politics.

"Don't worry. This isn't another letter to the editor. It's a letter of apology. I might have offended Judd."

"Why don't you just apologize face-to-face?" Pa Peasant observed the mass of crumpled balls around the desk, "For the sake of the environment, if nothing else."

"I just think a letter would be a bit more formal." Pet grabbed another sheet of paper for her next attempt.

"Oh, a letter's fine," her father conceded. "It's formal and polite and you don't have to look him in the eye. You just drop it off at his house and the next time you see him, you can pretend that it never happened. But somehow I think you're braver than that."

Pet scowled. She spent a lot of time trying to sound smarter and wiser than everyone else; she was not pleased when her father demonstrated that he was, in fact, just a little bit wiser than her.

"You're right," she sighed. "But my apology will have to wait till I go over the taxes one more time."

"That's nonsense. You've already filled out the necessary schedules and double-checked the figures."

"Triple-checked, thank you very much."

"My point exactly. The taxes are fine. Go out and do what you have to do to make this right."

Pet got up from the desk, hugged her pa and rushed to the front door. Pa Peasant was unique in the world for his ability to both scold and uplift at the same time. She flung the front door open and was greeted by a most unexpected sight.

Standing on the stoop, hand poised about to knock on the door, was a mountain of a man. He was bald, scarred and imposing. A pair of too-small spectacles perched on his nose, tilting across his eyes. He held a stuffed brief-case, miniature in his huge hand.

Not one to judge on appearance alone, Pet asked, "May I help you?"

"Greetings," the stranger responded with a hint of cheer. "My name is Frank. I'll be your tax auditor this evening."

CHAPTER THREE

Portraits generally disturbed Pet. It was something about the soulless eyes. Yet in other ways, this particular portrait of High Regent Evella was quite beautiful. She appeared dignified and regal.

The next portrait in the reception area featured the missing King Piotr. He appeared amazingly tall and handsome with a black beard. In his bejeweled hand, he held a scale to represent his dedication to justice. He was not known as King Piotr the Just for nothing.

It was at that moment that Mrs Kettlepot returned. "I'm sorry, but the magistrate is far too busy to see you today."

Forgetting the portraits, Pet responded, "You don't understand. My family has been stuck with a tax bill for a thousand gold pieces. There was a change to the fisherman's provision that, as far as I can figure, makes no sense."

The personal assistant gazed at Pet. "I haven't a clue what you're going on about. I just book the appointments here."

"If you don't let me see him, our local marine-based economy will be in ruins within three months," Pet insisted.

"My, that does sound serious."

"Deadly serious."

Mrs Kettlepot nibbled on her lower lip. Her job performance evaluations always said that she needed to demonstrate more initiative. "Come with me, dear. I'll see if I can squeeze you in." She knocked gingerly on the large oak doors and called in, "Excuse me, sir, may I come in?"

"Come in, come in," was the reply.

Mrs Kettlepot entered the large office with Pet trailing behind. Pet had expected to find Magistrate North surrounded by stacks of forms and government protocols, discussing high-level domestic security protocols with a lobbyist. She was a little disappointed by what she saw instead.

Magistrate North twirled a single fava bean between the prongs of tweezers, examining it intently under a magnifying glass. He hummed a tune to himself as he inspected every curve and twist in the bean's shape. Scattered across his desk were thirty or so little vials each containing their own bean. Without breaking his intense inspection of the bean, Magistrate North asked, "What is it, Mrs Kettlepot?"

"This young lady has a matter of utmost importance to discuss with you."

Magistrate North looked up to see Pet wave at him. Surprised by the sight, the magistrate loosened his grip on the tweezers. The fava bean fell away, bouncing off the desk and onto the floor. "Mrs Kettlepot!" he declared. "You shouldn't bring a member of the electorate in here when I'm..."

The magistrate couldn't seem to find the right words to finish his sentence, so Pet decided to help him out. "Ogling legumes?" she suggested.

"Who is this?" Magistrate North demanded of Mrs Kettlepot.

"This is Pet Peasant," Mrs Kettlepot informed him. "She's here to discuss the pending economic devastation of the Southern Province. It sounds awfully important."

He examined Pet and with a flash of recognition noted, "Aren't you at the same school as my son? You can't be more than sixteen."

"Seventeen, actually."

Magistrate North turned to his personal assistant, "Mrs Kettlepot, this is hardly the type of thing that should interrupt my private study time."

"I apologize, sir, but with respect, I do think you should listen to her. It sounds pretty dire."

Magistrate North shook his head. "I'm visiting the school next week. We can schedule some time then. Not more than twenty minutes though. You may both leave now."

Despite the heavy make-up Mrs Kettlepot wore, Pet could still see her face burn with embarrassment.

"Come along, dear. I was mistaken. The magistrate is too busy to see you now." Mrs Kettlepot turned to leave the room, but Pet stood her ground.

"You know, I think this would make an interesting letter to the editor of the *Seacrest Chronicle*."

That got Magistrate North's attention.

"Local politician uses office time for deviant bean voyeurism," Pet speculated. "Has a nice ring to it. Sure, it probably wouldn't be the end of your career, but you know how people talk."

The corner of the magistrate's mouth quivered. Pet could not tell if it was the beginning of a smile or a sneer. "Mrs Kettlepot, please leave us and close the doors behind you."

Once Mrs Kettlepot was gone, Magistrate North motioned to the chair in front of his desk. "Tell me, are they teaching blackmail in school these days or are you self-taught?"

Pet took the seat. "I needed to speak with you," she shrugged.

"The end justifies the means...yes, yes. It's just a little sad to see one so young already so cynical." The magistrate sighed. "You remind me of myself at your age. Have you ever considered a career in politics?"

Ignoring that terrifying notion, Pet placed the notice from Tax Auditor Frank on the desk. "Do you care to explain this?"

Magistrate North glanced at the figures, "My, my. That's a hefty sum you owe. If you need to apply for social assistance, you can do so on the third floor."

"What happened to the allowable marine maintenance deduction?"

To the magistrate, it was as if Pet was speaking a foreign language. "The what?"

"The allowable marine maintenance deduction," repeated Pet. "The provision that allows us to offset any amount we spend maintaining our boat against our taxable income. Tax Auditor Frank told me this all had to do with the recently enacted Tax Law 106. I haven't seen any coverage of it in the *Seacrest Chronicle* and from what I can tell it will be disastrous."

Anxiety gripped Magistrate North. He did not know or care about the differences between Tax Law 104, 105 or 106. He hoped that his face did not betray his alarm. Luckily for him, this was the first time Pet had met him and she just assumed he was always this pale and sweaty.

"These changes were announced in the last session of the House," explained the magistrate. "It was passed unanimously by all magistrates present."

"Were you present?"

"Umm…yes."

"And you voted in favour of these changes?"

Magistrate North nodded.

"You do realize that Tax Law 106 will mean the end of the Southern Province's entire marine-based economy?" Pet demanded. "The fishing industry accounts for forty percent of the gross provincial product. Unemployment will skyrocket. How could you agree to this piece of legislation?"

"Grand Vizier Lier made a very convincing case. In his speech, he delved deep into the heart of the socio-political construct that is modern governance." Magistrate North looked up to see if Pet had bought it. Most of his other constituents would flee in bewilderment from so many multisyllablic words, but Pet looked at him with stern eyes. There was something about her eyes that just compelled the truth. "He also offered me part of his time-share in the Kaimon Isles."

In school, Pet had learnt that all magistrates were required to make an oath on the realm to serve, using words over weapons, wisdom over wickedness and compassion over cowardice. Unfortunately, these days that oath did not seem to count for much. Despite her disgust with the inherent patronage rampant in modern politics, Pet opted not to carp about Magistrate North's dereliction of duty. Now was the time for solutions. "This is really bad. You need to stop it."

"I would if I could, but I can't. Since Tax Law 106 was unanimously passed by the House of Magistrates, the only way it can be reversed is by being made void by another bill. However, a new bill has to be drafted and then shopped around for consent from the other magistrates. This process takes about four months."

"In four months the damage will already be done!"

"That will be a shame."

Unable to sit any longer, Pet paced circles around the magistrate's office, "There must be a way to get out of this.

Could you somehow contact the Taxation Authority directly and ask them to hold off implementing Tax Law 106? Could you arrange some sort of deferred payment scheme till the legislation is overturned? Maybe the village could just refuse to pay till the new bill is passed?"

"No, no! And you definitely don't want to try that last option. You don't want to see what happened to the last village that upset Tax Auditor Frank."

"You must be able to think of something that can help us!" cried Pet. "Anything at all."

"Well, the high regent has the right to amend any piece of legislation at any time."

Pet leapt at this glimmer of hope. "So go tell her to repeal Tax Law 106."

"Well, I'd have to travel all the way to the Sapphire Palace. That's five days of grueling travel. Then I'd have to request an audience. She's notoriously picky and might not even see me. Even if I do manage to see her, she would probably say no. I'm not very convincing."

Pet's exasperation reached its peak. This man's constituency was facing economic meltdown and it was if he could not care less. Well, as they say, if you want a job done right...

"Fine. If you won't do it, then I'll just have to do it myself," announced Pet, and with that, she stormed out of the office with a plan already brewing in her mind.

CHAPTER FOUR

Protest after protest poured out of Ma Peasant's mouth: "You're too young! It's dangerous! You could get lost!"

Pet decided it best to address the latter point first. "It's easy enough to get to the Sapphire Palace. I just follow the Capital Road all the way there."

"You can't seriously plan on going to the palace by yourself. Do you know what happens to young girls travelling alone? They get eaten by wolves."

"I can take care of myself."

That particular counter-argument held little weight with Ma.

"Speaking of eating, what about food? You hate to cook. And where are you going to sleep? We can't afford to put you in an inn every night."

Pet glared at her father. Pa sat slumped at the kitchen table. He had been working on the waves all day and had been looking forward to a nice quiet dinner. Three minutes into their macaroni bake, Pet had put the kybosh on that by declaring her plan to travel to the Sapphire Palace to challenge the high regent.

She could not rely on Pa for support. Instead, Pet asked, "What if I take someone with me?"

Ma Peasant paused as her face contorted in contemplation. Though the expression lasted a tenth of second, Pet still saw it. If Pet worked hard enough she might be able to turn that inkling of consideration into approval, but it would require a lot of work.

"Who are you considering?"

"I was thinking about Candice." This statement was not entirely true. Pet had not envisioned sharing this journey with anyone, but if she needed to take a companion, Candice was the least objectionable person she could think of.

Ma Peasant rolled her eyes. "Great, so the wolves will have two girls to feast on. How's Candice going to protect you from a pack of hunting wolves? Give them flowers? Sing them a lullaby?"

"How about Judd Duncanson?"

Both Ma and Pet turned in shock to look at Pa Peasant. They knew that the words had to have come from Pa Peasant. He was the only other person in the room, but this represented a major deviation from established precedent. Whenever arguments like this occurred in the Peasant household, Pa Peasant kept his thoughts to himself.

"Excuse me?" was the indignant response from both Ma and Pet, overlapping in a disharmonic cascade.

"He's strong. He can handle himself in a difficult situation. He would look after Pet."

Pet was about to object vehemently, something to the effect that the big lug could not look after her any better than she could herself. However, Pet's better sense prevailed and she caught the words in her throat before they could escape.

Looking over at Ma, Pet was taken aback by her chilly glare. Luckily, Pa Peasant knew exactly what to say. "You know Pet. Once she makes up her mind about something, she won't change it for anything or anyone. I don't want to see her steal away in the middle of the night. The best we can do is make her passage as secure as possible."

Ma rose and went to her room without a word. She closed the door, plunging the kitchen into an uncomfortable silence. Pet glanced at her father and saw him staring at the table. After an eternity, Pa drew himself away from the table. "I'll go to talk to your mother. You make sure that Judd will go."

Pet followed his instructions to the letter. She left the half-nibbled macaroni bake and darted out the door. She knew just where to find Judd at this hour.

CHAPTER FIVE

Pitched duels echoed through Harling's Field. The sound of the clashing sabres was music to Pet's ears. That meant swordplay was still in session. Cresting the hill, Pet saw Sentry, with his purple cape and shaved head, cut an imposing figure as he stared at the dueling boys.

Sentry barely acknowledged Pet's arrival. For her part, Pet just ran by with a cordial, "Hi, Sentry!"

The most pressing task was to find Judd, but that was a little more challenging than Pet initially expected. All the boys were kitted out in armour and their protective headgear covered their faces. Luckily Judd's size gave him away. He stood about a head taller than all the other boys and twice as broad. He was dueling off to the left with another, much slimmer boy. Their sabres clashed together as they circled each other. If Pet did not know better, she would think they were dancing.

All of a sudden, the slimmer boy sprang like a cobra, swinging his blade at Judd. Judd just managed to get his sword in position to block the strike. Pet instantly recognized that attack. No-one else could spring with the same dexterity and speed as Lance North. Pet gulped. This could get a little awkward.

"Judd, I need to speak to you!" she called.

Judd's concentration deserted him as he looked in the direction of the voice. A silly error, considering Lance's blade was halfway to stabbing Judd's chest. He barely got his sabre up in time to parry the attack. However, Lance was not done and quickly swung again.

"I don't have all night. I need to speak to you now!"

This time Lance's sabre clashed against Judd's head. Even through the headgear, it hurt. Judd fell to his knees and dropped his sword. Lance pulled his blade away and stepped back. He whipped off his helmet. His hair was soaked with sweat and matted against his forehead. He smiled at Judd and offered him a hand up, "I know you were distracted. We'll have a rematch tomorrow."

Clutching his side, Judd scowled, "Just give me a sec, Pet."

Lance flashed his immaculate white teeth at Pet. Judd knew what Lance was doing. Judd had witnessed plenty of girls swoon at the sight. Lance picked up Judd's fallen sword and offered it to the approaching Pet. "Fancy a few rounds? You can show me your moves."

"Not now." Pet walked right by Lance and stepped over to Judd. "Look, I'm sorry about being rude to you in the market, but I need you to accompany me to the Sapphire Palace tomorrow."

Judd did not know quite what to make of this proposal. Was Pet Peasant asking him to run away with her?

As Judd tried to find the right words, Pet growled, "Aren't you going to say anything? What's wrong with you?" She then turned to Lance, eyes ablaze, and demanded, "How hard did you hit him?"

"Not any harder than he would have hit me," retorted Lance.

Clasping both hands around Judd's helmet, Pet yanked it off. She grabbed Judd by the cheeks, looked him straight in his eyes, and asked, "Are you there, Judd?"

"Don't do that," scolded Sentry who had suddenly appeared at Pet's side. "You could exacerbate any neck injuries."

Pet released her hold on Judd so that Sentry could examine the boy. In addition to serving as the regional guardsman, Sentry also doubled as the local medic. His training in the healing arts was limited, but since the closest properly qualified healer was far away in Thinsteps, Sentry was usually the first responder in medical emergencies.

Luckily, this was not a medical emergency. "He'll be fine."

"Yeah, I just needed a minute," Judd murmured as he released his chest plate.

"Well, hurry up. A minute is exactly what I don't have."

Lance approached Pet again with his signature smile. "Going to the palace are you? That's a long way. I could ask my dad if he can lend us the coach."

Sentry's ears perked up.

Pet angled her head towards Lance. "I didn't ask you. Anyway I'm not your dad's biggest fan right now."

"What about the Mariners' Day Dance? I heard that you were thinking of going with me."

This time Pet didn't even bother to face Lance. "Oh that was some kind of mix-up. I'll be gone by then."

Finally getting the hint, Lance picked up his gear and sulked away. Perhaps the Butler girl would be more accommodating.

Judd's senses were now fully restored. "Why do you want to go to the palace?"

Without pause, Pet leapt into an explanation: "Tax Auditor Frank says that my family owes the state one thousand gold pieces as a result of the marine maintenance deduction being dismissed because Magistrate North is incompetent and possibly corrupt. I want to go to the palace and persuade the high regent to repeal the legislation and ensure that our entire province does not slip into an economic black hole."

"You want to talk to the high regent? But she's a witch!"

"I'm going regardless. Are you coming or not?"

The speed of Judd's response surprised Pet. "Sure."

"Judd..." then she paused. Perhaps Pet had intended to thank Judd. Perhaps she had meant to scold him on his poor sparring technique, but when Judd looked at her, she simply smiled. "Nothing. I hope to leave first thing tomorrow."

"See you then."

As she watched Judd walk off, Pet felt a presence behind her. She did not have to turn around. She knew exactly who it was. "Sentry, what can I do for you?"

"So you plan on going to the Sapphire Palace. I hope you realize what a horrible idea that is."

Pet rolled her eyes. "You're not going to tell me that High Regent Evella is a witch too, are you?"

"The high regent is certainly not a witch, but that doesn't mean there aren't other terrible dangers in the palace."

As far as Pet was concerned, Sentry was a decent guardsman and a good swordplay instructor, but he had no authority to tell her how she should conduct her life. "This is not a trip to stoke my vanity. The entire economic well-being of the Southern Province depends on repealing this silly tax law."

"How about writing a letter to the Taxation Authority? They consider petitions against the current tax legislation as well. Running off to the palace is not your only option."

Pet was surprised by Sentry's knowledge of the tax code. It was a reasonable suggestion, but any petition to the Taxation Authority would take far too long. She opened her mouth to tell the Sentry all this and more, but then Pet paused. She reconsidered and instead said, "I'll think about it."

Sentry looked at her with doubting eyes. Pet stared straight back at him. A long, dubious moment passed which concluded when Sentry said, "Fine. See you next week."

Pet watched the guardsman leave and let out a deep breath.

Of course, Pet still had every intention of going. It was not that she was particularly proud to be lying, especially to a guardsman, but persuading her parents had been hard enough. She saw no reason to go to the same extremes with Sentry. After all, Sentry was just the regional guardsman; she did not have to justify anything to him. This was Pet's quest, and she was dead set on doing it her way.

CHAPTER SIX

Poised quietly at the back, Isabob stood watching his boss. His job was simple. He just had to listen out for anybody approaching and make sure no-one interrupted. The boss would do all the talking.

The boss stood in the dim light of the mirror. This was not any ordinary mirror for it was a magic mirror. Accordingly, this was not any ordinary reflection.

"Oh. You again. What do you want this time?" the Reflection asked with an irritated tone.

There was no time for idle chatter. The boss sucked in a deep breath and began.

Mirror Mirror, You're the Key.
I Need to Know, Where Is She?

The Reflection smirked and arched its eyebrows. "Who's '*She*' exactly? There are a lot of '*She*'s in the world. How am I supposed to know which '*She*' you're talking about?"

That is why most people did not bother consulting magic mirrors. Sure they could be limitless fountains of information, but they also had a well-deserved reputation for surliness. The rub was that the Reflections did not require anything. They do not need food, water, gold or love. Reflections only really liked one thing, and for some reason completely unknown to Isabob, that one thing was rhyming. But not just any old rhyming, that would be too easy. Reflections preferred rhyming verse. There was an art to the entire process called the 'Language of Mirrors.'

Mastering this language took decades. The boss was only now getting any good at it.

She Is the Princess of All the Land
Heir to the Forests, Water and Sand.

There was no obligation on the part of the Reflection to respond in verse. "Which one?"

Isabob rolled his eyes. How many princess could there be? There was only one. *The* Princess. The *Lost* Princess. Last of the Petros Bluebloods.

> *It's been Seventeen Years and a Day*
> *Since the Wind Came and Took Her Away.*

The Reflection was in a good mood that day and replied, "I know of whom you speak. What do you want to know about her?"

The boss chose the next words very carefully.

> *Tell Me Of This Innocent Pawn,*
> *Who She Is and Where She Has Gone.*

"Seacrest." The single word took both of them by surprise. The boss whirled around to look at Isabob. Their eyes met. Neither of them could believe it. Was that really a direct answer from a magic mirror? After all this time?

"The Princess is in Seacrest," the Reflection clarified, "But not for much longer."

Isabob did not need any orders. He leapt up from his seat and burst out of the door. Time was of the essence. He already knew what the orders would be: Find her. Bring her back. Use whatever means necessary.

CHAPTER SEVEN

"**P**lease be extra careful and remember to keep those extra pieces in a safe place." Mr Butler gave his daughter a big hug. "If the worst comes to the worst, you can always stay for a night or two at an inn."

"I know, Daddy." Candice smiled as she hugged her father back.

"I'll miss you, Princess. I am so proud of you, going off to stand up to a tyrannical government. You're a real chip off the old block."

Pet struggled to suppress her gag reflex. If Pet had known she would have to witness this schmaltzy moment, she might have reconsidered inviting Candice along. What did surprise Pet was how willing the Butlers were to let their precious little girl go on this trip. They considered it character building.

Pet's mother shifted uncomfortably. Ma had not said much to Pet since last night and this worried Pet. They might shout at each other more than Candice and her mother did, but at least they always knew where they stood with each other. This sudden muteness on the part of her mother changed that. Was she disappointed in Pet? Did she feel betrayed?

Pet went over to join Pa in tying on the last of the supplies to Mucker. Pet brushed a hand through the horse's coarse mane. "Are you absolutely sure I can't take Tucker instead? Mucker's so thin. He looks like he'll keel over at any moment."

"Hush your mouth," Pa chastised her. "Mucker is a lean and delicate animal. We're going to be one horse down as it is. And though Tucker's better at pulling carts, when things are at their darkest, Mucker is the one I would want by my side."

"Really? Why is that exactly?"

Patting Mucker's hide, Pa Peasant recounted, "In his best days, Mucker was the fastest ride in the province. He could easily outrun any of those thoroughbreds that Magistrate North breeds. Though it has never been tested, I do believe that Mucker is the fastest equine in the entire realm."

Pet looked at Mucker's meager form. She contemplated protesting further, but then she did not want literally to look a gift horse in the mouth. "You've convinced me. Mucker it is!"

Pulling the last strap taut, Pa declared, "We're about done here. Go say goodbye to your Ma."

There was no more avoiding it. Pet approached Ma and was relieved when her mother spoke first. "Take these with you. They're Sirius Salts." Ma pushed a small package into Pet's hands. "If you come down with a cold or something, breathe some of the vapours. You won't be able to smell anything for a couple of days, but it's guaranteed to clear up any congestion."

Pet kissed her mother's cheek. "Thanks, Ma."

"I didn't know what else to give you," Big tears were already welling up in Ma's eyes. "I know you think I'm not supportive of this trip, but I'm trying. I just find it hard to understand why you want to do all the things you want to do. But remember one thing for me," Ma Peasant's eyes narrowed, "it's a dangerous world out there. Not everyone is as nice as they are here. You need to be cautious, especially around the Shadowoods. Whatever you do, don't go into the Shadowoods."

"I won't."

"You have a good head on your shoulders. You've been raised well. I know that for a fact." Ma dabbed at her eyes with a hanky while Pet tried to fight back her own tears. "I'm really trying not to cry here…"

"Ahh, Ma." Pet gave her mother a big hug. "Judd will be with us."

"I always knew you were destined for great things," Ma whispered in her ear. "I knew it the moment we found you. Call it mother's intuition. I just didn't expect it to be this hard to let you go."

"Everything's all packed." Judd approached atop his horse, Bounds. "Candice is ready to move too. We ought to get going soon and not waste this daylight."

Pet was a little annoyed at his take-charge attitude. Perhaps it was for the benefit of the assembled parents, to give them the sense that their precious little girls would be safe with a strong, take-charge kind of man. She would have to put him in his place, but that could wait till later.

Ma looked up at Judd. "Judd, I want you to vow to me that you're going to look after the girls."

"I promise."

Reluctantly, Pet pulled away from her Ma and helped Candice climb up on Mucker. Then Pet pulled herself up and the three of them set off. Their departure was accompanied by waves and shouts of farewell.

After a few minutes of riding, the parents were out of sight and earshot. Pet breathed a sigh of relief. She had actually pulled it off. Sure, there were five days of travel ahead of them, but the hardest part was now certainly over.

"So here we are." Judd smiled. "Off on our big adventure. Exciting, ain't it?"

Pet turned annoyed eyes on Judd. She wanted to correct his grammar and any illusion he might have about who was leading this trip. As Pet opened her mouth to speak, she was interrupted by a familiar voice.

"Yoo hoo! I'm so glad you're still here. I hoped to catch up with you."

Mrs Kettlepot rode up on what Pet had to admit was a particularly proud-looking steed. Her face was flushed with excitement and she wore what looked suspiciously like a riding-hood. The supplies tied to the steed also gave Pet reason for concern.

"What are you doing here?" asked Pet.

"Why, Hubby and I are here to join you on your mission to the palace, of course."

And with that, Pet's suspicions were confirmed. "I'm not so sure that's a very good idea."

"What I think my friend is trying to say is," Candice interjected, in that delicate way she put things, "what will Magistrate North do without you by his side?"

"Oh, he'll make do." Mrs Kettlepot dismissed the objection with a wave of her hand. "This is much more important. The entire economic well-being of the province is at stake, you know."

"That's a pity," Pet lied. "During our meeting, Magistrate North told me how indispensable you were to the running of his office. He called you…what were those exact words…oh yes, 'the wind that drives his sailboat.'"

A puzzled expression fell over Mrs Kettlepot's face. "He said that? I never realized that there was such hidden depth in our relationship. Now I'm beginning to regret being so rude when I told him where to stick it."

"You quit?" spluttered Pet.

"After seeing you talk to Magistrate North, I was inspired. So I followed your example and told him exactly what I thought. It was so exhilarating. Then he fired me."

"What about Mr Kettlepot? Who will cook his dinner?" Pet was never one for gender-based stereotypes, but these were desperate times.

"He passed on last year." Mrs Kettlepot cast her gaze downwards.

"I'm so sorry," cooed Candice. Ever the comforter, she dismounted and approached Mrs Kettlepot.

"It's all right dear," sniffed Mrs Kettlepot. She then stared at Pet. "I know it might seem strange for an old woman to want to join a bunch of young people like you…"

"You're not old," soothed Candice.

"Yes I am, dear, but that's hardly the point. After Mr Kettlepot died, I got to thinking about what significance my life would have in the grand scheme of things. It didn't seem like much. But then I met Pet and she had so much fire in her, wanting to help people. I just want to be part of that."

"Her horse looks healthy," Judd noted. "Looks like it could carry some additional gear with no problem. We could take some of the load off Mucker and progress a bit faster than we had originally planned."

Mrs Kettlepot nodded. "Hubby is a very strong horse."

Pet did not like where this was going. "What skills can you contribute?"

"I can cook," Mrs Kettlepot responded. "I know how to pitch a tent and what berries are edible and what berries will give you a stomach ache. I know…"

"Your recipes," Pet cut her off, "do they all involve fish?"

Mrs Kettlepot flushed a little, "Truth be told, I was never one for fish. Too many bones and scales."

And that was that. "You may join us, Mrs Kettlepot. However I must warn you that we intend to maintain a brisk pace."

Mrs Kettlepot thanked Pet profusely, but Pet paid little heed. She was instead trying to figure out how exactly her solo journey to the palace had ended up being a four-person expedition. What a motley crew it was at that: the florist, the farmhand and the personal assistant. One could imagine the fear they would strike into the heart of the high regent.

At least she would not have to eat fish.

CHAPTER EIGHT

Proceedings went smoothly the first day. Spirits were high. To everyone's surprise, Mrs Kettlepot had some fairly raunchy stories which garnered uproarious laughs from her companions. Unfortunately, these good times would not last.

On the second day, new riding arrangements were made. Judd still rode Bounds, but Candice had moved over to ride with Mrs Kettlepot on Hubby. Mrs Kettlepot had some difficulty controlling the rambunctious steed and Candice was happy to help. This left Pet alone on Mucker. Ordinarily, she would have been pleased with the little extra room. However, contrary to Pa's hype, Mucker turned out to be quite lazy.

Try as she might, Pet simply could not get Mucker to accelerate any faster than a lackadaisical trot. She tried flattering and coaxing, but nothing inspired speed in her four-legged friend. Mucker just continued to clop along. Each clop served as a harsh reminder that, despite being the leader of this expedition, Pet was riding at the rear of the party. To make matters worse, it was Judd who was at the front.

Mrs Kettlepot and Candice tried to hang back with Pet. They spoke idly about different types of wildflowers. Pet could not decide what was more irritating, their inane prattle or the obvious effort it took to keep Hubby from darting ahead. All morning, Pet's dark mood brewed like a coffee-pot. Even Candice gave up trying to make small talk with her.

The noon sun shone high overhead as Judd brought Bounds to a halt. He dismounted and when Candice and Mrs Kettlepot caught up, they followed suit. When she caught up, Pet was not very impressed. "What's going on here?"

"This looked like a good spot for lunch," mentioned Judd as he tethered Bounds and Hubby to a nearby tree.

"It's too early. If we don't press on, we won't make it to Vale Alturin before nightfall." The fact that Pet felt like she was protesting dismayed her. Wasn't she the leader of this expedition? She was supposed to *make* the decisions, not protest against them.

"We should make it." Judd pulled out the map from the folds of his jacket. "The next few miles take us alongside Murky Swamp. A rest now will do us good before we trudge through all that muck."

"I don't care. We press on. I am the leader of this group, Judd Duncanson. It was my idea to go to the Sapphire Palace. I brought you along because I had to. You are not our pathfinder, not our scout, and certainly not our guide. I have my own map and I am certainly capable of reading it…"

At this point, Candice interjected, "Petunia Peasant! Stop this at once! Judd is just here to help you. He could have stayed home, but he chose to come along because he's a good friend. You had best remember that."

"But…"

"But nothing." Candice then turned to address Judd, "And you, this is Petunia's journey. She's in charge. She might be forced to bring up the rear on account of Mucker," she glanced apologetically at the pathetic horse, "who is slower than most, but she still calls the shots. If you think it's a good time to stop for lunch, you should check with her first."

Both Pet and Judd hung their heads, scolded. Judd mumbled, "She's right. I'm sorry. I didn't mean to take over."

He stuck his hand out in an apologetic manner. Pet took Judd's hand and clasped it. "I'm sorry too. I could do with a spot of lunch."

The four of them ate their lunch in relative quiet. Pet studied the map while she munched her cucumber sandwich. Having eaten his meal quickly, Judd used his extra time to sprawl out in the sun. He removed his jacket and closed his eyes. Pet briefly glanced up from the map and noted his bare chest.

As Candice absent-mindedly collected wildflowers along the side of the road, Mrs Kettlepot finished the last morsel of her sandwich and came to the conclusion that some tea was necessary. Unfortunately, the wood along the path was too damp.

"I'm just going to find some dry wood," declared Mrs Kettlepot, as she made her way deeper into the foliage.

"Don't go too far. We'll be leaving soon," a distracted Pet warned before returning to her intent study of the map. However, the sun was particularly warm and soon took its toll on Pet. She had meant to close her eyes for only a moment...

"Pet, wake up."

Always a heavy sleeper, Pet was happy to ignore the voice and instead return to her wonderful dream. It involved living in a tall tower and bossing people about. However, a gentle shake made that impossible.

"What is it?" Pet groggily asked.

"Mrs Kettlepot has been gone for quite some time," Candice informed her.

Along the side of the road, Judd was shouting into the dark foliage, "Mrs Kettlepot! Are you out there?"

The trio stood silently waiting for a reply, ears strained for the slightest response. Moments became minutes. Candice and Judd hesitated to say anything lest their words drown out Mrs Kettlepot's reply. Pet had no such hesitation. "We need to go in and get her. Candice, you stay with the horses!"

Though Candice made a face of disappointment, she was secretly relieved that she did not have to go trudging through the mud of Murky Swamp. Pet turned to Judd and asked, "Did you bring your sword?"

He nodded. With weapons in hand, Pet and Judd scrambled into the foliage. Soon, they were trudging through mud, doing their best to avoid the deeper puddles. Judd occasionally called out for Mrs Kettlepot, while Pet scanned their surroundings.

"Get away! Shoo!"

The cry punctuated the air. Judd and Pet looked at each with relief. The voice was distinctly Mrs Kettlepot's. Sure, the cry had a distressed tone to it, but Pet's heart loosened with relief. Mrs Kettlepot was alive.

Pet and Judd sprinted towards the source of the cry. They soon found a sight that they could not quite make sense of.

CHAPTER NINE

Perched in the lower branches of a tree was Mrs Kettlepot. Her collected kindling lay scattered on the swampy ground below. Her face was beet-red as she hugged the trunk for support. One of her legs violently kicked the air, missing its target by a good few metres.

The intended target was a hopping frog or at least what appeared to be a frog. To clarify, it was not that Pet doubted her ability to distinguish a frog and toad; rather, it was the fact that the creature-that-appeared-to-be-a-frog was quite obviously speaking to Mrs Kettlepot.

"Just one, milady," the creature croaked. "Bless me only once with what I desire and you may depart in peace."

"Never," hissed Mrs Kettlepot, still kicking away.

Pet turned to Judd to see what he made of the situation. She was dismayed to find that he was no longer beside her, but instead catapulting himself towards the talking frog.

"Hey, frog!" Judd brandished his sword. "Nobody messes with Mrs Kettlepot while I'm around!"

The creature turned to look at Judd, momentarily halting its harassment of Mrs Kettlepot. "Firstly, peasant, I am not a frog. Frogs have bulgy eyes. Do my eyes look bulgy to you? No. For I am a toad. Secondly, I have no intention of harming anybody, especially not this beautiful damsel."

"Beautiful!" exclaimed Mrs Kettlepot, "You think I'm beautiful?"

Though Mrs Kettlepot's face was already red from all the panic and exertion, Pet could still see the slightest hint of blush on her cheek. Was a talking toad really wooing Mrs Kettlepot?

Before any further cross-species flirtation could take place, Judd swung at the talking toad with the flat of his sword. The creature went flying through the air and smashed into a tree. Pet winced.

Pet grabbed Judd's arm. "What do you think you're doing?"

"Rescuing Mrs Kettlepot," was Judd's simple and obvious response.

Pet was about to respond, but the toad had a few words to say on the matter first. "This encounter would be comical, if it wasn't so tragically commonplace. A sophisticated and worldly admirer of the arts is wooing an angelic vision. Then some country bumpkin clops along and attempts to bully me out of my prize. To this, I say, 'NAY!'"

Before Judd could figure out what the toad was talking about, it leapt at him with lightning speed. "As fortune has it, the enchantment didn't specify a gender. Perhaps you may gift me with a brush of your lips in her stead, bumpkin."

The toad landed on Judd's face, knocking him down. Judd brought his hands up to pry the creature away, but the toad gripped his cheeks with surprisingly strong toes. "I am the Master of Murky Swamp," the toad announced. "Submit to my will!"

Meanwhile, Pet extended her hand to Mrs Kettlepot. "Are you alright?"

Mrs Kettlepot gladly accepted the help and slowly lowered herself down from her perch. "Did you hear that? He called me a damsel. Nobody has ever called me a damsel before."

Opting not to comment on the disturbing implications of that comment, Pet instead turned her attention to the titanic clash between man and amphibian unfolding in the muck before her.

"To smooth that rough touch with a tender kiss," quoted the toad. However, the words did not have any sort of reassuring impact on Judd. Instead he struggled with renewed ferociousness.

"Seems like we have an enchanted toad here," observed Pet. "Only a kiss will revert him to human form."

"Probably," agreed Mrs Kettlepot. "But that sort of curse has been unfashionable for about fifteen years."

Despite the amusing nature of their struggle, Pet wanted to get on with her day. "Okay, guys! This needs to stop."

Her words had little effect on their continuing struggle. So she tried again, but there was still no response. In exasperation, she cried, "I'll kiss the first person who stops this madness!"

Immediately, both the toad and Judd stopped. The toad hastily shouted, "I am no enthusiast of violence, but I felt conditions demanded certain actions be taken. My rash decision might have been in error. Please find it in your heart to forgive me, fine damsel."

Mrs Kettlepot scowled at how quickly the toad could re-direct its affections.

"You don't really intend to kiss that, do you?" asked Judd wiping a sour mixture of sweat and mud off his face.

Ignoring Judd, Pet kneeled down to address the toad. "What's your name?"

"Iago Von Klein the Third, the Master of Murky Swamp," announced the toad. "Well, that was my human name, prior to my misfortune."

"Who did this to you?"

With a dour look, Iago recounted, "A sorceress in a castle far far away from here. My father always warned me not to woo a sorceress."

Pet suspected that there was more to this story. "So she turned you into a toad for trying to woo her?"

"Did I forget to mention that she was an evil sorceress?" Iago glanced up and was confronted by Pet's doubtful eyes. "Indeed our courtship survived beyond the wooing stage and for a number of months we shared an intense romance…"

"Why are you asking its life story?" interrupted Judd. "Just skewer the frog and we can be on our way!"

Pet and Mrs Kettlepot simultaneously threw harsh looks at Judd, silencing him.

"I'm hardly a savage," protested Iago before looking directly at Mrs Kettlepot and intoning, "except when circumstances warrant."

Mrs Kettlepot giggled. Pet thought she might throw up. Struggling to keep things on track, Pet asked, "So you were dating this evil sorceress and…"

"The word 'dating' doesn't even begin to capture the magnitude of the passion I showered upon her. Every night, our love would re-shape this mundane world. The earth trembled in tribute, oceans gushed and the sky blazed with fire…"

"But then things went south," conjectured Pet.

"Yes. She became preoccupied with other matters. Night after night, I waited for her, but she would never come. I regret to say this, but I became lonely. I fully admit to being a man with substantial needs and my eye began to wander. To make a long and tragic story short, Evella found me kissing another woman and promptly cursed me."

"Wait a moment!" cried Pet. "Evella! Evella was the evil sorceress? Evella, as in the current high regent of the realm?"

"You mean that witch became high regent?!" croaked Iago.

This new information was a bit startling to Pet. Apparently the person she was going to talk to about overturning Tax Law 106 had a prior record for turning people into toads. She would have to take extra care to sharpen her argument as finely as possible.

"So about that kiss…," Iago prompted, giving Pet the eye.

"I'm not in love with you. Would my kiss still break the spell?"

"What is there not to love?" Iago rolled his short arms around his chest in what Pet could only guess was intended to be a seductive gesture.

"Actually," Mrs Kettlepot began, "transmogrifying curses are relatively simple as far as enchantments go. A kiss of true love is only required to break particularly powerful spells."

"Let's give it a try," Pet scooped Iago up and took a moment to consider his puckered expression. Being a bad boyfriend did not mean that he deserved to spend the rest of his life as a toad.

She then presented the toad to Mrs Kettlepot. "… Unless you'd like to."

Mrs Kettlepot gulped. "No thank you, dear."

Pet clamped her eyes shut and drew the toad towards her. She pressed her pursed lips against his for a fraction of a second. Iago suddenly became very heavy in Pet's hands and she was forced to drop him.

Her eyes sprang open and before her stood a fairly distinguished, grey-haired man. The man was nude and just a touch wrinkly. Pet, Mrs Kettlepot and Judd quickly averted their eyes.

"I'm back!" cried Iago in glee. He patted his hands all over his body to ensure that everything was in the right place. "Iago Von Klein the Third is back!"

"Bumpkin, hand me your jacket!" Though Judd had no special liking for Iago, he was more than happy to assist the ex-toad in clothing himself. "I surely cannot command an army in the buff."

Pet's ears perked up. "What army?"

"Isn't it obvious?" Iago wrapped himself in the jacket. "An evil witch has taken control of the realm! If she's capable of turning me into a toad, who knows what she did to gain that power? She probably used her black magic to unjustly seize the throne."

"Wait a moment," Pet objected. "You have no evidence of that."

Now somewhat clothed, Iago pronounced, "Evella is a usurper. She must be stopped. Raising an army and laying siege to the Sapphire Palace appears the most effective way of doing that."

"You're talking about starting a war! People will die!"

"Young lady," Iago addressed Pet, "leave this to the men. Women have no stomach for the sacrifice that matters of state require."

Pet's mind raced. What had she done? If she had not kissed the talking toad, there would not be a half-naked nobleman before her, planning a war. She certainly was not going to let him proceed. Pet had to think of a way to handle this and quickly.

Iago put an arm around Judd. "Bumpkin, I'd like to make you my first lieutenant. I terribly regret all that ugliness earlier, but I am sure you understand the necessity that motivated my actions. Reclaiming the throne is of far greater importance than any trifling ado between us."

Iago was interrupted by a kiss from Pet. It was a desperate gamble. She hoped that vestiges of the enchantment remained, vestiges that would be activated by another kiss.

The Master of Murky Swamp disappeared from sight. Only Judd's crumpled jacket remained on the muddy ground.

Pet sucked in a tense breath. Her kiss hadn't killed him, had it? Magic could be so unpredictable sometimes.

Then the jacket started to move. There was something crawling out from underneath.

"What did you do?" croaked Iago, as he revealed himself, once again a toad.

Relieved but not apologetic, Pet mumbled, "I'm sorry. You're simply too dangerous to be human right now. All you seem to want is war and bloodshed. I can't allow that."

"And you are an idealistic fool."

Pet regarded Iago with sad eyes, "Perhaps, but now I'm going to have to ask you to leave. Harass other unsuspecting travelers! Maybe one of them will give you what you need, but it certainly will not be us."

There was nothing left to say. Pet turned and started the long walk back to Candice and the horses. Judd inspected the muddy remains of his jacket and decided he would let the swamp keep it. Mrs Kettlepot gave Iago one last look before leaving the Master of Murky Swamp alone in his muddy kingdom.

CHAPTER TEN

Particular attention was paid to the rapidly approaching darkness. They had less than an hour before they would be forced to turn in for the night. Pet and her companions would not make it to Vale Alturin that day.

Pet sighed. She understood that schedules had to be adjusted, but so soon? This was only the second day of travel. Oh well, they could always make an early start tomorrow. Perhaps they would be able to catch up on some of the ground lost today. Pet spotted a nice enough clearing. "Let's pack it in."

Mrs Kettlepot quickly went about throwing together a cold dinner. She did not want to go in search of kindling, particularly considering what had happened last time. So cucumber sandwiches it was. Fortunately, Pet had grown quite fond of Mrs Kettlepot's cucumber sandwiches. After dinner, Mrs Kettlepot and Judd retired almost immediately. Judd had been particularly quiet during the meal.

All of a sudden, Pet saw a blur of movement out of the corner of her eye. She turned to Candice and asked in a hushed whisper, "Did you see that? There was something on the road."

"What do you think it was?"

Pet's heart started to race. But she quickly scolded herself. There was no reason to panic. They were in the woods, sometimes things moved. "I have no idea. I'll be right back."

Pet crept up toward the road. It was only a matter of metres. Halfway, Pet wondered if she should have brought her sword.

"Do you see anything?" asked Candice, following close behind.

Pet strained her eyes through the gathering gloom. "It's just a rider going past. He appears to be on his way to Seacrest."

Now, this was no typical rider. Riders rarely rode so fast in the dark. Perhaps more disturbingly, the rider and his horse had made no noise. Considering their pace, Pet should have heard the sound of galloping. Instead, there was only ghostly silence.

Regardless, the rider was gone now. Pet and Candice returned to the campsite and lay in the grass by the final embers of their fire. The stars were beginning to shine through overhead. "Beautiful, aren't they?" Pet observed.

"Never mind that." Candice had something else on her mind. "You have to tell me what happened in the swamp."

Though Pet did not particularly want to recount the entire sordid mess, Candice did have a right to know and had been patient all day. So Pet told her of the encounter from beginning to end, adding a touch of embellishment when it came to the struggle between Judd and Iago in the mud.

Once Pet was done, Candice commented with a mixture of relief at not having been involved with such a muddy affair and disappointment at missing out on the action, "Oh. That's why Judd looked so embarrassed."

"Yes," Pet muttered. Judd, Judd, Judd. What was she going to do about Judd? His actions in the Murky Swamp were troubling. He had gone in with a bludgeon-first-ask-questions-later mentality. Trusting Judd's judgment was going to be an issue.

If today's experience had taught Pet anything, it was that, despite any amount of planning, unpredictable situations were going to arise. When they did, Pet had to know that she could rely on her companions.

"But in the end, I did realize something."

"And that is?" Candice asked.

Pet guiltily glanced over at the sleeping forms of Judd and Mrs Kettlepot. This was going to be the hard part. She crept close to Candice and whispered in her ear, "We have to leave one of them behind."

CHAPTER ELEVEN

Plush cushioning did little to soothe Lance North's mind as he sat in the reception area. Today was not Lance's best day. He was in danger of having to go stag to the Mariners' Day Dance. His intended date, Pet Peasant, had rejected him and run off with Judd Duncanson. If word got out about that, he would never hear the end of it. He needed to discuss the situation with his father, but Magistrate North was currently in a breakfast meeting with the vice-magistrate of something-or-other.

The edge of a billowing cloak suddenly brushed his knee. Lance was not alone. It was as if this Cloaked Man had appeared out of thin air.

The angle of the cloak's hood prevented Lance from getting a good look at the man's face. However, he did get a look at something else. The cloak shifted for a moment, revealing a large and heavy axe strapped to his side. There was a faded red stain on its blade. Was that blood?

The Cloaked Man placed his hand on the doorknob to the magistrate's office. A man with blood on his axe was walking in on his father! Lance felt compelled to take some sort of action and announced, "His assistant quit. I think he's in a meeting."

The Cloaked Man opened the door and slipped into the office.

Lance sat there, unsure what to do. As of yet, there were no screams from his father's office. That meant the Cloaked Man was probably not chopping his father and the vice-magistrate of something-or-other into tiny bits. That was a good thing. He might just be some local farmer or woodsman. There was no need to panic.

The door of the office swung open. The vice-magistrate of something-or-other scampered out. His face was sweaty and pale. He gave Lance a pitying look before hurrying away. This did little to ease Lance's mind.

At this point, a new visitor strode into the reception. Sentry was certainly a heroic sight in this situation. The guardsman immediately asked Lance, "Did he come through here?"

Lance pointed at the door. "He's in there."

"Are you armed?" asked Sentry.

Lance shook his head. Sentry pulled a dagger from his belt and handed the butt end to Lance. "Stay behind me. If anything happens to me, your job is to get your father out of there and then keep running."

It was quite a surprise to Lance to find he was now standing, wielding the dagger, and nodding. Sentry unsheathed his own sword and put his hand on the doorknob, "On your marks, one, two... THREE!" Sentry flung the door wide open and leapt in. Lance tumbled in after him, taking care not to trip over Sentry's cape.

The Cloaked Man sat in one of the chairs opposite Magistrate North, holding a porcelain tea-cup between his large fingers. He turned to look at Sentry and Lance with raised eyebrows.

"What is the meaning of this rude interruption?" asked Magistrate North.

"Your visitor did not register at the gate." Sentry sheathed his sword. "I thought you might be in trouble."

"My visitor is an emissary from the Sapphire Palace. He is here on important business."

"This the boy?" inquired the Cloaked Man.

"Yes. My son, Lance." Magistrate North beckoned for Lance to take one of the chairs. Lance crept out from behind Sentry and took the seat.

Sentry inspected the Cloaked Man, "He doesn't look like any emissary I've ever seen."

"I appreciate your concern," the magistrate responded, "but he carries orders bearing the Royal Seal. Please leave us."

After the door closed behind Sentry, Lance felt a shiver travel down his spine as he realized that he and his father were now alone in this room with the Cloaked Man. Predictably, it was the magistrate who broke the silence, "Sentry will be harshly dealt with."

The Cloaked Man shrugged, "Dogs bark."

Magistrate North turned to Lance and explained, "The emissary here has been tasked with locating a person of importance."

"A girl." The Cloaked Man's gravelly whisper commanded attention. "Seventeen, black hair, adopted."

One name came immediately to Lance's lips but he suppressed the urge to release it. "Could be any number of people."

"Unlikely." The Cloaked Man had a point. Most Seacrest Folk were blonde. There are a few red-heads and brunettes, but girls with black hair? You could count them on one finger.

"It sounds like that girl who came to visit me recently," Magistrate North mentioned. "She's one of your school chums. Loud and opinionated. I forget her name..."

Lance North was many things, but he was not one to give up a friend without good reason. "What do you want with her?"

The Cloaked Man sniffed the air, "Not your concern."

"I will not answer your question until you tell me exactly why you want her."

Magistrate North's mouth fell open. His throat flexed as if to object to Lance's rude treatment of a guest, but the Cloaked Man quieted the magistrate with a quick wave of his hand. "You want to join the Royal Guard?"

Lance stared crossly at his father. Lance had wanted to join the Royal Guard ever since he could remember. They were the pinnacle of armed forces in the realm. One of the reasons that Lance trained so regularly with Sentry was to develop all the necessary skills. There was no reason this Cloaked Man should know that though.

"I might have mentioned it in passing," admitted the Magistrate.

"The Royal Guard requires complete devotion to the regent," reminded the Cloaked Man.

The boy gulped. The threat was clear. One word to a recruiter about Lance not assisting an emissary of the regent and he would be black-listed. No matter how many championships he won or top marks he attained or damsels he rescued, his application would never be considered. All of a sudden, all of his dreams were on the verge of becoming dust.

Lance's mind spun in doubt and confusion. Was it selfish to betray his friend for a career in which he would undoubtedly help even more people? How did he even know he was really betraying his friend? This man, despite his caustic demeanor, was an emissary from the Sapphire Palace and the high regent would never have ill intentions towards one of her subjects, would she?

"Her name is Pet Peasant," Lance spluttered. "She left two days ago..."

And Lance continued to spill the beans about Pet. It distracted him from the increasingly sinking feeling he had in the pit of his stomach. He told the Cloaked Man everything he knew. Each word felt like a betrayal, but try as he might, he could not stop himself from speaking. Once Lance had exhausted his knowledge on the subject of Pet's departure, the Cloaked Man nodded and rose to his feet.

Magistrate North offered his hand to the emissary, "Apologies for the theatrics earlier. You know boys can sometimes have a misplaced sense of loyalty."

The Cloaked Man did not take the Magistrate's hand. Instead he strode out of the room, leaving a quietly destroyed Lance.

Magistrate North smiled a warm smile at his son. "Between you and me, I'm glad that man is gone. Emissary or not, he made me uncomfortable. However, you did the right thing. He does represent the high regent."

Lance disagreed. He had definitely not done the right thing.

"Was there something you wanted to speak to me about?"

"Nothing," Lance murmured.

"Is everything all right?"

There was no way Lance could answer that question. He thought he might have heard his father calling out to him as he left, but he could not be sure. All that Lance could hear was the intense, guilty beating of his heart. He slumped out into the morning light and tried to work out what to do next.

"What did that emissary want?"

Lance turned to find Sentry behind him and told him, "He was looking for Pet."

Sentry scowled. The Cloaked Man had just left Seacrest via the Capital Road. If Pet had decided to go to the Sapphire Palace despite his protests that is the road she would have taken. "What did you tell him?"

It occurred to Lance that he could just lie to Sentry. However, there was something about Sentry's piercing glare that made Lance realise that only the truth would do. "Everything."

Sentry considered his options. "I'm going after him. There's something about him that makes me think he does not have Pet's best interests at heart. Will you join me?"

Lance's face lit up. This was his chance to redeem himself. He had made a mistake, but now he could atone for it. A triumphant scene flashed before the boy's eyes: he and Sentry riding into battle with matching purple capes. They would be fighting the Cloaked Man with his bloodstained axe. The axe would swing wildly in the air. Then Lance imagined the axe sinking into his chest and the sucking sound the wound would produce. He saw himself falling to the floor in a bloody pile of guts and gore.

"I can't."

"Suit yourself!" Sentry replied as he departed.

Confused and numb, Lance walked off without any particular destination. To see Lance at that moment with his hunched posture and bereft eyes, you might think him one of the living dead. And you would not be entirely wrong.

CHAPTER TWELVE

Pleasant rays of daylight shone through the leaves and dappled against Judd's face. He opened his eyes to find the bluest sky he had ever seen. Today was to be a fine day and Judd was going to make the most of it. Then he stretched.

Judd could stretch his arms easily enough and crook his neck, but a distinct problem arose when he tried to stretch his legs. They would not move. Concerned, Judd looked down at his feet.

Oh! It all made sense now. His feet were tied to a tree.

This must be some sort of joke. He lightly kicked his feet, expecting the rope to come undone. It did not loosen the slightest bit. Judd kicked harder. It did not help. In fact, it seemed to Judd that, with every movement he made, the rope binding his feet to the tree became tighter.

Bending down, Judd took a look at the knots binding him to the tree. Someone had used the Seacrest Special to tie these knots. The Seacrest Special was developed by the long nautical tradition among the Seacrest Folk. One Seacrest Special was virtually unbreakable. Whoever had done this had used nine.

Whoever had tied this must have had some sort of seafaring background, like perhaps an adopted father who was a fisherman,   "Very funny, Pet, but I need to pee. Can you untie me now?"

Looking around the campsite, Judd was dismayed to find everyone had packed up and appeared ready to go. Mrs Kettlepot sat on Hubby looking in the other direction. Candice and Pet stood beside the other steeds looking at him warily. Why weren't they saying anything to him?

"What are you guys up to? What's going on?" Judd asked with a half-laugh.

Pet crouched down beside him, "We need to talk."

"Talk about what?"

"It isn't you," sighed Pet, "It's me. This isn't working for me at all. You're a nice guy, but this was a mistake. We should nip it in the bud before doing something we regret later."

"Huh?"

Pet shook her head. Why did Judd have to look so bewildered and innocent? It felt like she was leading a baby lamb to the slaughter. She gritted her teeth, "We're leaving you behind, Judd."

There was no response. Had he even heard her?

Finally, he mumbled, "I don't get it."

Pet began her well-rehearsed response, "Your actions yesterday disappointed me. You attacked Iago without thinking. It was a situation that could easily have been resolved with diplomacy, but instead you went in with your sword swinging."

"I was just trying to protect Mrs Kettlepot. That was the right thing to do, wasn't it?"

"You have the wrong idea about this mission. This isn't about adventure or heroics." Again Judd tried to interrupt, but Pet would not let him.

"I'm not looking to start any trouble. I'm just looking to appeal to the government to change a boring tax law. It's actually pretty mundane. I don't think you get that."

The more Pet spoke, the more she was almost able to fool herself into thinking she was doing the right thing, "The point is that we're travelling along a safe road. We have no need for an armed escort, especially the type of escort who gets us into further trouble, rather than delivers us from it."

"I thought we were friends."

"We were… are..."

"But I promised your ma," Judd reminded her.

"Someone should come along soon enough. They will be able to cut you free. We're only a day from Seacrest, so you should be able to walk or hitch back."

There was no response from Judd.

"Unfortunately, we have to take Bounds with us. If we leave him here, you'll try to follow us."

Judd's hand darted to his belt. He could not believe he had not thought of it earlier. His hand was surprised to find an empty scabbard. Where had it gone?

"I hid your sword in those bushes over there." The bushes in question were just out of Judd's reach. "Do you have any questions?"

Judd looked at Candice. So far, she had not said a word. "Do you agree with all this?"

Candice could not make eye contact with Judd, "This is for the best…"

"Any other questions?" inquired Pet.

None came. He just looked at her with his bewildered eyes. Pet had expected Judd to say something. The silence was eerie.

This was it. This was farewell.

"I hope one day you'll understand. Take care, Judd."

As the others left, there was still no response from Judd. He was still trying to wrap his head around what had just happened.

CHAPTER THIRTEEN

Perturbed silence filled the rest of the day. Of course, there was the clip-clop of the horses as they padded along the Capital Road, but that had become background noise – a heartbeat for their journey. At least their journey still had a heartbeat, Pet mused, despite her actions.

In particular, Candice had never appeared more distant. Her head lung low and her gaze seemed fixed on Mucker's mangy mane. Pet had wisely opted to ride Bounds herself, rather than make either Candice or Mrs Kettlepot do it. Strangely, even though she was now riding Bounds, Pet somehow still managed to trail behind the others.

Pet wanted to clear the air, "Candice, I…"

"Not now, Petunia." It was not what Candice said, but rather how she said it that disturbed Pet. Her tone was as dead as her gaze.

"Shouldn't be much further to Vale Alturin," piped up Mrs Kettlepot. She was riding in the front, with the map in her lap. She looked back at Pet and gave her a smile.

Mrs Kettlepot's innocent enough words spurred Candice to speak. "We shouldn't have done that to Judd. He was our friend!"

Pet wanted to sound like a leader who made the tough choices and did not look back, "What's done is done."

"What's done is done?! We didn't spill a pint of milk, Petunia. We trussed up one of our best friends and abandoned him by the wayside!" Candice gave Bounds an exaggerated look, "Without a horse, I may add."

"We hardly trussed him up," protested Pet. "We just tied his leg to a tree. You should know. You chose the tree."

Candice returned her gaze to Mucker's mane. "I know."

Why was Pet trying so hard to defend her actions? Her very best friend was in pain. Pet had to do something about it. "We did the right thing."

"You're the one who always says that dialogue is the key to resolving conflict, but did you discuss your problems with Judd? No. You didn't. Instead you tied him up. You abandoned him."

"He made a promise to my mother! You can't make a leopard change his spots or Judd Duncanson change his overprotective ways."

Candice glared pointedly at Pet, "The point is that you didn't even try."

"Do you think I liked abandoning Judd? It had to be done and since I'm the leader here, the hard decision fell to me."

"You just seemed overly eager to make this particular hard decision."

Pet opened her mouth to respond, but nothing came. What could she say to that? How could she convince Candice she was right?

Silence returned in its deafening glory. The horses continued to clop along. Mrs Kettlepot continued to lead the way. Candice returned to staring at Mucker's mane. Pet returned to her musings. It was strange. There Pet was, riding with two other people, but never in her life had she felt quite so alone.

CHAPTER FOURTEEN

Perfect grass undulated under a brightly shining sun in the cerulean sky. This was Vale Alturin and it was everything that Candice had hoped it would be. The meadow exploded in colour. A light warm breeze blew in from the east. Everything was so vibrant and alive.

As she usually did when depressed, Candice overcompensated. She removed her shoes and stretched her legs out in front of her. Her feet played with the grass, letting the blades slide between her toes. She delicately held a single purple finger and slowly plucked off the petals. One by one, she released the petals and watched the breeze capture them.

Despite nature's best efforts, Candice's dark mood did not improve. Trying to trick her mind into thinking she was having a good time was not working.

About half a mile away, Pet sat on the hill watching Candice. She munched her cucumber sandwich as she tried to figure out what to do. Pet was not too keen on the idea of letting Candice wander off by herself, especially considering what had happened to Mrs Kettlepot, but Pet had not dared to raise her concerns with Candice. At least here at Vale Alturin, Pet could still keep an eye on her.

Behind Pet, Mrs Kettlepot was cleaning up the plates from lunch. Pet asked her, "Do you think I made the wrong decision?"

"Oh, I don't know, dear. You're the leader and sometimes you have to make hard decisions. I don't question that."

"Come on, Mrs Kettlepot. I decided to leave Judd tied to a tree in the woods. You don't have an opinion on that?"

"You had your reasons," Mrs Kettlepot responded. Then, changing the subject, "It's a beautiful day isn't it?"

Pet continued to press the issue, "I know it was drastic, but I couldn't think of any other way to stop him. He could have ruined everything."

The old lady took in a resigned breath and gathered her thoughts, "Candice's been picking a lot of purple flowers."

"What do flowers have to do with anything?"

"Purple is the colour of shame."

Mrs Kettlepot had a point. Candice was feeling pretty bad about what they had done. Of course, Pet could justify her position, but what had she really done about addressing Candice's feelings? The girl felt she had betrayed Judd.

"I'm more partial to yellow myself," smiled Mrs Kettlepot, "It's the colour of hope, you know."

"So you're saying that I've been so focused on being the leader and justifying those actions that I've forgotten that I'm also her friend," Pet frowned. "The trouble is that I don't know what to say to her."

"I can't help you with that, but as far as I can gather, you've been best friends for a long time. I can think of no-one more qualified to help her through this rough time. You'll think of something."

Who would have thought Mrs Kettlepot had such wisdom behind her? There was certainly more to this lady than the doddering old woman that met the eye.

CHAPTER FIFTEEN

Plump fingers clumsily pulled on the threads of the rope every which way. Try as he might, Judd's hands could not figure out a way to untie these knots. It did not help that he was seething with rage and every failed attempt was just making him angrier.

Judd took a deep breath. He was getting himself worked up. Every time he got angrier, he got clumsier too. To get this knot undone, he needed to remain calm. Judd looked down the Capital Road towards Vale Alturin. He half-expected Pet and Candice to come riding back at any moment, apologizing profusely for their bad judgment, but alas, they never came.

"This is for the best..."

Candice's parting words to him echoed through his mind. Whose best? Hers? His? Pet's? Fine! They were going to have it their way. He would eventually get this knot undone and go home. He would return to his fishing and pretend this had never happened. If he ever saw Pet or Candice again, he would not look at them. He would not even say a word. He would just keep walking by.

No. No. No. He could not do that. Judd shook that thought out of his mind. He had promised to protect Pet. Once he got this darn knot undone, he would head towards the palace. He had at least to try to catch up with them or how could he look himself in the eye again?

Judd had just bent down to work on the knot for the umpteenth time when, from the corner of his eye, he noticed a flash of movement. He dropped the rope and looked down the road. Was that them? Unfortunately not. It was coming from the direction of Seacrest. Oh well, Judd mused, hopefully whoever it is will be able to cut me free.

It was a cloaked rider on a horse. The tense look of the man's body and the way he repeatedly kicked his horse's flanks gave the distinct impression that this Cloaked Man was a man on a mission. He was riding very fast. A vague hope swept through Judd. If this man would give Judd a lift, he would be able to catch up with Pet and Candice in no time.

Contemplating the possibility of catching up with the others, Judd overlooked one odd fact. As hard as this Cloaked Man was riding his horse, there was no sound of galloping.

Judd waved the man down. The Cloaked Man slowed down. As he got closer, Judd was taken aback by his forbidding presence. Without greeting or introduction, the Cloaked Man asked, "Pet Peasant. You know her?"

"She's a friend of mine." Judd promptly corrected himself, "She was. How do you know her?"

"I have to find her," the Cloaked Man responded as he dismounted his horse.

This sounded awfully important. "I wish I could help you, but they tied me to this tree and went on without me."

The Cloaked Man took a moment to regard Judd's current predicament. If he was surprised that Judd was tied to a tree, he did not let it show. Suddenly, with a speed that defied description, the Cloaked Man had an axe in his hand. Judd gulped.

The axe came down swiftly and severed the rope binding Judd. The Cloaked Man did not give Judd any time to express his gratitude. "How long ago?"

"This morning," Judd absent-mindedly responded as he flexed his newly-freed leg.

"What are you doing?" asked the Cloaked Man with his gravelly voice.

Judd was peering beneath the Cloaked Man's hood. "I'm just trying to remember your face. Next time you come to Seacrest, I'll give you a bucket of fish on the house."

"That's unfortunate."

It was not one particular thing that caused Judd's blood to freeze. Perhaps it was a combination of the gravelly voice, cruel smirk and big axe. In the end, it did not matter. It only mattered that Judd suddenly had a feeling that his very life was in danger.

Judd glanced at the bushes. Pet had stashed his sword there. Now that he was free, he could reach it. Without warning, Judd launched himself towards the bushes. If he was quick enough, he could get to his sword before the Cloaked Man knew what was going on.

The Cloaked Man was quicker. He grabbed Judd by the arm with a vice-like grip. Then, with a strength that eclipsed Judd's own, he slammed Judd against the tree.

When Judd's senses returned, he found the Cloaked Man pinning him against the tree and an axe blade pressing against his neck. Judd's eyes widened. Was this it? Was he going to die here?

The Cloaked Man whispered, "I can't allow witnesses. It's nothing personal." And with that the Cloaked Man stepped back and swung the blade into Judd's chest. Not that Judd was aware of his. All he really felt was an enormous force penetrating his chest, accompanied by a cacophony of cracking bones. The boy buckled to his knees. The Cloaked Man pulled his axe away and Judd brought his hands up to his fresh wound. His fingers instantly became slick with his own blood.

With that, the Cloaked Man mounted his horse and rode away towards Vale Alturin, towards Pet.

Judd did not even notice him leave. His vision blurred. There was a high pitched buzzing in his ear and a terrible taste in his mouth. He crumpled to the ground, his arms wrapped around his bloodied chest. Everything throbbed.

As the blood flowed from his body, Judd felt guilty about the stain it was undoubtedly leaving on the ground. What an odd thing to worry about, he mused. This was certainly not how he had envisioned his death. He had always supposed he would die in bed an old man surrounded by his children and grandchildren. Judd certainly did not expect to die alone here in the woods, so very far from his beloved sea.

The darkness was coming. Judd could not be sure if it was the day passing into evening or death finally coming to claim him. It mattered little to him. This was it. He was ready for it.

Judd's struggles came to an end. His eyes went hollow and empty. He hoped Pet and Candice would be okay.

CHAPTER SIXTEEN

Plates were cleared and the cups cleaned. Pet had initially planned to talk to Candice over dinner, but it never happened. There was a glance here or there, but nothing resembling actual communication. And now the meal was over. Perhaps sometime tomorrow Pet could try again?

That was not enough for Mrs Kettlepot. She had endured an entire day of quiet and decided that now was as good as any for some idle chit-chat, "I bet you're all wondering why my horse is called Hubby."

Pet had not given the matter much thought. Horses (and boats too for that matter) had a whole array of strange and silly names. It was as if each owner was trying to be slightly cleverer than the last. "Let me guess. Your late husband gave it to you."

"Why yes. How did you figure that out? You're a very clever girl." It was hard for Pet to believe that Mrs Kettlepot was the same woman who had given her such sage advice that very afternoon.

Mrs Kettlepot leaned back and waited for the conversation to start flowing. She had broken the ice; certainly the others had something they wanted to share. Mrs Kettlepot waited and waited, but nothing came.

Apparently they needed more prompting, "I just thought of a funny story. Do you girls want to hear it?"

She did not wait for a response, "Once upon a time there were two songbirds. They were the very best of friends. One day the songbirds got into a fight. I can't remember what the fight was about, and if you asked either songbird, they wouldn't be able to remember either."

Pet rolled her eyes. Did Mrs Kettlepot think she was fooling anybody?

"Regardless of the fact that they couldn't remember what the fight was about, the two songbirds still refused to talk to each other. They let all the resentment they felt brew up inside them. Pretty soon neither songbird could sing. After a while longer, they couldn't fly either.

"These two songbirds had lost the two things that had made them special, their beautiful song and their ability to fly."

There was a slight rustling in the leaves behind Mrs Kettlepot. She paid it little attention, "The ironic thing was that there was an easy enough solution. A simple conversation to clear the air between them, maybe with an apology or two would have cured everything. Both songbirds suspected this, but neither of them wanted to be the first to say anything.

"Each feared that if they said the slightest conciliatory thing, the other would simply rebuff them. A silly fear considering they had nothing to lose and everything to gain." Mrs Kettlepot gave Pet and Candice a knowing look. "There's a moral to that story."

Pet looked over at Candice. Mrs Kettlepot smiled broadly. This was going to work. The power of her story had managed to heal the rift between these girls.

"Not yet," murmured Candice with nary a glance at either of them. Abruptly, she stood up and walked over to her bedroll.

"Whatever," Pet muttered before calling it a night herself.

Mrs Kettlepot leaned back and shook her head. At least she had tried. That was the ultimate folly of age, she supposed, you could see where the young were going wrong, but lacked the power to correct their course.

"I thought it was an inspired story that should echo down through the ages."

Startled, Mrs Kettlepot threw her head from side to side. Where had that voice come from? Pet and Candice were both asleep.

"I love the way you enunciate your words," the voice cooed. "It's so delicate and full of passion. It's a shame that such wisdom is wasted on the young."

Just like that, it all clicked into place for Mrs Kettlepot. It should have been obvious from the start. Mrs Kettlepot hissed, "Go away. I'm still not going to kiss you."

"Though the thought of our lips pressing fills me with rapturous longing, such thoughts have to be put on hold. For now you must run away with me."

"There's no chance of that happening. How did you catch up with us anyway?"

"Did you really think I would let such an object of rapturous beauty as you just slip through my fingers? Also I am not restricted to roads like you."

Despite the flattery, Mrs Kettlepot's resolve remained strong. Of course, she liked to be called an 'object of rapturous beauty.' Iago might have been a toad, but he certainly had a way with words.

"I assure you that this is a matter of the utmost gravity, my love," Iago pressed her. "There is someone after you. A very dangerous someone."

This worried Mrs Kettlepot, This could be just a silly game on Iago's part, but she couldn't chance it. "Who's after us?"

"A dark arrow of a man riding a dark horse. He's coming straight to this location and he's riding very fast. He'll be here soon."

Mrs Kettlepot went to wake the others. They needed to hear this.

"Wait," Iago whispered. "This man will be upon you in mere moments. He must be an expert tracker to be able to find you here so quickly. If all three of you came with me, this man would undoubtedly be able to find us. Your only chance of survival is to come with me now, alone."

"You don't know me as well as you think. If you think that I would even entertain such a notion."

"Alas, I feared as much," Iago sighed with melancholy, before changing to a more commanding tone. "Come now!"

If only she was thirty years younger, "I can't."

"You don't understand. He's already here."

CHAPTER SEVENTEEN

Panicking eyes darted from side to side. Pet and Candice were still sleeping. The last embers of the fire crackled away. Mrs Kettlepot peered into the darkness beyond, but could not make anything out. She heard nothing other than the pop and fizzle of the fire. As far as she could tell, they were alone.

"What are you talking about, Iago? We're alone."

The toad did not respond. She was about to scold him and recount the story of the boy who cried wolf, when the words fell silent in her throat. The hair on the back of her neck stood on end and she turned slowly back to the campsite.

Then she saw him.

The Cloaked Man crouched above Pet. He brought his hand down to touch her dark hair. Pet was such a heavy sleeper that she did not even notice.

Without thinking, Mrs Kettlepot grabbed one of the spluttering logs from the fire. The heat seared the flesh of her palm, but she did not feel the pain. She lobbed the log at the Cloaked Man, "Get away from her!"

The Cloaked Man turned to face Mrs Kettlepot. He said nothing as he put one hand beneath his cloak and pulled out his axe. It collided with the lobbed log, splintering it into toothpicks and spluttering sparks everywhere.

Mrs Kettlepot instinctively threw a second log which in turn was again struck away. This time Pet woke up. She lazily pried her eyes open to find a large Cloaked Man above her. With a gasp, she tried to roll away.

Unfortunately, the Cloaked Man brought his foot down on her stomach hard, knocking the breath right out of her. As Pet squirmed, Mrs Kettlepot continued to throw log after log at the Cloaked Man, while he continued to bat them away with his axe.

Mrs Kettlepot realized that her strategy was not working, but could not think of any other way to distract him. It did not help that her supply of logs was running dangerously low.

"What in the realm's name is going on here?" asked Candice as she ran up to Mrs Kettlepot. "Who is this man? Why are you throwing logs at him?"

"He's trying to kill Pet!" declared Mrs Kettlepot before lobbing another log at the Cloaked Man.

Candice instantly grabbed the cast-iron kettle sitting next to the fire and threw it at him. She would be damned if she let someone else kill Pet first.

The Cloaked Man swung his axe around and managed to swipe the log away, but was in no position to block the kettle. It smacked hard into his forehead, snapping his head back. Pet tried to take advantage of the Cloaked Man's disorientation to shove his leg off her.

It did not work. The Cloaked Man reached down and pressed the blade of his axe against Pet's neck. Candice and Mrs Kettlepot froze. The message was clear. Pet tried to crane her neck so that she could make eye-contact with the Cloaked Man, "What do you want with us?"

His dark eyes narrowed on Pet. "I only want you."

In hindsight, Pet wished that she had written down her thoughts on Tax Law 106. "Fine. Kill me and let the others go."

"I need you alive." His revelation only slightly relieved Pet.

"How much?" asked a meek voice. It belonged to Candice. "How much would it cost for you to walk away and forget you ever saw us?"

The Cloaked Man paused. "How much do you have?"

"Five hundred gold pieces." In reality, she had seven hundred, but she thought leaving herself some room for negotiation was not a bad thing.

"I'm being paid ten times that."

The next words out of the Cloaked Man's mouth were certainly not what Pet expected. "What's that smell? Is it bleach?"

"I don't know what you're talking about," Pet responded.

The Cloaked Man continued to sniff the air and wove his head around trying to trace the smell back to the source. Candice gulped as the Cloaked Man's eyes locked in on her. "Not a natural blonde beauty, are we?"

Candice was so terrified that she could not speak. All she could do was shake her head.

"What's your natural hair colour?" the Cloaked Man pressed.

Beads of sweat dribbled down Candice's face. Pet wanted to tell this Cloaked Man to back off, but was afraid what he would do in response.

"Black," Candice responded.

"You come with me too!" The Cloaked Man beckoned Candice to come over to him.

What was this guy's game? What did having black hair have to do with anything? Did he have some sort of fetish for raven-haired maidens? Either way Pet did not like where this was going.

The Cloaked Man pulled Pet up stiffly by the collar, "Get up. The old lady lives on one condition; neither of you cause any trouble on the ride to the palace."

"We'll be good," Pet conceded.

However, Mrs Kettlepot had other ideas.

CHAPTER EIGHTEEN

Predictably, Mrs Kettlepot had her own objections to this preposterous arrangement. Was she supposed just to sit back and allow Pet and Candice to run off with the Cloaked Man, all in the name of protecting her life? That was certainly not going to happen.

Pet cooed, "Come, Candice. We need to go now."

Candice was terrified out of her mind. She certainly did not want to go off with the Cloaked Man, but felt compelled to. Mrs Kettlepot's life hung in the balance. Candice took a hesitant step forward.

Mrs Kettlepot grabbed Candice's arm and tugged her back.

Pet's eyes flashed at Mrs Kettlepot, "What do you think you're doing?"

Mrs Kettlepot still had one last piece of firewood in her hand. She gripped its hot bark tightly, "The right thing."

In a swift movement, Mrs Kettlepot raised her last log like a club and charged at the Cloaked Man. Sure he still had his axe pressed up to Pet's neck, but he had said himself that he needed Pet alive. Still it was a bit of a gamble. The Cloaked Man could slice Pet's neck open at any moment.

Luckily, the gambit paid off. The Cloaked Man shoved Pet to the ground and swung his axe around. Mrs Kettlepot was not the quickest opponent he had ever faced. He had plenty of time to orient his position and plan his strike. It would take only one clean stroke to decapitate this old nuisance.

A familiar voice boomed from within the woods. "Craven foe, you crept up on my fair maiden in the middle of the night. You attack her with an axe. You threaten her life. You have incurred the righteous fury of Iago Von Klein the Third!"

There was a blur of green motion as Iago leapt out of the bushes arching towards the Cloaked Man's face. The Cloaked

Man had no time to react, and before he knew it, a rather large toad was attached to his face, knocking him backwards.

The Cloaked Man stumbled backwards till he ended up against a tree. Falling to one knee, he dropped his axe and brought both hands up in an effort to pry Iago off. However, the toad held on with all his strength as he tried to crush the Cloaked Man's face was his powerful legs.

Mrs Kettlepot grabbed Pet and helped her scamper away. Pet went straight for her bed roll and thrust her hand in amongst the soft folds.

"Are you hurt?" asked Candice as she ran over to check on Pet.

"Only my pride," declared Pet as she whirled around with her sword raised. She was now ready to assist Iago as necessary.

Then, without warning, the Cloaked Man dropped his hands away from the toad on his face. He twisted his body around and grabbed the trunk of the tree. His hands gripped the bark as he threw his face against the trunk with tremendous force. Pet winced as she watched the brutal display. Poor Iago bore most of the brunt of the blow and his body convulsed. His legs released their grasp on the Cloaked Man's face and his body fell limply to the ground.

"Iago!" cried Mrs Kettlepot.

"Enough is enough!" screamed the Cloaked Man. His hood had fallen back revealing a crimson face with crazed eyes, "Contract be damned! I'm going to kill you all!"

His hand fumbled on the ground looking for his axe.

"Looking for this?" asked Mrs Kettlepot. She had picked up the Cloaked Man's axe when she helped Pet escape.

The Cloaked Man threw back his cloak. Candice gasped. Mrs Kettlepot gulped. Pet swore. Tied to the inside of his cloak were at least a dozen additional axes. The Cloaked Man was soon brandishing two new axes in his hands.

"On the ground!" shouted Pet.

All three fell to the ground just as the first two axes whizzed through the air.

"Roll!" commanded Pet. "Just keep moving."

Mrs Kettlepot tried to move, but found she could not get very far because the end of her dress was nailed into the ground by one of the axes. With a jerk, she tore the fabric and rolled away.

Thankfully she rolled when she did, because the moment Mrs Kettlepot moved, an axe sliced into the ground where she had been. Scrambling behind a tree, she braced herself as she rose to her feet. The trunk provided some measure of protection, but she could not see how the others were faring.

Mrs Kettlepot poked her head around the tree. She was dismayed by what she found. Candice had managed to find cover behind a tree at the other end of the clearing, while Pet hugged the ground behind a log in the middle of it. The Cloaked Man was hurling axes at the two girls. Each additional axe splintered a part of their respective cover.

Those girls were about to die right before her eyes, unless she did something about it.

A plan flashed through Mrs Kettlepot's mind and she boldly stepped out from behind the tree. "Here I am. Do you think you can hit me?"

The Cloaked Man held one axe high in the air and aimed at Mrs Kettlepot.

"What are you doing?" screamed Pet.

The Cloaked Man released his axe and it came spiraling towards Mrs Kettlepot's head. In that second, she suddenly wished she had spent a little more time thinking about her plan.

"Get down!" yelled Pet as she darted across the clearing and tackled Mrs Kettlepot's kneecaps.

As Mrs Kettlepot fell backwards, her head tilted back. The axe continued its deadly velocity right over her face. The tip of her chin was slightly grazed by the axe's blade.

The old lady crashed into the ground as the Cloaked Man once again took aim and released another axe at the prone Mrs Kettlepot. Pet swung her sword, knocking this axe out of the air. She rolled to her feet and brandished her sword at the Cloaked Man. "I've had just about enough of this," she exclaimed.

"What are you doing?" cried Mrs Kettlepot. "He'll kill you."

"I'm sure he'll try," Pet responded. She hoped that her confident-sounding voice did not betray her inner anxiety.

The Cloaked Man chuckled. "I hope you put up a better fight than your tied-up boyfriend."

Boyfriend? What was he talking about? Then all colour drained from Pet's face, "Are you talking about Judd? Is Judd dead?"

The Cloaked Man threw his axe. Pet's mind came alive and she swiped her sword, deflecting the axe. A calm fell over Pet. The Cloaked Man was trying to put her off her game. Judd might be dead. That was terrible, but if she did not keep her wits together he would soon have some company. Pet took another step towards the Cloaked Man, "Why do you do this?"

The Cloaked Man ignored the question and threw another two axes.

Pet knocked those away as well, "Was your mommy mean to you growing up? Is that why you find satisfaction in terrorizing women?" Two could play at psychological warfare.

The smile had disappeared from the Cloaked Man's face. He dropped his hands further into his cloak.

"Does it make you feel like a big man?"

It was at that point that the Cloaked Man's hands reappeared gripping the hilt of the biggest axe that Pet had ever seen. This battle-axe was almost as tall as her.

"How's this for big?" the Cloaked Man asked as he swung his battle-axe in the air. "I save this one only for special occasions."

"Knowing Pet," came a voice behind the Cloaked Man, "She's terribly flattered."

The Cloaked Man turned around and the cast-iron pot smacked into his face with all the might Candice could muster.

The Cloaked Man crumpled to the ground, dropping the battle-axe.

For a moment, nobody dared to breath. Had they done it? Had they defeated this monster? Candice gingerly prodded the Cloaked Man's body with her foot. No reaction. He was out cold. Pet could not help but smile broadly. They were going to do it. They were going to live through the night.

CHAPTER NINETEEN

Promptly, Pet tied the Cloaked Man to the tree. She used twice as many Seacrest Specials as she had with Judd. As she worked, Pet examined the Cloaked Man's unconscious face. It was odd. In this state, he looked so ordinary. What could turn a man like this into such a cold-blooded killer? Despite all her bravado, there was still so much she did not understand about people.

Off to the side, Mrs Kettlepot cared for the slightly broken Iago. He had regained consciousness, but was sore all over. One leg in particular was twisted in an unnatural fashion. Admittedly, Mrs Kettlepot was not a specialist in amphibian physiology, but she did her best to care for the injury. Meanwhile, Candice introduced herself to the groggy man-toad. She wanted to thank him for his daring antics.

Mrs Kettlepot cooed to Iago, "You were so very brave."

"I would brave any danger for the sake of my love," responded Iago. Mrs Kettlepot blushed like a schoolgirl. Candice took this as her cue to leave.

"You certainly deserve that kiss now," Mrs Kettlepot brought her lips down towards Iago. She did not think that Pet would mind terribly if she restored Iago to his human form. He had risked his life for them and deserved some sort of reward.

"No, my love. Not now."

Mrs Kettlepot jerked her lips away. "What's the matter?"

"The spell. If I transfer back to human form with a broken toad leg, the magic might not align my human form properly. I might end up mutilated."

The explanation made sense, but Mrs Kettlepot was still disappointed. She actually wanted to kiss Iago Von Klein the Third, despite his toad form. It was kind of thrilling how he was able to make her so ambivalent to his species.

With a broad smile, she picked up Iago and cradled him in her arms. "Until your leg gets better, I will just have to take the very best care of you."

"I have no objections to that," murmured Iago as he fell into a weary slumber in the warm comfort of Kettlepot's arms.

Across the clearing, Pet patted down the slumped form of the Cloaked Man. She found a heavy purse which she promptly pocketed. As Candice walked up, Pet inquired, "How's the toad doing?"

"Just a broken leg, as far as I can tell. We fared much better than… "

Candice could not bring herself to say his name

"We don't know for certain that the Cloaked Man was telling the truth." Pet was grasping at straws and she knew it, but what was the alternative? … Admitting Judd was dead because Pet had left him tied up beside the road?

Pet looked over at Candice to see what she was thinking. Pet was shocked to see Candice picking up one of the Cloaked Man's axes.

"What are you doing?"

The voice that came out of Candice's mouth seemed so distant that Pet at first thought that a stranger had answered. "I'm going to kill him."

"We can't do that," spluttered Pet.

The same cold distant voice responded, "This man killed Judd. He deserves to die."

When had everything gone upside down? A stranger had assaulted them in the dead of night. Judd was dead. Candice wanted to play the part of executioner. But no matter how topsy-turvy everything seemed, Pet knew that this was not a solution.

"Don't do this."

"What do you intend to do with him, then?"

"I imagine we leave him tied up here. We then go to the nearest town and report to the Regional Guard what happened. They will come back and arrest him."

"What if some unsuspecting travelers come along," Candice hypothesized, "and he convinces them to release him? He would kill them and then come after us again. This time he'd be better prepared and he would probably succeed in killing all of us."

"If you execute him in cold blood," Pet stared deeply into her friend's eyes, "you will never forgive yourself. Let the Regional Guard put him on trial. Let them decide his fate."

Candice shrugged, "I could live with it, for I'd be safe in the knowledge that this monster was never going to terrorize anyone else again."

"I won't let you do that, Candice."

Candice parted her lips as if to say something, but no words could escape. Tears welled up in the corner of her eyes. She could no longer hold it in. Grief overtook the poor girl. The time for words was over.

Pet hugged her best friend. Candice began to cry and cry. Between sniffles and sobs, she was trying to say something, but the only words that Pet could make out were, "Why Judd?"

The immediate course of action became obvious to Pet. She barked at Mrs Kettlepot, "We leave now. Pack up everything you can."

As they departed, Pet could not help but think how unfair it all was. Judd was gone and the Cloaked Man was going to live. It occurred to Pet that maybe her desire to let the Cloaked Man live was in some ways a very selfish one. She simply could not bear to have any more blood on her hands.

CHAPTER TWENTY

Preliminary rays of the morning light washed over Pet. She closed her eyes and welcomed the dawn. She hoped the fresh light would provide some sort of relief for her tired body and her racing mind. Taking in the crisp morning air, Pet waited for the relief to kick in, but it never came.

Since the Cloaked Man's attack, they had been riding through the night without stop. They wanted to put as much distance between themselves and the Cloaked Man as possible. The plan was a simple one. Frontier Keep was only a few hours away. They would report what had happened to the Regional Guard there and then figure out their next move. By all accounts Frontier Keep was one of the safest places in the realm, second only to the Sapphire Palace.

Pet brought her hand up to shade her face from the bright morning sun and peered into the distance. Frontier Keep in all its walled glory sat on the horizon. It looked so sturdy and safe.

"In less than two hours we'll be in Frontier Keep," Pet declared to the others. "We can rest there."

Nobody responded. They were all drained, physically and emotionally. Well at least Candice and Mrs Kettlepot were. The newest member of their party, Iago, actually seemed quite comfortable cradled in Mrs Kettlepot's arms.

Pet already knew how she was going to spend the two hours. For the umpteenth time, she was going to go over what had happened with the Cloaked Man and try to figure out some semblance of a reason why he had done what he did.

This had not been a random attack. Pet had been specifically targeted. Someone had paid a large amount of gold for him to kidnap her. Why? What was so special about her? Apparently her hair had something to do with this mystery, but many people had dark hair. There simply were not that many in

Seacrest. Perhaps the dark hair thing was just a means of identifying her. Maybe it was more to do with who Pet was.

Could somebody consider her a threat? Were her proposed changes to Tax Law 106 going to uncover some sort of conspiracy? Pet's mind raced through the list of people who knew about her interest in Tax Law 106. Candice. Judd. Mrs Kettlepot. Her parents. Magistrate North... Could Magistrate North have hired the Cloaked Man to attack her?

That notion was laughable. The Magistrate could not tear himself away from his bean collection long enough to talk to his own son, let alone hire a mercenary. Anyway who would care enough about an obscure tax law to go to such desperate measures?

The Cloaked Man had mentioned something about taking them to the Sapphire Palace. Who was in the palace? Well, the high regent for starters. Iago disliked her, but the idea that the high regent had hired the Cloaked Man to prevent Pet from proposing her changes to Tax Law 106 was even more ludicrous than thinking that Magistrate North was behind it. Evella would not need to go to such ludicrous extremes. All she had to do was say, 'No.'

Still Pet was in danger and anybody travelling with her was in danger too. Judd's unfortunate fate was proof enough of that. Poor poor Judd... Pet imagined his sprawled body lying there ravaged and undignified. Judd Duncanson had deserved better, in both life and death.

Pet glanced over at Candice, Mrs Kettlepot and Iago. Nobody else was going to die on account of her.

The remaining ride to Frontier Keep passed quickly. It was an easy matter to gain access to the keep and once behind its tall walls, Pet finally felt she could breathe easily for the first time that day. They were safe now, if only for the moment.

CHAPTER TWENTY-ONE

Precise directions were always appreciated by Pet. The guard on duty had told them exactly where to find the best inn in town. Candice and Iago went in to secure some rooms, while Pet and Mrs Kettlepot went to make their report at the Royal Guard Station.

Mrs Kettlepot worried that the station might not be open yet. Pet decided to knock on the door anyway. It did not hurt to check if anyone was home.

The door swung open and there stood perhaps the most attractive boy that Pet had ever laid eyes on. His brown hair was short but unruly and a single sultry curl dangled down over his left eye... oh and those eyes. They were the most unusual shade of silver. It was if they could see right into Pet's soul and burn all her troubles away. She was so taken aback, Pet scarcely heard it when he asked, "Can I help you?"

With no response forthcoming from Pet, Mrs Kettlepot stepped up, "We're here to see the Regional Guardsman. We have to report a crime."

"You've come to the right place," said the-most-attractive-boy-ever as he ushered the two ladies into an office. He sat behind the large desk and gestured to them to sit down. "I'm Dashing."

"You certainly are," mumbled Pet.

"No, you misunderstand. My name is Guardsman Dashing."

The blue of Dashing's uniform really brought out the silver in his eyes. Guardsmen really did look better in blue rather than in that depressing purple Sentry always wore.

"You can't be a guardsman," cried Mrs Kettlepot, "You're far too young."

Mrs Kettlepot had a point. He did not look a day over seventeen.

"I may be young, but let me assure that I am sufficiently qualified to serve as the Royal Guardsman for Frontier Keep. Now what was this crime you wanted to report?"

Mrs Kettlepot explained how they were on a political mission of great importance and reported the events of the prior night. Perhaps she lauded Iago's cunning and bravery a bit too much, but apart from that it was a pretty accurate recounting of their ordeal.

After Mrs Kettlepot concluded, Dashing's brow furrowed, "So you believe that this Judd Duncanson has been murdered by this... Cloaked Man?"

"Exactly," nodded Mrs Kettlepot.

"But you didn't witness this murder?"

Mrs Kettlepot nodded again. Pet felt a bit uneasy about the tone Dashing employed.

"And this Iago Von Klein the Third you mention...." Dashing hesitated for a moment to find the right words. "He's a frog?"

"A toad," corrected Mrs Kettlepot, "and a very becoming one at that."

Pet could see where this was going. "Wait a moment. You do believe us don't you?"

Dashing smirked again. This time, Pet's heart did not swoon, in fact she found that condescending smirk quite ugly.

"Your story has elements which are frankly unbelievable. I have better things to do than chase around after your illusions."

"You think that we just made this up? Why would anybody do that? Just to get the attention of an incredibly attractive boy? Don't be so full of yourself." In hindsight, Pet wished she had not included that part about him being incredibly attractive. It did not underscore her point particularly well. "This is actually your fault. That we were attacked so brazenly in your jurisdiction makes it clear that you're not doing your job well."

Dashing's handsome face scowled. "Wait just one second. That's not fair..."

"If fair had anything to do with it, we would not have been attacked..."

...and Judd would still be alive.

"As we speak, there's an evil dangerous man tied to a tree," Pet stared pointedly at Dashing. His good looks were not going to spare him from her rancour. "We told you where you can find him. If you choose not to go arrest him, any further blood he sheds will be solely on your hands."

And with that, they left. Once outside, Pet turned and asked Mrs Kettlepot, "Can you believe that he didn't believe us?"

"It was very rude," Mrs Kettlepot glumly observed. "It's a shame, though. He's very handsome, isn't he?"

Pet did not say a word. The last thing she wanted to do was dwell on how good-looking Dashing was. He might be incredibly handsome, but he was also incredibly frustrating.

CHAPTER TWENTY-TWO

Picturesque, clean and comfortable. The inn certainly ticked all of Pet's boxes. It even had a small stable which put up their horses for a nominal fee. The room rate was a bit pricier than Pet would have expected, but they could afford it. After all, they also had the Cloaked Man's gold now. Pet had paid for two rooms with the ill-gotten coinage and did not feel the slightest twinge of guilt doing so.

It was worth the extra expense to give Mrs Kettlepot and Iago each their own room. This would give Pet and Candice time to talk privately. Unfortunately, Candice was not in a talkative mood. Fair enough. It had been a very long night and nobody had had enough sleep. Some rest would do them all a world of good. Pet lay down on her bunk and closed her eyes. Sleep quickly consumed her.

It was late afternoon by the time Pet woke up. She had not meant to sleep quite that long, but she had to admit, it certainly felt good. Pet stretched her body and looked over at Candice's bunk. It was empty.

Pet went downstairs to the lobby and found the innkeeper, "Excuse me, have you seen my travelling companion?"

"She's out back," responded the innkeeper. "Are you going to be staying a while in Frontier Keep?"

"We're just stopping off," Pet informed him. "We are on our way to the Sapphire Palace."

"The Sapphire Palace? Why would you want to go there?"

"I'm going to protest against a tax law."

The innkeeper nodded in approval. "Good for you. That high regent is just gouging us all with taxes these days. It's shameful. The realm needs more people like you willing to stand up to her."

That was certainly a nice change. It was not often that people appreciated Pet's efforts. She thanked the man and went in search of Candice with a little extra bounce in her step.

The moment she stepped outside, Pet was taken aback by what she found. There was her best friend, the kind and gentle Candice Butler, brandishing an axe. With a mighty swing, Candice threw the axe at a nearby tree. The axe smacked into the tree and its blade sunk deep into its bark.

"What are you doing with the axe?" Pet asked casually as if it was no big deal that Candice had suddenly turned into a deadly axe-thrower.

Candice walked over and tugged the axe out of the tree. "I thought I should learn to protect myself."

"Are you sure you're okay? You never struck me as the axe- throwing type."

"I'm doing better now," Candice said as she threw the axe again. "This is therapeutic. It's made me realize a few things."

Candice did seem a lot more relaxed. The difference between this Candice and the listless Candice who had gone to bed was like night and day. It was almost like having the familiar happy Candice back, except now with an axe.

"For the longest time, I thought people were inherently good," explained Candice. "Even the dirtiest, rottenest scoundrel; if you peered down hard enough, you would see that there was a kernel of goodness inside them. At least that's what I believed."

She took a brief pause to throw her axe again. "But with that Cloaked Man, as much as I tried, I couldn't find the slightest hint of anything good or nice. All I saw was evil. Pure and simple evil." At this point, Candice let out a sour laugh. Pet felt a very slight chill run down her spine. "I was so naïve. That man was evil and I know he's not the only one. The world is a dangerous place. It's as simple as that. I've got to learn to be more realistic about things. Not every story ends with happily ever after."

Candice threw the axe again. Pet really wished she would stop throwing that stupid axe at that stupid tree. "I've decided to become more like you. I'll learn to defend myself. I won't take crap from people. I won't be silly and sentimental. I won't be scared any more."

Is that really how Candice saw her? As some sort of heartless warrior? Then it hit Pet. This was all about something much simpler.

"I was scared too," admitted Pet.

The axe came to a sudden stop mid-swing. Candice dropped her arm and turned away from Pet. "No you weren't."

"You think I wasn't scared? I was terrified."

"But you were so brave," protested Candice, "the way you tried to talk him out of it."

Pet was not following Candice's logic, "But you were the one who knocked him out. You weren't too scared to do that."

"But do you know what I was thinking? I was repeating over and over how I didn't want to die, how I didn't want to end up like Judd." Tears began flowing freely from Candice's eyes. "And when it was over and the Cloaked Man was defeated, I was so ashamed and angry, I wanted to make him pay. That's why I wanted to kill him. It had nothing to do with Judd. I was being so selfish. You were right to stop me…"

Pet put an arm on Candice's shoulder. She flinched slightly at the unexpected touch. "I think you're one of the bravest people I know."   Candice was about to object, but Pet would not allow it.

"You are so willing to love people. If somebody disappoints you, you don't give up on them. You let them have as many chances as they need to get it right. That isn't easy. It takes guts to have that much faith in people."

"Judd's still dead," observed Candice. "He's dead because of what we did."

"No, he's dead because of what the Cloaked Man did. The Cloaked Man is the one who killed him." Pet hoped that sounded convincing even though she did not quite believe it herself. If anyone should shoulder the blame for leaving Judd in the woods, it should be Pet.

The two friends sat there holding each other for a while. They deserved this moment of calm. However, Pet was about to ruin it.   "What's this about you dying your hair blonde?"

"You didn't know? I had black hair until the second grade. I'm surprised you don't remember."

Pet's memories of elementary school were hazy at best. "Why did you do it?"

"According to my mother, I came home from school one day and insisted that I dye my hair blonde so I could be like the other girls. I was never as happy being different as you were Pet." Candice took a strand of her hair and twirled it around her finger. "Now I just like it like this. It's part of who I am."

Pet ran her fingers through her own black hair. It was a tell-tale sign to anyone who met her that she was not born in Seacrest. It had not always been easy, but finding out now that there was someone else with black hair this entire time and Pet had not known about it!... It would have been nice to know earlier than this that she was not alone.

"That's fine, I guess. I'm just wondering if there's anything else you haven't told me."

Candice looked away. "We still have a lot to do. Somebody has to tell Judd's parents. We have to make sure he's properly buried."

"I know, but let's start dealing with all that tomorrow."

Pet winced. It felt dishonest to keep a secret from Candice. The secret was that Pet did indeed have a plan. It was for the best. Hopefully, Candice would one day forgive her for it.

CHAPTER TWENTY-THREE

Predicaments were expected in the Cloaked Man's line of work, but nothing had prepared him for this. As consciousness slowly returned to him, the first thing that occurred to him was his inability to move.

His memories began to piece themselves together. The details were still a little vague, but now he remembered the two girls, the toad and the old woman. That one girl did have a sweet right hook. How long had he been out for? The Cloaked Man chuckled at the irony of it all, before he noticed that the chuckling caused his already sore face to burn with pain.

The Cloaked Man struggled against whatever bound him. They were ropes and they were tied tight. He had certainly under-estimated those women. When he was first offered this contract, he was inclined to turn it down. Where was the challenge in kidnapping a dark-headed Seacrest girl? What had caused him to change his mind was the sheer amount of gold being offered for the job and the unusual source of the job.

He had never actually met his employer, nor had he expected to. Arrangements such as these were always handled through an easily disavowable intermediary. But the coinage? There was no denying that. It was royal coinage, straight from the mint and shiny as the day it was pressed. It was a handsome enough reward for what had initially seemed to be an easy job.

It was at that moment that the Cloaked Man heard the approaching footsteps. A smirk flashed across his face. There were two distinct footsteps coming towards him. He recognized one of them right off the bat. This game was suddenly about to get more interesting.

"Hello, dog," shouted out the Cloaked Man, "You're far from home."

Sentry stepped into the clearing with his purple cape flowing in tatters behind him, "Here I was thinking that I was going to have to defend the girls from you, but I should have realized that it was going to be the other way around."

"Untie me," commanded the Cloaked Man. "I am an emissary of the palace."

All whimsy vanished from Sentry's voice, "I saw what you did to the Duncanson boy. It was not very brave of you, striking down an unarmed boy."

"I had nothing to do with that."

"Funny. That's not what he says."

Out of the underbrush came Judd. His chest was covered in makeshift purple bandages and each step he took caused him to wince, but otherwise he was much more alive than the Cloaked Man would have expected.

The last time Judd had seen the Cloaked Man, he had tried to kill him. Despite changed circumstances, Judd's body shivered as their eyes met. His mind flashed back to the crackling sound as the axe plunged into his chest. If it had not been for Sentry coming upon him when he did, this Cloaked Man would have killed him.

Sentry put a warm hand on Judd's shoulder. He was going to take care of this, "Who sent you after Pet Peasant?"

There was a long pause before the Cloaked Man responded. During that time, all he did was peer at Sentry with examining eyes. When the Cloaked Man did respond, it was not to Sentry's question. "I thought there was something familiar about you. It is you, isn't it? What are you doing in Seacrest?"

"What is he talking about?" asked Judd, but Sentry did not say a word.

"I saw him once in his old life," the Cloaked Man continued. "I get it now."

Judd looked over at Sentry with questioning eyes. Judd had always trusted this man completely. The entire town held him in the highest regard, but how much did they really know about him? Sentry was a notoriously private man and never spoke of his life before coming to Seacrest. Perhaps there was much more to him than met the eye.

Sentry said to the boy, "Don't listen to him. He's trying to sow confusion. The only question you need to ask yourself is this: who do you trust more? Me or him?"

"You!" The answer came easily. Sentry had never left him to die by the side of the road.

Sentry unsheathed his sword and handed it to Judd, "Would you like the honour then? He wounded you worst of all."

"But the laws of the realm…" stuttered Judd. "They say he should get a fair trial before any punishment is carried out."

Judd knew that Sentry needed no education on the laws of the realm. After all, his life's purpose had been to enforce these laws… or so Judd had assumed up to now.

"A black-haired girl in Seacrest?" squawked the Cloaked Man. "But of course. It all makes sense now. Does she even know who she is?"

Judd knew that he should not pay the Cloaked Man any heed. He would say anything at this point to save himself from death, but still Judd felt himself compelled to ask, "What doesn't Pet know?"

"Ignore him!" commanded Sentry.

"You haven't figured it out for yourself yet? I guess you're a little young," laughed the Cloaked Man. "Your beloved Sentry has a secret. He's actually…"

The words never made it out of the Cloaked Man's throat. Instead Sentry slashed it. The Cloaked Man's eyes grew wide and dollops of blood poured out of his neck. Judd gulped as he watched the man spit and splutter. The Cloaked Man was dying and he realized it. The smirk had disappeared from his face and now he looked so afraid. Judd almost felt sorry for him.

For his part, Sentry remained cool and collected. He pulled back his sword and plunged it straight into the Cloaked Man's heart. In an instant, the dying man was dying no more. The execution was complete.

The body of the Cloaked Man hung limply against the ropes. Its head tilted strangely to one side and the eyes looked out at nothing at particular. Judd had never seen anybody die before.

"It is done." Sentry sheathed his sword. "Let us be on our way. We have to find the girls."

Still shell-shocked, Judd complied. He did not say a word as he got on the steed behind Sentry. He was still trying to process what he had just seen. Perhaps Sentry was justified in his slaying. The Cloaked Man was an evil man without mercy or compassion, but there was something else going on.

Sentry had a secret. That was fine. Lots of people had secrets. What was worrying was that Sentry was willing to kill in order to keep his.

CHAPTER TWENTY-FOUR

Potatoes were not Pet's favourite food, but they were filling. This gathering had little to do with the meal anyway. Pet took a last sip of her juice and looked at her companions. Mrs Kettlepot was breaking off pieces of bread to feed to Iago, while Candice finished her plate. For the most part they looked content. It was as if the assault of the Cloaked Man and Judd's murder had never happened. If only Pet herself could forget for just one moment.

She could not wait any longer. Pet blurted to the table, "Maybe we should call this off!"

A piece of stew fell indignantly from Candice's mouth. "You mean the trip to the palace?"

"It's not going well," Pet reasoned.

"That would be the understatement of the year," murmured Iago. He was swiftly slapped on the bottom by Mrs Kettlepot.

"What about Seacrest?" countered Mrs Kettlepot. "Tax Law 106 will drive the fishery industry under and bring economic devastation to the entire Southern Province. The stakes are too high just to give up."

It appeared that at least someone had been listening to all her tirades about Tax Law 106. Pet could not suppress a glum smile.

"I'm just saying it would be easy to go back. Just follow the Capital Road all the way back to Seacrest."

Candice's eyes narrowed on Pet. This was not how her best friend reacted to challenges. There was something else going on here.   "But we are going to keep going, right?"

"I guess you're right. I'll keep going." Pet did not like lying to her friends, so her response was technically truthful.

The four of them made their way upstairs and retired to bed. However, Pet did not sleep. She got under the covers, but just lay there, eyes wide open and listening. She was waiting for Candice to fall asleep. Pet dared not even roll over, lest she disturb Candice. After a while, the familiar sound of deep breathing filled the room. Candice was finally asleep. Now was the time for action.

Pet crept out of bed. She moved slowly; aware that some of the floorboards were creaky. In her slumber, Candice looked so happy and innocent. Pet could not see the fear, doubt and sadness that this journey had caused. Should she really do this? Would Candice ever forgive her for leaving her too?

Pet shook her head and reminded herself to remain resolute. This was nothing like when she had left Judd behind. Pet was doing this for Candice's own protection. Somebody was after Pet. If Candice and the others stayed with Pet, they would be putting themselves into danger. They would eventually understand. They would have to. This was the only way.

Without any further consideration, Pet scurried into the corridor and gingerly tiptoed towards the staircase. Soon she was in the dark dining-room. Moonlight gleamed through the windows, casting shadows across the room. Then a voice asked, "Where do you think you're going?"

Pet screamed.

"Calm down, child. You'll wake the entire building." The sound of a match striking was quickly followed by an illuminating gleam of fire. A grumpy looking Mrs Kettlepot lit the wick of a nearby candle and gave Pet a cross look.

Only then regaining her composure, Pet gasped, "Have you been waiting in the dark for me all night?"

"I prefer my tea in the dark." Mrs Kettlepot poured another cup of tea. "Why don't you sit and have a cup with me?"

Though Kettlepot's words had been formed as a suggestion, Pet knew they were not. She hesitantly took a seat and blew on her hot tea. "It's for the best you know."

"How so?"

"Too many people have been hurt. Judd is dead. Iago is wounded. Candice is all messed up. This trip has been a disaster."

"It hasn't been easy," agreed Mrs Kettlepot.

"But you were right at dinner. This mission is too important to just give up. It makes no sense endangering everyone. I can complete the mission on my own."

"Really?" Mrs Kettlepot replied. "If it weren't for us, you'd be the prisoner of the Cloaked Man right now. God knows where you would be then."

Pet took a sip of her tea. "It'll be harder for people like the Cloaked Man to track me if I'm on my own."

"Did you ever consider that this isn't all about you? This is too important to leave in just your hands. All of the Southern Province depends on you getting to the Sapphire Palace. The chances of you getting there are greater if we are with you."

"Do you really think Candice or Iago care about Tax Law 106?" replied Pet, "They are here because of us. Why should they put themselves in any more danger for a cause they don't even understand? I'm sorry. You won't make me change my mind."

Mrs Kettlepot had had enough of this. "Go ahead. Be a silly young girl. I can't help you with that. But if you can't see how we can help you, can you at least see how you can help us?"

"I don't follow," Pet admitted.

"Candice, your best friend in the whole word is mourning and your plan is to abandon her? Iago needs to learn what it means to be a responsible leader, that violence isn't the only solution to problems. Who's the best person to teach him that? And what about me?" Tears begin to brim in Mrs Kettlepot's eyes. "I was lost. I needed something to believe in... And I found it... Do you plan to just take that away from me?

"Give us a little credit," Mrs Kettlepot sniffed between the occasional dabbing of her eyes. "None of us want to abandon the mission. We all decided to join you on this mission knowing there would be some risks. Granted, we didn't expect the risks to be quite so dire, but we're all still here."

"Judd isn't."

"Listen to me. You don't have the luxury of wallowing in that guilt any longer. You have a mission to lead. You learn from your mistakes and don't repeat them."

An almost unheard of event was about to happen. Pet was on the verge of changing her mind, but first she had to make sure Mrs Kettlepot fully understood her plans. "Somebody sent the

Cloaked Man after me. I don't know who and I don't know why, but someone definitely wants to stop me. I wasn't planning to stick to the Capital Road. It's too obvious and if anyone else came after us, we'd be sitting ducks.

"Instead, I want to go directly through the Shadowoods. It will cut the travel time by at least a day and it will be harder for anybody to find us. I know that the Shadowoods is a dangerous place, but I don't see any other way. I also know that it's a huge risk. Are you ready to take that risk with me?"

"Yes."

Pet murmured, "Thank you."

They sat in the dining-room wordlessly, sipping on their now cool tea. It was a comfortable moment of quiet shared between friends. However, Pet could not help but feel that this was the quiet before the storm.

There was one last thing on Pet's mind. "The others must understand the risks of going through the Shadowoods."

"They'll understand," yawned Mrs Kettlepot. "We should go get some rest. Apparently, we have a very exciting day ahead of ourselves tomorrow."

CHAPTER TWENTY-FIVE

Positions like that of the First Guardsman were expected to involve a strong measure of discretion. Usually it was easy enough. Bribing some magistrate's mistress or blackmailing some overly critical voice rarely presented a challenge. This entire affair with the Lost Princess was another matter altogether.

The Cloaked Man had been instructed to send daily updates on his progress. The last message had been sent yesterday morning and had indicated that the Cloaked Man had arrived in Seacrest. The girl had left the town and was en route to the Sapphire Palace. The Cloaked Man had written of his intention to circle back and capture her. A day had passed and no subsequent message had arrived.

Isabob would ordinarily wait just a bit longer, but this was a matter of upmost importance. Accordingly, he reported this development to his boss right away. The boss was not pleased. Evidently, the Cloaked Man had failed. Fortunately, there was another option.

Isabob could not believe his ears. How could the boss consider sending such a monster after the Lost Princess?

Still, orders were orders and a guardsman always followed orders. Isabob chastised himself for his doubt. Nobody wanted a murderer free, but if such an action benefited the realm more than it hurt it, perhaps it was right.

Upon his arrival in the dungeon, a lone Junior Guardsman saluted Isabob. At least there would be only one witness to his shame.

"Take me to the Big Bad," ordered Isabob.

Isabob handed the Junior Guardsman the prisoner release form. The boy inspected the sheet of paper carefully. It contained all the appropriate approvals and specified that the Big Bad was to be released into the First Guardsman's custody. If the Junior Guardsman was at all surprised by Isabob's request, he had the wisdom to disguise it. Isabob took care to take the copy of the form back. He did not want a paper trail.

The Junior Guardsman brought Isabob to a large door. Isabob promptly gave the instruction, "Open it!"

In a voice cracking with anxiety, the Junior Guardsman inquired, "Are you sure? It eats everything that goes in there."

This boy was not helping.

"Just let me in."

The Junior Guardsman unfastened the multitude of locks on the door. People had gone to a lot of effort to ensure that whatever was behind that door was not getting out. The door creaked open and the first thing Isabob noticed was the moist air escaping, cascading over him. Then he heard the heaving. Something very big was breathing on him.

Isabob grabbed a torch from the wall and approached the open cell, "Lock the door behind me. Don't open it until you hear me ask you to."

The door slammed shut behind Isabob. The locks made a symphony of scraping metal. Isabob hoped this was not the last music he'd ever hear.

The cell was very dark. The torch did a little to illuminate the cell, but also served to cast large shadows amongst its many crevices. In one particularly dark corner, Isabob could make out a pair of bright yellow eyes.

"I take it that you're the Big Bad." There was a slight flicker of movement and Isabob prayed that the creature was not licking his lips. "Let me introduce myself. My name is…"

"I'm about to eat you," growled a voice from the darkness, "Unless you give me a good reason not to in the next five seconds."

In the bravest voice he could muster, Isabob responded, "I'm here to set you free."

A hearty fearsome laugh filled the cell. "Set me free? I'll never be set free. I've eaten over two hundred children."

As the creature slunk out of the shadows, Isabob looked at it carefully. For the most part, it looked like a wolf. It had the same yellow eyes, mangy fur and large teeth that one would expect from a wolf. What differentiated this creature from other wolves was its massive size.

"Circumstances have arisen that have forced certain interests to consider releasing you on early parole. Given certain conditions are met, of course."

"A catch?" chuckled the Big Bad. "I love it. What do I have to do?"

"Find a girl and bring her to me." Isabob tried to be as explicit on the next point as possible. "We need her alive."

The Big Bad quickly turned around. Isabob could not help but marvel at how quickly the creature could move despite its large frame. "Then you've come to the wrong monster. I eat little girls. I don't escort them to places."

"I disagree. You will find this girl and bring her to us because you will be given what you most desire in the world, your freedom." Isabob was a little pleased with how bold he was with this giant wolf. "Anyway, our reports indicate that this girl is travelling with some other children. You can eat them as you see fit."

It was hard to make out, given the Big Bad's lupine features, but it appeared to Isabob as though it was smiling. "I'll do it."

Isabob was pleased. Given the Big Bad's reputation, just the simple fact that Isabob still had all of his limbs was cause for celebration. However, the next item on the agenda might change that. Isabob pulled out a collar. "You will also be required to wear this."

"You must be joking. I am the Big Bad, the most feared predator of the realm and voted number one in a recent poll of people's worst nightmares. I do not wear collars," scoffed the Big Bad. "For my kind, a collar is an evil totem. Put a collar on us and we become pets. We become slaves. It's undignified. I should eat you where you stand for even suggesting it."

"Given your previous murderous rampages and your demonstrated inclination towards betraying everybody and everything, the interests I represent are not entirely certain they can rely simply on your word," Isabob explained. "This collar is our insurance policy. The collar is enchanted and once attached to your neck, it will gradually shrink. You probably won't notice anything till about the twelfth hour of wearing it. It might be a little uncomfortable at that point. From about the twentieth hour onward, it will become quite bothersome. From then on, you will be slowly suffocated and by the end of a day and a half, you will be dead."

"So you plan to release me," asked the Big Bad, "just so the collar can kill me?"

"If you find the girl and return her to us alive within thirty hours, I will remove the collar and let you be on your way," Isabob replied. "Do you think you're up to it?"

There was a mischievous glint in the eyes of the Big Bad. It might have been offended by the collar itself, but it was certainly drawn to the idea of how it slowly suffocated people to death. That was classy.

"You should also know that the collar has been modified to take into account your…" Isabob paused for a moment to gather the right words, "…unique abilities."

In the end, when it came down to choosing between rejecting the shame of wearing a collar and the possibility of freedom, the choice was clear. "I will comply," the Big Bad said.

Isabob pulled out an envelope containing several documents. "In here I've provided you with a description of the girl. She has dark hair…."

"Put those away!" The Big Bad shook its massive wolf's head. "I rely on one thing only when it comes to tracking prey… their scent. Do you have anything which belonged to this girl?"

"I do." Isabob removed a small folded piece of fabric from the envelope. It was a small pink blanket with a monogrammed P on it. "Will this be enough?"

The giant wolf pressed his large, moist nose into the fabric. He took a massive sniff, "Exquisite. She smells like turquoise wildflowers and cinnamon with a dash of petulance."

So, even a savage beast like the Big Bad could find poetry in the world, mused Isabob. Perhaps he was not such a monster after all. Then the Big Bad asked, "Can I eat her after you're done with her?"

Isabob promptly reverted to his initial opinion of the giant wolf.

As quickly as he could, Isabob attached the collar. Upon exiting the cell with the Big Bad, Isabob promptly turned over an hourglass. The thirty hours had begun and there was to be no tarrying. He explained to the Junior Guardsman that the Big Bad was to be released and that no mention should be made of this in the records. The boy nodded, but his eyes looked far from convinced.

Isabob escorted the Big Bad to the gate. No parting words were exchanged. The moment the gate opened, the Big Bad was off like a shot. As the monster ran off into the purple hue of the early morning, Isabob could not help but wonder what it took to be considered a monster.

CHAPTER TWENTY-SIX

Positive thoughts infused Pet's being. An hour ago, she had outlined her plan to go through the Shadowoods to Candice and Iago. Both of them had agreed to the risks without hesitation, just like Mrs Kettlepot. They had such faith in Pet. It was quite uplifting.

Candice was packing her gear onto Mucker. She looked up and briefly smiled at Pet before returning to her final preparations. It was nice to see Candice smile again. Mrs Kettlepot and Iago sat on Hubby patiently waiting for the others. Mrs Kettlepot shifted back in the saddle so that Iago could have the spot just in front of her.

Looking down, Pet checked that her scabbard was firmly in place. The sword was to be worn for at least the duration of the trip through the Shadowoods. Having her sword hidden away in her bedroll had not done much good against the Cloaked Man. Who knew what they might encounter in the Shadowoods?

Once Candice was ready, Pet swung herself onto Bounds. As they set off towards the gate, Pet took a moment to admire her companions. They might look like a motley lot, but Pet could not think of a braver, more loyal group of friends.

Just as they reached the East Gate, a familiar luscious voice called out, "Pet, may I have a word with you?"

Pet cursed her heart for swooning at the sound of Dashing's voice. Before turning around, Pet steeled herself. She knew that the chances of Dashing having become spontaneously ugly overnight were remote. "What do you want?"

"I'm surprised to see that you're leaving," replied Dashing's still handsome face.

"I did not think I was a prisoner here."

"Of course you're not. I wanted to apologize for the way I treated you yesterday. It was wrong of me to doubt your account

of what happened. I sent some men to investigate your claims…
It's just that, sometimes I speak before I think."

Pet knew that sensation all too well. "Apology accepted.
When will your men be back?"

"They should be back in a few hours. If you care to stick
around, we could grab some breakfast in the meanwhile."

Did he really just ask me out on a date, Pet wondered.

"Thanks, but no thanks. We're about to set off for the
Sapphire Palace." Pet was careful not to go into just how she was
planning to get to the palace. She imagined Dashing would have
quite a bit to say if she revealed her plan to travel through the
Shadowoods.

"Yes, for that tax appeal…," Dashing remembered. "I'll be
going to the palace myself tomorrow afternoon to make some
reports to the First Guardsman. Perhaps if you're still there, we
could meet up."

Meet up? Did that mean that he wanted to see her again?
Maybe he was just being polite or maybe he wants to follow-up
on her charges against the Cloaked Man. Either way the
possibility that this was not a final good-bye thrilled Pet.

"Pet," shouted out Iago, "We should get going."

Pet spun around, "I'm coming. Just wait!"

It then occurred to Pet that it had not perhaps been the most
ladylike reaction in the world. She turned back sheepishly to
explain to Dashing, but he was preoccupied with something else
entirely. He eyed Iago and asked, "Is that a talking toad?"

"Yes. Yes, it is."

There was a pregnant pause. Dashing and Pet just looked at
each other. There were people waiting for her. She couldn't just
sit there gawking at the-most-attractive-boy-ever all day. Pet
opened her mouth. She had to say something. Anything…

Luckily, Dashing beat her to the punch. "Sorry, I'm usually
better at this."

Pet was secretly delighted. That was the best reaction she
could have hoped for. He was just as nervous as she was. That
meant only one thing. Dashing liked her! The most-attractive-
boy-ever liked her! There was only one thing to do.

She had to get out of there as soon as possible.

"'Till next time!" Pet smiled as she rode off to join her companions. She was none too pleased to see the giant grins plastered on everyone's face.

"So that's Dashing!" observed Candice. "His name fits."

Pet did not dignify the observation with a response. She knew, if she did, she would open herself up to all sorts of questions that she did not feel like answering at that moment.

"Oh look, he's waving good-bye," noted Mrs Kettlepot, frantically throwing her arm in the air. Candice and Iago quickly joined in waving Dashing goodbye. Pet did not.

Instead Pet rolled her eyes. "Come on. Enough of this. Let's go."

The others sighed and turned around, heading towards the gate. Pet nonchalantly stayed at the rear of the party. When she was confident none of the others was looking, Pet turned to return Dashing's wave and gave him one last smile.

CHAPTER TWENTY-SEVEN

Prior to departing from Seacrest, Pet had promised her Ma that she would avoid the Shadowoods. Pet had not been lying when she made that pact. At the time, this was supposed to be just a simple trip to the Sapphire Palace. Circumstances had certainly changed. Pet hoped Ma would understand.

It had taken fewer than three hours to reach the edge of the Shadowoods. Pet called the group to a halt and looked towards them. From here, the Shadowoods did not appear nearly as forbidding as the name indicated. Actually, they were quite beautiful. The sky was bright and blue and the overhanging branches strained the sunlight, speckling the path with patches of sunshine.

"Mrs Kettlepot," asked Candice, "Why do they call it the Shadowoods anyway?"

"Oooooh. I don't think this is the best time for that story."

Pet always preferred knowledge over ignorance. "Tell us!"

"Several decades ago, before you were born, the realm was unified by Mart the Mighty. Back then these woods were known as the Songtrees because of the way the wind whistled through the trees making the most beautiful melodies. Unfortunately, Mart had been so busy nation-building that he never had time to have children, so when he died nobody knew who would be the next King. Two different claims were made on the throne. One was by Petros, Mart's cousin and the other by a mad sorcerer called Rile."

Pet listened attentively. The Great Unrest was considered the darkest moment in the realm's history.

"Petros's claim on the throne was considered more legitimate and had the support of the people. Rile didn't accept this and hoped to march on the palace and take it by force," continued Mrs Kettlepot. "However, he couldn't find anyone to join his army. Instead Rile turned to the gentle animals of the Songtrees. He used the darkest of magics to twist these poor animals into the darkest of monsters. With his army of twisted creatures, Rile lay siege on the palace."

Mrs Kettlepot gave Iago a brief glance. "My late husband was among the palace's defenders. He said the monsters he faced that day defied description."

Candice gulped.

"It was a fierce battle." Mrs Kettlepot's eyes turned sad. "Mr Kettlepot got his left foot bitten off by one of the creatures. He was one of the lucky ones. Hundreds of young men died that day. After a great deal of bloodshed, the guardsmen managed to defeat Rile and drive his creatures back to the woods, but that wasn't the end of it.

"The wind was too terrified of the twisted creatures that now lived amongst the trees, so it never came back and never whistled between the branches again." Mrs Kettlepot's face saddened. "Thus the Songtrees became the Shadowoods."

Pet turned to look at the Shadowoods again. The forest did not look so innocent anymore.

"Those dark and twisted beasts," piped up Candice, "What happened to them?"

"Why, they remained in the Shadowoods, dear," explained Mrs Kettlepot. "Why do you think no-one in their right mind ever comes in here?"

"Brilliant," mumbled Pet. And with that, Pet rode into the forest. Hesitantly, the others followed suit. Mrs Kettlepot's story did not change anything. They still had to cross the Shadowoods and that was that.

CHAPTER TWENTY-EIGHT

Packs of small cuddly kittens do not usually present much of a danger, but in the Shadowoods, this was not quite the case. Of course, one could not necessarily tell that at first glance. Candice squealed, "Oh look! A pack of cuddly kittens!"

"Careful!" warned Pet.

"We need to take them with us." Candice dismounted Mucker. "We can't just leave them behind. Some monster might eat them."

When Mrs Kettlepot saw Candice approaching the cats, she cried, "Wait! Those aren't ordinary cuddly kittens. They're murder-kittens."

It was just then that the first murder-kitten lunged for Candice's throat with a mouth full of large fangs. Candice barely managed to knock the bloodthirsty cat away in time. Then the remaining murder-kittens stalked towards her, hissing an unholy hiss. Candice scampered away as quickly as she could. As soon as she was back atop Mucker, the group quickly rode off.

Luckily, the next few hours bore no further encounters with the dark and evil monsters of the Shadowoods. Pet was beginning to feel fortunate. If murder-kittens were the worst they were going to have to face in the Shadowoods, that would be fine by her.

Then as the group was approaching the River Finch, Iago asked, "What is that thing on the bridge?"

Words failed Pet. The creature looked like somebody had taken the most dangerous parts from different animals and sewed them together. It had a lion's head, a serpent's tongue and a scorpion's tail.

"That is a manticore," Mrs Kettlepot identified it easily. "They served as the main cavalry in Rile's army. Their keen sense of smell makes them fantastic hunters. They are renowned for their fiercely territorial tendencies and taste for human flesh."

The only consolation in this situation was that the manticore appeared to be sleeping. However, its massive frame blocked most of the bridge. To make matters worse, the bridge itself looked rather tenuous. The wooden slats had seen better days and the rope binding it all together was frayed.

"We're still going to have to get across that bridge," Pet declared, to the others' dismay. The River Finch was far too violent and fast-moving to cross by any other means and going to the next bridge would mean a three-day extension to their travel time.

"Look at the grey hairs on the mane and the cracked condition of its scorpion tail," noted Mrs Kettlepot. "This must be a quite an old manticore. Though age does little to temper a manticore's fury, it does strengthen the depths of their slumber. Perhaps we could creep by without waking it."

"Did I mishear?" Iago piped in, "Do you really plan to sneak around a sleeping manticore with all of our horses?"

Pet's only answer was, "Yes."

"Being a manticore's lunch is such an undignified way to go," sighed Iago.

The group slowly trotted down towards the bridge. The manticore had left room for one horse to pass by at a time. They decided to dismount and guide the horses one-by-one past the sleeping manticore. Then Pet announced who would go first.

"Why me?" cried Candice.

"You're the lightest and you'll be taking Bounds across with you. He's a very well-mannered horse. Out of all of us you have the best chance of getting across safely." Pet then pressed a scroll into Candice's hands. "If the rest of us don't make it, you must complete the mission."

She looked down at the scroll, "What is this?"

"This document outlines all my arguments against Tax Law 106. You would have to deliver it to the high regent personally," explained Pet. "This mission is bigger than us alone. It's about saving Seacrest."

Taking Bounds's reins in her hand, Candice let out a sigh, "Fine. Let's do this." Candice had no parting words to the others. She just wanted to get this done as quickly as possible. Gingerly, she took her first step onto the bridge…

"Stop!" Mrs Kettlepot whispered loudly.

Candice spun around, "What is it?"

Mrs Kettlepot promptly plucked a small purple flower from Candice's hair and threw it to the ground.

"What are you doing?" Candice scolded. "I picked that at Vale Alturin."

"That was a Tinkerbloom flower!" scolded Mrs Kettlepot.

"I know what a Tinkerbloom flower is," retorted Candice. "I am a florist."

"Then you should know that the scent of a Tinkerbloom drives manticores wild."

Candice frowned. She actually did not know that.

With all the Tinkerbloom flowers removed, Candice once again began her trek across the bridge. Pet, Mrs Kettlepot and Iago did not dare to breathe as they watched her tip-toe towards the dozing manticore. Bound's hooves clip-clopped against the wooden slats of the bridge, but luckily the noise did not in the slightest disturb the manticore's sleep.

Candice came alongside the sleeping manticore. She took her first step beside the manticore and then another. Time oozed by. Pet's heart beat loudly in her chest and her palms began to sweat profusely. Mrs Kettlepot sucked in a deep breath. Then just like that, Candice and Bounds were through. She turned back and silently waved at them. Pet had never been prouder of her best friend.

Despite not being nearly as stealthy or quiet, Mrs Kettlepot, Iago and Hubby still managed to get by the manticore without incident. Pet began to wonder if this manticore was really sleeping at all or if it was dead.

Pet took a tight hold on Mucker's reins and gingerly took her first step onto the bridge. The manticore suddenly moved and Pet almost jumped out of her skin. Relax, Pet. It had just wagged its scorpion tail. It's still asleep.

Closing her eyes, Pet took in a deep breath. All she had to do was creep past and then everything would be alright. Though not entirely convinced, Pet recognized that she could not just hang out there in the middle of the bridge indefinitely.

Accordingly, she took another step and another. Pretty soon she was approaching the manticore's side.

Mucker was doing fine. The lucky horse was not fazed by the manticore's presence one bit. All he had to do was get by the monster and they would be home free. Of course, that's when Mucker stumbled.

His front left foot fell between two slats. Mucker's three other legs helped him regain balance, but also caused the bridge to swing violently. Pet grabbed the rope of the bridge with one hand to steady herself. With her other hand, she gripped the hilt of her sword. Pet heard a loud collective gasp. She glanced up and saw Candice, Mrs Kettlepot and Iago, their eyes wide in fear.

It occurred to Pet that the manticore had not done anything. Mucker had stumbled. Pet had steadied herself. The others had gasped. Still the manticore just lay there.

Pet promptly helped negotiate Mucker past the rest of the manticore. They had done it! The most difficult part was over. They had successfully sneaked past the manticore! It was then that she trod on the manticore's tail.

The manticore let out a loud yelp. As the beast began to shudder with energy, its tail and its large stinger came alive, lifting off the bridge and waving through the air.

"Uh Mrs Kettlepot, it's waking up," Pet half-whispered/half-yelled. "What do I do?"

"Sing it a lullaby. Manticores love music."

"I don't sing."

"What do you mean, you don't sing? Just sing anything."

Candice put an arm on Mrs Kettlepot's shoulder. "It's true. She won't sing to save her life."

Without any other options, Mrs Kettlepot told Candice, "We'll just have to do it ourselves. Do you know Stay Little Princess?"

Candice nodded and the two promptly began to croon:

Stay Little Princess. Don't Go Away.
The King Will Love You Day After Day.

Pet couldn't believe her ears. Were they really singing? Here she was, trying to evade a giant scorpion tail and they were singing!?
Tell the Wind, You Won't Go.

The King Wants To Sit and Watch You Grow.

All of a sudden, the flailing scorpion tail began to sag. The manticore yawned and snuggled up against the bridge once again. It was working! It was actually working!

Tell the Sea, You Don't Dive.
The King Wants You Dry and Alive.

At this point, Iago was chiming in with the occasional alto croak.

But If You Choose to Disappear,
The King Will Find You. Don't You Fear.

That last measure had done the trick and the manticore had fallen back asleep. After a few delicate steps, Pet finally reached the other side of the bridge.

The party clasped each other in quick embraces before stealing away into the forest. Once there was a safe distance between them and the manticore, they had a celebration. Mrs Kettlepot and Candice each congratulated each other on the melodic beauty of their respective singing voices. Iago declared that the worst was definitely over. Pet smiled and hoped that Iago was right.

He was not.

CHAPTER TWENTY-NINE

Persistent was not the first word that jumped into Pet's head when she thought of Mrs Kettlepot. That was about to change. She was simply not letting this go.

"Everybody can sing, Pet," insisted Mrs Kettlepot. "Even you."

It had been a long day. This was the last thing in the world that Pet wanted to be talking about. "I have a larynx and a voice-box. I suppose, ostensibly, I could sing. I've just never done it."

"Not once? Not even as a small child?"

"Never," responded Pet. Candice confirmed Pet's admission with a simple nod.

Mrs Kettlepot made a sympathetic grimace. "Did something happen when you were a child? Some scarring incident that caused you to vow that you would never sing again?"

"It's just that I never saw the point. There are lots of other things to do in the world and standing around making silly tones with my voice just ate into the time I could be doing something more productive."

"You came to this conclusion as a small child?" asked Mrs Kettlepot incredulously.

Candice explained, "She was a very opinionated small child."

"That won't do." Mrs Kettlepot rose to her feet. "Singing is certainly not a waste of time. Singing is important. As humans, we don't sing to warn off predators or communicate with each other. Instead we sing so that we can bask and celebrate in the beauty that is all. We sing to remind ourselves that we are alive and that that is a very good thing. We sing to affirm our very own existence..."

"I'm simply not breaking into song," interrupted Pet, "No matter how perky you get."

With a humph, Mrs Kettlepot sank down into her seat, "Mark my words, Petunia Peasant, you will sing before this journey is over."

"I'll sing with you," Iago offered and so the two of them went off to sing softly in a corner of the campsite.

"I'm off to bed," muttered Pet. "I'll take the second watch with Candice."

Pet got into her bedroll and tucked her hands underneath her cheek. She laid her head down and closed her eyes...

...but sleep wasn't coming. There were too many thoughts swimming around in her head. One particularly nagging thought was a line from that nursery song.

Stay Little Princess. Don't Go Away.

Why was she repeating that lyric over and over in her head? It was just a silly song. Pet had heard it plenty of times growing up. There were much more important things to think about. Who had sent the Cloaked Man after her? Was Candice really okay? What was Dashing doing at that exact moment?

Stay Little Princess.

Why did she keep on going back to that song? Unless it was all connected somehow...

Had Mrs Kettlepot's choice of lullaby been a coincidence or was it something more?

Wait. Was that it?

No way.

There was no way that little old Petunia Peasant was the Lost Princess.

The simple fact that Petunia Princess had dark hair did not mean that she was the long-lost daughter of King Piotr the Just. Never mind the fact that Pet was the right age, there must be lots of girls her age with black hair... but then how many of them were adopted?

Her parents had never hidden the fact that Pet was adopted. In fact, they celebrated it. Ma and Pa had so wanted to have children, but no matter how hard they tried, they could not. They were about to resign themselves to a childless life, when one day, like a blessing, Pet had come into their lives.

Growing up, Ma had regaled Pet with the story of her arrival. It had been an unseasonably breezy summer night. Ma at first thought it was just the whistling and howling of the wind. But the knocking persisted. In a hurry, she went to the door and found the baby Pet, swathed only in a pink blanket. It had been like her prayers had been answered.

Ma and Pa had done their civic duty. The next day, they had reported to Town Hall that they had found a baby. Nobody came forward. Since it was known in Seacrest that the Peasants were good people, but unable to have a baby, the general consensus was that some unwed mother had decided that her child would be better off with them.

Pet had always wondered where she came from, but never felt a need to press any further. Despite looking a little different from the Seacrest Folk, Pet always felt she belonged and she loved her parents.

This was not the first time Pet had contemplated the notion that she was the Lost Princess. However, the last time was when she was nine and every nine-year-old girl in the realm hoped that she was the Lost Princess.

But her name was Petunia. It fit with the others. King Piotr. Queen Polly. King Piotr's father was King Philip. King Philip was married to Queen Penelope. King Philip's father was King Petros. It made a certain amount of sense, didn't it?

Stop right there, Pet told herself. What a silly, silly goose she was. The Cloaked Man could have been insane or made some sort of mistake. How could she use the actions of a madman to justify the idea that she could be the Lost Princess? It was preposterous.

But if it were true…

CHAPTER THIRTY

"Purpose of your trip?" the guard called down from the high walls of Frontier Keep. Judd had never seen walls like this. Walls in Seacrest were mostly for holding buildings up. These walls seemed primarily designed to keep people out. It all seemed a tad hostile for such a beautiful morning.

Sentry did the talking, "We are travelling to Martstown and seek to spend the night here."

"Come in," the guard instructed them. "Check in at the Regional Guard Station once you're through."

The gates creaked open and the two men rode through. Sentry whispered to Judd, "Try not to look quite so guilty."

Judd flashed with anger. Why did Sentry insist on lying about their journey? After all he was addressing a fellow law-enforcement officer. Lying to a guardsman was a serious offense. Now, because of Sentry's actions, Judd was complicit in another crime. Of course, telling a few fibs paled in comparison to executing a man in cold blood.

Perhaps he shouldn't rush to judgment. Sentry might have taken a life, but he had also saved Judd's. If it were not for Sentry and his first-aid skills, Judd would be dead.

Outside the Regional Guard Station, Sentry removed his tattered purple cape. Judd was relieved. It would probably make a better first impression. If only Sentry had time for a shave too. A few black hairs were now poking out of his chin.

They soon found themselves seated opposite a young guardsman. "Hello. My name is Dashing. I just need to ask you a few questions about your journey. First of all, I'm going to need your names."

Judd scowled at this 'Dashing.' He was one of those pretty boys, like Lance North. This Dashing was probably just as arrogant and insufferable as well.

"My name is Azor," Sentry lied, "and this is my boy, Trusty."

It took a massive effort on Judd's part not to interrupt. What kind of name was 'Trusty'? 'Trusty' was a dog's name. It did not matter how much Judd owed him, Sentry would hear about this.

Dashing made a mark on a form in front of him and asked a litany of additional questions. Lie after lie poured from Sentry's mouth. Right before Judd's eyes, the man spun an entire fictional existence for them. He was a blacksmith and was currently training his son in the fiery arts. They were going to Martstown for a family reunion. 'Trusty' had never been to his father's town before. Judd was careful to memorize each and every detail, lest he got asked any follow-up questions.

This Dashing fellow was getting a detailed synopsis of their supposed lives. Were all visitors to Frontier Keep asked quite so many questions? Or was there something suspicious about 'Azor' and 'Trusty'?

"And what road did you take to get here?" Dashing examined Sentry closely as he asked the question.

Again Sentry lied. "We took the Coastal Road."

"We've had some reports of vagabond activity on the Capital Road. Did you by any chance meet any unscrupulous characters on your journey here?"

Sentry shook his head. "I didn't notice any on the Coastal Road."

Dashing made another note. "Does the name Petunia Peasant mean anything to you?"

It took everything Judd had not to jump out of his chair. How did this guy know about Pet? Sentry remained stoic. "No."

A smirk flashed across Dashing's face. This guardsman knew something. Judd had no idea how he knew something, but Dashing did.

Sentry stood up. "I think we've been very cooperative and have answered quite enough of your questions. We have supplies to purchase and accommodations to arrange, so if you would not mind excusing us…"

"I will have no problem excusing you," smiled Dashing, "once you start answering my questions truthfully."

"Get up!" Sentry barked at Judd, "We're going."

Judd did not need to be told twice. He jumped to his feet and spun around, only to find three guardsmen barring his way out. Their weapons remained sheathed, but were prominently displayed. Frantically, Judd looked over at Sentry. He'd better have a plan for getting out of this one.

Sentry eyed the three guardsmen between him and the door. He tensed his muscles and moved his hand towards his belt. Judd shook his head in disbelief. Was he really considering the prospect of fighting his way out? Sentry himself was a guardsman. Why didn't he just tell them this?

"What is the meaning of this?" Sentry asked. "We have done nothing to warrant this."

"That remains to be seen, 'Azor.' I do know that you've been dishonest with me. Now please sit so we can discuss this further."

Wordlessly, Sentry sat back down. Judd followed suit, acutely aware of the three pairs of guardsman eyes watching him as he took his seat again.

"You should know that the Coastal Road has been particularly rainy the last few days," Dashing explained. "Your horses and clothes don't appear damp in the slightest."

"The sun dried them," responded Sentry.

"Perhaps," smiled Dashing. "But if you lied about which route you took, it makes me wonder what else you lied about. However, you did tell me some things whether you meant to or not. 'Trusty' here doesn't do as good a job at disguising his accent as you do. I imagine it's from the Southern Province. Thinsteps or Seacrest... Which is it?"

"Seacrest," admitted Judd, which instantly got him a rebuking stare from Sentry.

"Now we're getting somewhere," smiled Dashing again. This guy was smiling way too much, Judd thought to himself.

Dashing turned to Sentry, "Do you have anything to say for yourself?"

Sentry's lips remained clamped shut.

Judd had sat there silently and let Sentry play this his way, but now he was losing badly. Going to prison meant they would be unable to catch up with Pet, Candice and the others. It was time for Judd to take matters into his own hands. "Is Pet all right?"

"Yes, she is," Dashing answered. "Does that upset you?"

"Upset me? Why would it upset me?"

Checking his notes, Dashing said, "When you rode up to our gates, 'Azor' here was seen wearing a tattered purple cape. Do you know what strikes me as odd? How similar capes and cloaks can look."

What would a cloak have to do with...? Oh, the Cloaked Man! Pet must have reported the assault of the Cloaked Man and Dashing must have thought Sentry was the guy who attacked Pet.

Judd was about to explain the entire situation when Sentry interjected, "We have nothing further to say on this matter."

Dashing nodded to his fellow guardsmen, "I will have some questions for you later. Accordingly, I've arranged a place for you to stay this evening."

One guardsman came up behind Judd and gently put his hand on the back of Judd's shoulder. It was not a particularly aggressive gesture, but Judd knew what it meant, "Wait! Where are they taking us?"

"The holding cells." Dashing did not even bother to make eye contact.

Judd could not believe his ears, "But you don't understand..."

A look from Sentry said it all, "Just comply, boy."

And that was that. Judd and Sentry were escorted out of Dashing's office and to the cells. In Judd's entire life he had never had any trouble with the law, and here he was being led to a cell. All the while, Pet and the others were still out there unprotected.

CHAPTER THIRTY-ONE

Prostrated eyes watched night slowly melt away. This was the dawning of the sixth day of their mission and their second in the Shadowoods. They should be able to make it out of the Shadowoods today and reach the Sapphire Palace before dark.

Pet yawned deeply. With all the thoughts running around her head, she had not got much sleep before Mrs Kettlepot roused her to take her turn on shift.

Sitting idly next to her, Candice stared silently into the ebbing darkness. Pet turned to her friend and asked, "Would you like to be a princess?"

Candice shrugged, "That's an odd question. What brings that on?"

"I'm just curious."

"I guess all the shoes would be nice," Candice mused. "Princesses have a lot of shoes right?"

"C'mon, Candice. Be serious. Would you or would you not like to become a princess?"

Candice took a moment to whirl the thought around in her head. "No. I don't think I would. Everybody would be watching and judging your every move. That would be very unsettling."

"But one could do a lot of good as a princess," replied Pet. "I could... I mean, one could shape policy, enact beneficial laws and generally improve the quality of living of those in the realm."

"I suppose, but that's always been your forte and not mine. I wouldn't like telling people what do all the time. I'm not one for making big decisions that affect other people. I'm much more suited to a simpler life. Just me, my flowers and maybe one day a big, strong husband."

Pet was about to admonish Candice gently about her plans. Candice was one of the smartest girls Pet knew. She could do anything she liked. Why would she settle for just flowers and a husband?

Pet stopped herself short, "I thought I heard something."

"Of course you heard something. These are the Shadowoods. Life is teeming here. Birds sing, deer run, murder-kittens hunt. You can't jump at every little noise, you'll drive yourself nuts."

Pet frowned, "This sounded different, like…"

"Help!" The sound had been faint, but clear.

"Just like that," Pet scrambled to her feet.

Candice took a moment to contemplate the sound, "It sounds like a little girl… Wait! What are you doing?"

Pet was strapping her saddle to Mucker's back, "I'm going to check it out. Wake the others up and wait for my return."

"You can't run off by yourself," objected Candice.

"That girl could be injured or dying."

"It could be a trap."

Pet paused. Candice made a good point. This would be a good way to take advantage of her better nature. But could Pet ignore someone's pleas for help?

"Please help me." There it came again.

Pet made up her mind, "I have to go to her. Once the others are up, you can follow."

"We're already up and ready to go," announced Mrs Kettlepot.

Pet and Candice twirled around to see Iago and Mrs Kettlepot saddling up the horses and securing the baggage to them. Iago explained, "It was impossible to sleep with you two shouting at each other like hooligans. So are we off to rescue that damsel in distress now?"

The four of them set off towards the sound. Pet tried to get Mucker to speed up a bit, but given all the branches, close trees and random rocks, he refused to go any faster than a brisk trot.

"Please, can anybody hear me?"

"We're on our way," shouted Pet into the woods. "Please stay where you are and continue to call out."

"I'm over here," responded the voice.

"Look left!" exclaimed Candice. Not too far to the left, a small swathe of purple made its way through the woods.

Pet leapt off Mucker and barged through the trees shouting, "Help's here!"

The purple stopped moving.

"Do you require any assistance?" asked Candice.

"Yes," replied a quiet voice.

Finally, the foliage gave away and Pet come face to face with a little girl with long dark hair, dressed in a purple riding-hood. She looked tired, but her face lit up when she saw Pet and Candice.

"You're here to help me?" enquired the girl with a parched voice.

Pet wondered if this was what being a hero felt like, "Yes, we are." Candice looked carefully to see if the girl was wounded in any way, "What's your name?"

"Lilac." It was a fitting name.

It occurred to Pet that it was odd that the girl was not really looking either at her or at Candice. Instead, Lilac kept her eyes on the bushes as if she was expecting something else. After a while she turned to look at Pet. "Is it just you two?"

Pet answered, "Well there's Mrs Kettlepot and Iago back with the horses."

"This Iago is a man?"

"He's more of a toad," responded Candice.

Lilac shook her head. "Then you won't do at all. I'm sorry to have wasted your time."

"What do you mean?"

"It's just that you're girls," the little girl observed.

"So are you," retorted a mystified Pet.

"I'm in terrible danger," cried Lilac, "I need real help."

"What do you mean, we can't help? What kind of assistance were you expecting?"

"Oh a knight or perhaps a guardsman or two." Lilac brought her hands up to her mouth and shouted deeply into the woods, "Will somebody else help me, please!"

"I'll have you know that I'm a champion swordsperson." Pet unsheathed her sword and raised it high in the air, "and my friend over there is pretty handy with a throwing axe. Whatever your problem is, we can solve it."

This revelation gave Lilac temporary pause. "Are you like girl knights?"

"Sort of," was the best Pet could muster.

Lilac studied Pet and Candice. "I don't know. You're not much older than me."

"We're old enough to know that you shouldn't be in the Shadowoods by yourself." Candice put a hand on Lilac's shoulder, "What are you doing out here anyway?"

"It's a long story." Lilac leaned her face against Candice's arm. She pressed her nose against the back of Candice's palm, "I appreciate the offer for assistance, but I don't think you can help me. In fact, it's possibly best if you keep your distance."

This girl was starting to exasperate Pet. "Why don't you tell me what the problem is and I can tell you if we can help or not."

"Something's following me."

"What's following you?" asked Candice.

Suddenly, a tremendous roar echoed through the forest. It was so loud that it seemed to be coming from everywhere at once. Candice turned around wide-eyed, trying to find the source, brandishing one of her axes.

"That!"

CHAPTER THIRTY-TWO

Pain coursed through Pet's face. One particularly spiteful branch had slashed her forehead, but she clenched her teeth, gripped her sword and focused on cutting away the other branches as best she could. At least the pain meant she was still alive, but there was a strong possibility that she might not be much longer.

Pet patted the galloping Mucker and glanced back at the others to check that they were still with her. Candice rode high on Bounds, using her own body to shield poor Lilac from the branches. Mrs Kettlepot and Iago brought up the rear on Hubby.

None of them had actually seen the creature yet, but they could certainly hear its sickening roar and the snap of the unfortunate trees that fell in its path. It kept getting louder and louder.

It was gaining on them.

The Shadowoods were not helping matters. The trees themselves were getting closer and closer together, making it harder to ride around them. It was as if the forest itself was closing in like a trap.

Glancing up, Pet noticed that a tree had toppled and now rested against its neighboring tree. The massive trunk stretched diagonally across their path. It was too high to leap over so the only alternative was to go under, though it would be tight.

"Bear low and left!" shouted Pet as she pulled the reins accordingly. She pulled in her arms and turned her body as Mucker rushed past the trunk.

Without stopping, Pet turned around to see how the others fared with the tight passage. Candice pushed Lilac down with one hand and artfully dodged her head around the trunk as Bounds ran under. Now only Mrs Kettlepot was left.

Mrs Kettlepot feared she would not be able to squeeze her body under that tree. Unfortunately, there was no way of getting out of this. With that monster behind them, Hubby would not stop for hell or high water.

The weird thing was that Mrs Kettlepot was strangely accepting of the prospect of dying in the next few moments. In these last few days, she had found adventure and true romance. What more could an old lady ask for? At least she would be going out in a blaze of glory.

There was just one thing Mrs Kettlepot wanted to do before she died.

Impulsively, she turned and kissed her man-toad paramour.

It was the worst thing she could have done.

CHAPTER THIRTY-THREE

Physics being what they are, a relatively light toad suddenly becoming a significantly heavier old gentleman creates a significant force. Disoriented, Iago's now-human legs flailed in the air as his now-human fingers gripped for balance. He was on the verge of falling off Hubby and taking Mrs Kettlepot with him.

Iago's wrinkled nude body impacted against the tree first. A large thwack echoed through the forest, as he fell off Hubby pulling Mrs Kettlepot down with him. Both slammed against the forest floor and did not move.

Now unfettered by any riders, Hubby ran under the fallen trunk and sped off further into the Shadowoods right past a horrified Candice and Pet. Candice turned to Pet in a panic, "What do we do?"

"I'm going back. You have to keep going."

"I'm not leaving…" began Candice.

"You need to get Lilac away from here. She doesn't deserve to die here and you're the faster rider."

Candice knew Pet was right, but it certainly did not make the prospect of continuing on without her feel any less cowardly.

"You've still got the parchment?" Pet asked. Candice nodded. "Good. After Lilac is safe, you must complete this mission."

Candice knew this was not the time to argue. She gripped the reins of her horse. "I love you, Petunia. Now you go show that monster who's boss." And with a shake of the reins, Candice and Lilac were off.

Arriving back at the fallen tree, Pet was relieved to find that Mrs Kettlepot at least was moving. Iago was still unconscious. However, the shadowy form was gaining ground   Pet leapt to the ground. "Can you stand?"

Mrs Kettlepot grabbed her head. "I'm so sorry. This is entirely my fault. Take Iago. I'll face it alone."

Pet tried to help Mrs Kettlepot to her feet. They got about halfway up before Mrs Kettlepot fell back down. She was not able to go anywhere.

"Go," mumbled Mrs Kettlepot, "No sense in you dying needlessly too."

"I'm not leaving anyone again," Pet declared.

A tremendous roar snapped Pet's head around. The creature loomed in on them. Its growling grew louder and more hideous than before. Pet held up her sword and adopted a fighting stance. Fleeing was no longer an option.

"Whatever this is," worried Mrs Kettlepot, "I don't fancy our chances."

"We have a chance, that's all we need." Pet could not see the creature clearly yet through the dark and the crashing debris of the falling trees, but the monster was definitely getting closer. She tightened her grip on her sword. If Pet was going to go out today, at least she was going to go out swinging.

Another shriek filled the air. Only one remaining tree remained standing between her and the monster.

Pet's sweaty palms slipped slightly on the hilt of her sword.

The last tree fell and the monster come into view. Pet would recognize that cracked scorpion tail anywhere. It was the manticore from the bridge yesterday. What was it doing here? Why would such a territorial beast be pursuing them over such a long distance?

The manticore had no hesitation. It was intent on laying waste anything that stood in its path. At this moment, that included Pet. The beast leapt at Pet with its long claws extended and fanged jaw wide.

The manticore had just given Pet a way to win this fight. By leaping as high in the air as it did, Pet could duck under the beast and stab it in its soft underbelly. If she was lucky, she would hit something vital.

Pet instinctively moved forward to stab the manticore, but pulled herself short.

Was this really how she wanted to live another day? Throughout her life Pet had fervently believed that there was always an alternative to violence. Why was now any different?

Pet let her sword drop down. She had hoped it would not come to this. She opened her mouth, took in a huge gulp of air and began to sing.

CHAPTER THIRTY-FOUR

Perhaps singing was a bit of a generous description. Pet's song had no words. It was composed of just one simple sound, "Laaaaaaaaaa." She was belting out the loudest note she could. Luckily, it had the desired effect.

The manticore was not eating her. Instead, it paused. Its lion's face stood only inches away from Pet's. Its hot breath washed over her cheek. If Pet had not been in full voice, she would have gulped.

Mrs Kettlepot could not believe her eyes or her ears. Which was more bizarre? Pet's singing or the manticore's reaction?

Pet's terror was palpable. Was it more frightening when the manticore was pouncing at her or now with the beast towering over her, regarding this strange singing thing before it?

It occurred to Pet that she could not maintain this single note indefinitely. She was running out of air. Hopefully she would pass out. It was probably best to be unconscious if a manticore was devouring you.

Pet glared at Mrs Kettlepot and noticed she was trying to mouth a message to her. However, Pet could not figure out what the seemingly random movements of Mrs Kettlepot's lips were seeking to communicate. Pet's face flushed as her knees started to buckle. Mrs Kettlepot watched Pet's collapsing body with horror.

"Sing it a lullaby!" shouted Mrs Kettlepot.

The manticore growled at the interruption. The beast appeared increasingly agitated as Pet's note quavered. Mrs Kettlepot was right. She needed to lull the manticore into a slumber and singing a single note would not do the job. There was just one problem. Pet did not know the words to any lullaby.

Well, that was not exactly true.

There was one. Pet's eyes blazed with panic. It was now or never.

Pet stopped singing.

The manticore roared and lifted a paw as if to strike her head clean off.

Pet gulped in air and began to sing.

Stay Little Princess. Don't Go Away.
The King Will Love You Day After Day.

The paw paused menacingly in the air, but the new song had given her a stay of execution.

Tell the Sky Not to Snow.

These were not the right words, but the manticore did not seem to mind. Its paw slowly returned to the ground.

The King Wants To Sit Back and Row.

Perhaps the manticore was not the one Pet had to be scared of. Mrs Kettlepot stared daggers at Pet. How dare she butcher such a time-honored lullaby with the wrong words?

Tell the Boys, You Won't Jive.

Mrs Kettlepot tried to join in, but the moment the slightest sound escaped her lips, the manticore roared at her. Mrs Kettlepot abruptly stopped. The manticore seemed interested only in hearing Pet sing.

The King Will Ensure They Won't Survive.

The manticore's eyelids began to droop.

But If You Ever Drink Beer

Pet was getting the hang of it. The melody never really changed. She could just repeat it forever and just string a series of rhyming words together. It was not as if the manticore cared if they made sense.

The King Will Come and Find You Dear.

Pet continued like this for about ten minutes. Her lullaby had descended into a recitation of nonsensical words that happened to rhyme. She was particularly pleased with rhyming 'manticore' with 'great big bore.'

It did the trick. The manticore fell asleep. Pet could not believe it. She had managed to soothe the savage beast with her music.

By this time some of Iago's senses had returned. Though he was far from fully aware of his surroundings, he seemed to comprehend the importance of being quiet. With Mrs Kettlepot proping him up, Iago was able gradually to limp away from the manticore.

Once they were a distance away from the manticore, Mrs Kettlepot looked back at the sleeping beast that had caused them so much trouble. This silly manticore was behaving like no other manticore she had ever heard of. Wait... Why was Pet now approaching the manticore?

Were her eyes playing tricks with her? They were not. Pet was taking careful steps towards the manticore. That silly girl should have been doing the opposite. The only thing Mrs Kettlepot could do was watch in horror as Pet delicately drew her fingers below the beast's nose. The manticore squirmed slightly, its massive frame shuddering for a moment. Luckily, it did not wake. Pet withdrew her hand and stealthily crept back. "What did you do?" was Mrs Kettlepot's obvious question.

"I applied some Sirius Salt under its nose. That ought to block its sense of smell till we get far enough away," explained Pet in a hushed tone. "So, what did you think of my singing? Was I any good?"

"Well..." Mrs Kettlepot struggled to find the right words, "I've never seen someone with your natural talent for rhyming."

Pet was unsure if that she was actually a compliment or not. However now was not the time for further enquiry. Candice and Lilac had gone off ahead and Pet was eager to catch up with them.

CHAPTER THIRTY-FIVE

Parts of the path up Deadman's Finger were lined with loose rubble that made Bounds's hooves slip. At any moment, Candice, Lilac and Bounds could slide off the side of the mountain and plummet to the floor of the Shadowoods far below. Gazing down at the sharp rocks below, Candice wondered if that was how this mountain got its name. Still, the dangerous trek over Deadman's Finger was the quickest way out of the Shadowoods.

Lilac was riding behind Candice on Bounds. Her small arms held tightly onto Candice's waist. Candice glanced back at her travelling companion. This strange girl had just showed up out of nowhere and Candice knew little about her. "Lilac, what was that thing that was after you?"

"I don't know. I just heard its roars and it terrified me." Lilac could not have been more than ten, but she spoke very well for her age.

"What were you doing in the Shadowoods?"

Lilac frowned, "I was with my mummy and I wandered off. I tried to find her but I got lost."

"What town are you from, Lilac?"

"Frontier Keep."

Candice frowned. That was on the other side of the Shadowoods. Candice had hoped she could drop off Lilac before continuing her journey to the Sapphire Palace, but there was no way Candice was going to go back to Frontier Keep and then back to the palace. Pet had made it clear that the mission to the palace was of the upmost importance.

Pet...

Candice reined Bounds in to a halt. Was she really okay with never seeing Pet again? To leave her to die in the Shadowoods? "What's wrong? Why did we stop?"

"You're getting off here."

"You're leaving me?!" cried Lilac.

Normally, Candice would have been a lot nicer, but Pet was in danger. She grabbed Lilac and hoisted her off Bounds. "You can hide in the cave over there. You'll be safe there. I need to go back."

"Don't go!" Lilac stared at her with big sad eyes. Candice knew this trick. She had done it herself many times growing up. This was a look intended to elicit sympathy, but it was not going to work. Candice was going back to help Pet. Her mind was made up.

"I'm sorry." Candice handed Lilac some food. "One day I hope you love someone enough that you understand why I'm doing this."

No response, just more staring.

"I'll just be a few hours. You stay out of sight till then." Candice took Lilac's hand in hers and noticed a small bracelet of purple flowers was attached to the girl's wrist. "Where did you get these flowers from?"

"I picked them myself. Do you like them?"

Candice dropped Lilac's hand. "Do you know what these flowers are? Do you know what they do?"

Lilac's tone suddenly turned. "How else was I going to get the manticore to follow me?"

Candice gasped.

"You're too late you know," Lilac smirked at Candice. "The manticore is probably already gnawing on Pet's bones as we speak."

Now Candice did not feel any guilt about leaving this scary little girl. She took a few steps back towards Bounds. "Lilac, I'm going now."

"No, you're not. I won't let you."

CHAPTER THIRTY-SIX

Prison certainly did not agree with Judd. The cell was very small, especially for two big men. It certainly did not help matters that Pet and the others were in terrible danger and Judd was unable to help them. Judd turned to Sentry. "We have to get out of here."

There was no response. Sentry just sat there staring out into nowhere and scratching the short black bristles on his chin. If they were going to get out of there, Judd was just going to have to arrange it himself.

That insufferable Dashing had asked a good question. Why did Sentry abandon his post in Seacrest to follow Pet and the others? Sentry had told him that the appearance of the Cloaked Man had given him cause for worry, but couldn't he just have notified the Regional Guard here in Frontier Keep? They would have been in a better position to do something about it. It was as if Sentry had some personal stake in Pet, but for the life of him, Judd could not figure out what it was.

Judd wandered over to the steel bars and shook them. They did not budge. He also tested the cement that held them in place. The guards had confiscated their weapons, so he scraped at the cement with his fingernail. Perhaps if he scratched hard enough he could get one of the bars loose…

"Please stop that," Sentry spoke up. "If they didn't move the first twenty times you did that, they're not going to move now."

"At least I'm doing something."

"If you had just left the talking to me in the first place, we wouldn't be here in this mess."

"Really?" asked a skeptical Judd. "Dashing saw straight through your lies."

Sentry nodded. "Dashing is a good guardsman."

"Maybe once we get out of here, you can ask him for some pointers." Usually, Judd was never this sarcastic, but then, for that matter, he usually did not find himself in a cell. Apparently it was true. Prison did change you.

At this point a third voice joined the conversation. "Excuse me, I was hoping to have a word with both of you, but if you'd like me to come back later?" The voice belonged to the Warden standing on the other side of the bars with a folder in his hand.

Sentry asked, "Where's Dashing?"

"Guardsman Dashing had some business to attend to at the palace. I am in charge until his return."

Judd pleaded, "What will it take to convince you that neither of us is the Cloaked Man who attacked Pet?"

"We don't think that any longer. Some of my men just returned and we found this Cloaked Man tied to a tree." A sigh of relief escaped Judd's lips. They must realize then that Sentry and the Cloaked Man were two different people. This was a step in the right direction, "This Cloaked Man had had his throat slashed. He was already dead by the time we found him."

This time Sentry responded. "That's unfortunate, but from all accounts he was a violent man. I am sure society will survive his loss."

"It's interesting that you say that," the Warden noted, "Because we tested the blood on your sword and it was a conclusive match to the Cloaked Man's blood."

Judd could read the writing on the wall. They were about to be charged with the murder of the Cloaked Man. It did not seem fair, especially considering how the Cloaked Man had tried to kill him and Judd had had nothing to do with Sentry's decision to execute him. Judd turned to look at Sentry with desperate eyes. "Just tell him everything. He'll understand."

Sentry remained stoic. "No."

"They might be willing to release me," pleaded Judd. He knew what he was about to propose would sound like a betrayal. "I can go after Pet and the others and make sure they get home safely. It's better if one of us gets out rather than neither of us."

"I have a better idea." Sentry removed his gauntlet.

"Oh and what would that be?" asked the Warden.

Sentry examined the Warden. "You look like you're in your mid-forties. That means you would have completed your initial training about twenty years ago, right?"

"Close enough, but why does it matter?"

"Then you would recognize this." Sentry had fully removed his gauntlet at this point. He wore an ornate ring on his right hand with a sparkling sapphire in it. It was not the most masculine piece of jewelry that Judd had ever seen, but it looked expensive.

All colour drained from the Warden's face, "Is that what I think it is? How could it be? Are you…"

"Hush," whispered Sentry. "I must insist that you make an oath on the realm to keep this knowledge to yourself and reveal my secret to no-one."

Without hesitation, the Warden solemnly made such an oath. Sentry eyed up and down the corridor to make sure there were no other guardsmen present, "We need to get out of Frontier Keep as soon as possible. We will need our horse and weapons returned to us. Tell no-one of this. Is that understood?"

"Yes sir," responded the Warden. "I will return when everything is ready for your departure."

Judd watched in amazement as the Warden scurried off. What was it about Sentry's ring? Did it have some sort of enchantment? Sentry anticipated the obvious questions. "Don't bother asking. I won't tell you."

Soon enough the Warden was back with their weapons and opened the cell door for them. Sentry strode purposefullly out of the cell and the Warden helped Sentry put on his tattered purple cape. Judd had no idea why he did not just throw that thing out.

Soon, Judd and Sentry were back on their horse on the outside of Frontier Keep. They would now contine their quest to catch up with Pet and the others. That was all that mattered. Any other questions could wait. Even the numerous questions about Sentry.

CHAPTER THIRTY-SEVEN

Pressing on, Pet strode through the forest at a ferocious pace. Iago and Mrs Kettlepot followed on Mucker. With Hubby having run off, there was only one horse left between the three of them, which meant that one of them had to walk. Pet had no problem with being that person. Being on the ground meant she could follow Bounds's tracks easier. If they hurried, they might be able to catch up with Candice and Lilac.

Iago would have liked to take things a bit more slowly. His human form felt stiff and strange to him. When he had been knocked off the horse, he had reinjured his ankle. It certainly did not help that he was clothed only by one of Mrs Kettlepot's shawls, draped over his privates. To make matters worse, the ground was uneven and Mucker was unsure of his footing. After his third trip and stumble, Iago called out in irritation, "Do we have to go at such a ridiculous pace?"

"Yes." Pet's tone implied there would be no further discussion on the matter.

There was a rustle in the woods ahead. Something was rushing towards them. Mrs Kettlepot asked in a hushed tone, "Is it the manticore again?"

"I don't think so," Pet responded as she unsheathed her sword.

The source of the noise appeared and everyone breathed a sigh of relief. It was Bounds, but if Bounds was here, where were Candice and Lilac?

"Easy boy, easy," Pet cooed into the horse's ear. Bounds was frantic but calmed down slightly at the sound of Pet's voice as she asked him soothingly. "What are you so worried about? Where's Candice?"

Hoisting herself on top of Bounds, Pet noted to the others, "This is good. If I ride Bounds, we can pick up our pace a little."

It took less than an hour to reach the path up Deadman's Finger. The climb up was arduous, but Pet had no intention of slackening the pace.

With the Shadowoods stretched out beneath them, Pet took the opportunity to shout out at the top of her lungs, "Candice? Lilac? Are you there?"

Her words echoed for several minutes across the valley.

"I think I heard something," Mrs Kettlepot said.

"That would be the ringing in your ears from Pet's yell..." But Iago cut himself short, "I think I hear it too."

There it was again, "We're up here."

"That's Lilac," Pet declared and spurred Bounds forward. It took only a few minutes to reach her. Lilac's clothes were ripped, her hair tousled and there was a spot of some blue liquid on her lips.

"Lilac!" Pet dismounted from Bounds. "What happened to you?"

"We were attacked," Lilac replied in a numb voice.

"Where's Candice?"

Lilac pointed to the cave behind her. Pet ran into the cave, paying no heed to the puddle of blue, goopy liquid that she hurried through. She was unprepared for the sight that greeted her. Candice lay on the dusty floor of the cave, barely conscious, gripping her stomach and coated in that same blue liquid.

"Candice!" Pet cried. In a flash, she was by her side and Candice's hand was in hers. It was slick and blue.

"Pet? Is that you?" Candice mumbled.

"Yes it's me. What happened to you?"

"Don't trust Lilac," gasped Candice, "She's evil."

Mrs Kettlepot rushed up alongside Candice, "What happened to her?"

"I... I..." Pet tried to find the words, "I don't know."

Mrs Kettlepot tried to examine Candice's chest, but one of her hands still gripped her stomach. As Mrs Kettlepot moved her hand, Candice's face contorted in pain. Her other hand gripped Pet's like a vice. Mrs Kettlepot exclaimed, "Something's slashed her. It's pretty deep."

"What's all this blue stuff?" asked Pet.

Mrs Kettlepot guessed, "I think it's blood."

Blue blood?

Mrs Kettlepot pressed a bandage against Candice's stomach with one hand and riffled through her sack with the other. Pet marveled at Mrs Kettlepot's calm demeanour. It frustrated Pet that she could not contribute to helping Candice, more than holding her hand.

There was something she could do. She whispered into Candice's ear, "I'll be right back."

"Where are you going?" inquired Mrs Kettlepot.

Brandishing her sword, Pet responded, "Lilac and I are going to have words."

CHAPTER THIRTY-EIGHT

Prizing his returned human form, Iago had not noticed all the action in the cave. He was instead going through Mrs Kettlepot's pack to see if she had any clothes that he could wear. He was after all a gentleman of advanced years. It would be vastly inappropriate to spend the rest of the journey with a shawl tied around his waist, especially in the company of much younger girls.

Without warning, Pet's voice rang out from the cavern, "Where is she?"

Lilac had been sitting at the mouth of the cave watching the events inside unfold. As Pet came storming out, the little girl stumbled backwards. Upon laying eyes on Lilac, Pet promptly pointed her sword at the girl.

Iago asked, "What's going on here?"

"Help me!" shrieked Lilac. "She wants to kill me."

Pet could be sanctimonious and quite bossy, but she never struck Iago as a murderer. He pushed himself off the rock and approached her, "Pet, you need to calm yourself."

"Out of my way, Iago," Pet declared coldly. "This is between me and her."

Suddenly, Lilac's eyes brimmed with tears, "We were attacked by this gigantic wolf and I ran away! Perhaps if I had stayed, Candice would be okay. I'm so sorry!"

"Are you happy now?" Iago glared at Pet. "She's upset. Let's put our weapons down and calmly discuss this situation."

Pet took a good look at Lilac. She certainly looked like a scared little girl. Her face was dirty. Her cheeks were stained with tears. Her lips and hands trembled. Her hands were shaking so much that the loose bracelet of purple flowers on her wrist seemed like it was about to slip off...

Purple flowers?

"Tinkerbloom!" gasped Pet. "She's wearing Tinkerbloom flowers! The manticore was following the scent of the Tinkerbloom flowers when it attacked us. She did this on purpose. Sick a manticore on us, separate us, and then pick us off one by one."

"You sound paranoid, Pet," Iago exclaimed.

"I am not!" Never had Pet spoken with so much fury. "Candice is dying in there and Lilac is responsible."

"That's a relief," gasped Lilac. "I am supposed to deliver her alive, but I couldn't resist a taste. Especially given her unique vintage."

Iago turned to look at Lilac. "What?!"

"Oh be quiet!" Lilac's face was now plastered with a sick grin. "I'm evil. Shouldn't that be obvious to you by now?"

Pet went to skewer Lilac with her sword, but Iago held her back, "She's still a little girl, Pet. No matter how sick and twisted she is, you can't just stab her."

"Don't worry about me, Iago," Lilac sneered, "I can take care of myself."

Pet had figured it out. "A little girl can't do the kind of damage I saw inflicted on Candice. You're something more, aren't you?"

A horrible laugh erupted from Lilac's mouth. Iago promptly released Pet. His eyes darted around, desperately searching for something he could use as a weapon.

"Tell me what you are," Pet demanded.

"It's easier if I just show you." Lilac closed her eyes and began to change.

CHAPTER THIRTY-NINE

Primal fur sprouted out all over Lilac's body. She grew from three foot something to a towering seven feet. The dress and flowery bracelet fell in tatters to the ground. Her small child's teeth grew into bright white fangs. Her nose became a snout. Her ears elongated. The transformation was as quick as it was startling. The only constant was the red scarlet collar adorning its neck.

Simultaneously, Pet's and Iago's mouths fell open. Iago managed to stammer, "You're... a... wolf?!"

The creature took a mocking bow. "I am indeed. My name is the Big Bad and I will be your murderer this evening."

"Run, Pet!" Iago shouted. "Run for your life!"

"No!" Pet was not about to let Candice's attacker walk away from this. This monster had to pay.

"I have free reign to feast on you lot," the Big Bad smiled. "So who's first?"

Ignoring the pain in his leg, Iago charged at the beast. He ducked low and launched himself towards the monster's legs. While Iago tackled the Big Bad from below, Pet ran forward swinging her sword.

Deftly, the Big Bad evaded both the tackle and Pet's attack. Then in a flash, the wolf pinned each of them down beneath a large paw. Pet was being crushed beneath its enormous weight. She kicked vainly in the air, but her legs were too short to connect with the Big Bad's body.

"Don't you realize how futile this is?" laughed the Big Bad. "You live your whole lives thinking they have purpose, thinking you're going to make something of yourself. But here you are in your last moments, and guess what? This is it. This is what your life has been building up to. You're going to be my appetizer."

"You talk too much," Iago uttered as he kicked. Fortunately, his legs were longer than Pet's and he managed to connect his foot with the Big Bad's body. Unfortunately for the Big Bad, it was pinning Iago down in a position where his adrenaline-fueled kick connected with its groin. Despite being half wolf and of dubious gender, the blow still hurt.

The Big Bad promptly swept them both away. Iago landed against the side of the mountain with a tremendous wallop. He fell into the dirt floor of the road and his hand instinctively felt the back of his head. It was damp. Not again, was Iago's last thought before he lost consciousness.

As air rushed past her ears, Pet realised that she had been thrown over the side of the cliff. Pet's hands scrambled desperately for something to grab onto. Her fingers managed to grab onto a stray root. Her hands gripped harder than Pet had ever gripped anything in her life. Her chest thumped hard against the cliff side, knocking the air out of her, but her hands held on. She glanced down and saw only the forest floor far below.

Looking up the cliff, Pet realized that she had to haul herself up. She stretched and reached for the edge of the cliff. She pulled valiantly and soon had a good grip on the ledge. With all her might, she pulled herself up to the ledge. I'm going to survive this after all, she told herself. Then Pet looked up. The Big Bad was standing above her.

At this point, Mrs Kettlepot emerged from the cave. What she found horrified her. Her love lay bleeding and unconscious and Pet was dangling over a cliff with some horrible monster towering over her.

"Get away from her," cried Mrs Kettlepot. She picked up a rock and lobbed it at the Big Bad. The rock missed.

The Big Bad ignored Mrs Kettlepot. It was having much more fun with Pet. "I can't decide whether to let you fall or eat you."

All colour drained from Pet's face. She screamed, "No! Don't do it."

The Big Bad smiled, "As much as I enjoy hearing you beg for your life, it won't do you any g..."

The monster's sentence was interrupted by a mighty wallop against its back. It suddenly occurred to the Big Bad that Pet had not been talking to it.

Mrs Kettlepot slammed into the Big Bad. It might not have been the strongest tackle in the world, but the Big Bad was not standing very strongly given his recent groin injury. It was enough for Mrs Kettlepot to successfully charge the Big Bad over Pet's head and off the cliff. Unfortunately, Mrs Kettlepot followed the monster over. There was simply no way of escaping the momentum.

Pet clenched her eyes shut. She could not believe what was happening. Maybe her eyes were playing tricks on her. Maybe…

A sickening thump echoed up from the forest floor, confirming Pet's worst fears.

Mrs Kettlepot was gone.

CHAPTER FORTY

Perishing in such a way was unfathomable to Iago. Even so, there was no way Mrs Kettlepot could have survived such a drop. Still he scrambled down the rocks with the utmost urgency. He could not allow his love to lie twisted and exposed on these rocks for any longer than absolutely necessary.

A shape on an outcrop caught Iago's attention. Lilac lay there with her neck twisted at a particularly precarious angle. The monster was dead. It struck Iago as odd that the Big Bad had reverted to its Lilac form upon death. Had that horrible wolf been a sick twisted little girl all along? It didn't really matter now, did it?

There were more important matters to be dealt with. Soon enough, Iago found the body of an older woman, battered, bloody and caked with dirt. Iago knew this had to be the body of Mrs Kettlepot, but something within him refused to concede that this broken form in front of him had once belonged to his love.

She had been such a beautiful woman. The kindness she had shown a lowly toad was proof enough. But where had her beauty and kindness got her in this cruel world? An open grave at the bottom of a cliff.

"Ia…"

In a flash, Iago was by her side. "My love, you're alive!"

"It is you." Her eyes remained shut and her lips barely moved.

"Open your eyes for me, dear."

"I… I can't."

Tears from Iago's eyes spilled onto her face, unsettling some of the grime. "We need to get you out of here."

With much effort, Mrs Kettlepot was able to pry open her eyes slightly. They were cloudy. "I'm dying."

"No you're not. Don't say that."

"Please." Her hands gripped his arm lightly. "It's not so bad."

"What can I do?"

"Do you mind…" Her battered body previously so still, suddenly convulsed. "Do you mind staying with me?"

Iago smiled a sad smile. – To think that she thought comforting her in her final moments would be some sort of imposition! Iago lay down on the stone next to her and cradled her in his arm. With his mouth pressed against her ear, he whispered, "I love you, Mrs Kettlepot."

She could not say anything in response, but a brief smile did twitch across her face. As he held her in his arms, Iago desperately tried to feel every final movement. She was so still now. Her eyelids slowly closed. Her breathing became ever more shallow and slow. Wordlessly, Iago moved his lips away from her ear and brought them towards her lips.

With a sudden jolt, Mrs Kettlepot's eyes darted open. "Don't," she rasped.

Iago looked deeply in her eyes and again drew his lips closer.

"You'll turn back…" she weakly intoned, but the strength to finish the sentence escaped her.

Undetered, Iago pushed his lips against hers. She murmured softly in response. He felt, if anything, his love deserved one final kiss before dying. He would gladly accept his amphibian form, if it gave Iago the opportunity to comfort his love in her final moments.

Mrs Kettlepot smiled, closed her eyes again and breathed her last breath.

Strangely serene, Iago croaked, "I love you" for the final time.

CHAPTER FORTY-ONE

P articles of sand ceased to flow. The last grains of sand in the hoursglass slipped through to the compartment below. The thirtieth hour was over and the Lost Princess had not been delivered. How was this possible? At least the Big Bad was now dead. Isabob could take at least a small measure of satisfaction from that.

"I'm making some tea," Isabob announced as he walked over to the kettle. Fortunately the dungeon did not lack that particular amenity. "Would you like any?"

The Junior Guardsman was worried. "People will ask questions. What do I say when they ask what happened to the Big Bad?"

Isabob returned holding two cups of tea. He took his place at the table and instructed the boy, "Drink!"

The boy took a sip. He hoped it would do a little to calm his nerves. It did not.

Isabob sighed. He knew he had to do this, but he took little satisfaction in it, "I'm going to have to tell you something about modern politics. Whenever there's a screw-up, like in this case, the escape of the Big Bad…"

"But it wasn't an escap…"

Isabob's cross look quickly silenced the boy. "Like the escape of the Big Bad, the reaction isn't always as constructive as one might wish. The reaction isn't, 'What went wrong and how do we ensure this does not happen again?' I wish it was. Things might be better then. No, the reaction usually is, 'Who screwed up and how do we punish them?' Do you understand what I'm saying?"

The Junior Guardsman gulped.

"It must be obvious to you who the scapegoat is going to be." Despite the conviction in his voice, Isabob did regret the fate that was going to befall this boy. "If it's any consolation, I suffered a similar setback in my career when I was your age."

The Junior Guardsman could not stop himself from yawning.

"I look at you," Isabob continued, "and see such strength of character. I don't imagine that you would allow yourself to be party to a cover up."

The boy's eyelids began to droop. He fought to keep his head up but was swiftly losing the battle.

"That's why I've poisoned your tea. You might think me cowardly in your final conscious thoughts, but let me assure you that this is an act of mercy."

The boy's head now rested on the table. His eyes were shut. By all appearances he was asleep. Regardless, Isabob continued, "If I didn't do this, you would endure years and years of humiliation and disrespect."

A gentle snore escaped the Junior Guardsman's mouth. Isabob scribbled a suicide note for the boy. Something about being unable to take the loneliness any more of working the night shift in the dungeon and then taking responsibility for releasing the Big Bad. Isabob would use his influence to ensure that the investigators would not look too closely at the note.

Unfortunately, Isabob could not stop there. There was still much to be done. The Lost Princess was still out there. She had to be found, but this time Isabob was not going to take any chances. The use of agents had failed twice already. This time Isabob was going to take matters into his own hands.

CHAPTER FORTY-TWO

Peaceful murmurs escaped Candice's lips belying the horrible damage done to her body. Brushing a lock of hair away from Candice's sleeping face, Pet could not help but think how pretty she still looked, despite her recent mauling. Candice always looked good, no matter the circumstances. That was one of the things that used to irk Pet about her. Now she treasured it more than anything.

Pet double-checked the straps she had used to secure Candice to Bounds's back. She had padded the straps with all the blankets, clothing and additional padding she could find. Discarded dishes, food and personal items lay scattered on the ground around her, but Pet had no inclination to clear up the mess. After all, one friend was dying and another was already dead.

Candice was in dire need of further medical attention. Mrs Kettlepot had done a good job bandaging Candice up, but she was not out of danger yet. The girl's skin was still very pale and she had yet to regain consciousness. The only option was to continue over Deadman's Finger and complete the ride to the Sapphire Palace. Whatever other intrigue the palace had in store for Pet, she knew there would be healers there.

"Where is Iago?" Pet thought aloud. "We need to get going."

"Right here," a familiar voice croaked from below.

Pet looked down at Iago again in his toad form. If he was an amphibian again then he must have found Mrs Kettlepot and kissed her. Pet could not think of happier news, "You found Mrs Kettlepot?! She's alive!"

The sudden happiness drained from Pet's body with Iago's reply, "Not anymore."

Pet collected Iago in her arms and swung on top of Mucker. Wordlessly, they departed.

As Mucker picked a delicate path down the other side of Deadman's Finger, Pet asked Iago, "Did you bury her?"

Resting in her lap, Iago murmured, "Yes, but I couldn't manage a marker."

Pet briefly marveled at the effort it would have taken for a toad to single-handedly bury a fully-grown woman, let alone erect a marker. The tone of his voice was so uncharacteristically hollow that Pet was left wondering how much of Iago had died along with his lover.

"I could kiss you, to change you back, if you wanted." Pet could feel Iago's body stiffen on her lap. She hoped that she had not offended him.

"No. No thank you," Iago eventually whispered. It was not that he did not want to be human again. For a very long time, that had been the one thing that he wanted most in the world. However, right now all he wanted was for that last kiss from Mrs Kettlepot to linger on his lips for as long as possible.

The rest of the journey down Deadman's Finger was conducted in silence. They soon found themselves at the start of the Hashram Plains. Pet for one was happy to see them. The Hashram Plains were wide, flat and had very few trees for monsters to hide behind.

A crack from the left snapped Pet out of her trance. Instantly, she scolded herself for being irresponsible. Just because they were out of the Shadowoods, it did not mean they were out of danger. Pet whispered to Iago, "Did you hear that?"

"Yes."

"Could it be Lilac again?"

Iago's memory flashed with blood and rubble. The memory gave him a measure of grim satisfaction, "Lilac won't be bothering us again."

"So it's something else." Pet spurred Mucker on. "I should be paying better attention. We definitely don't want to get sneaked up on again."

"That sounds like a good idea," said a creaky voice behind Pet. Shocked, Pet twisted around quickly, losing her balance in the process. Both she and Iago fell off Mucker and tumbled into the mud,

Grasping the hilt of her sword, Pet scrambled to her feet. She drew out her sword and directed the point at the owner of the voice. "State your purpose. Friend or foe?"

"Hahahahahaha." Before Pet was a big laughing lady with knotted hair and simple clothes. She was quite old, older than Mrs Kettlepot.

"What are you trying to be, girl? A big scary guardsman?"

"Who are you? How did you sneak up on us?"

"You don't live next to the Shadowoods without picking up a trick or two." The stranger gestured at the wounded Candice. "Who's this?"

The woman put out a hand to touch Candice.

"Don't touch her!" shrieked Pet.

The strange woman regarded Pet with compassionate eyes, "Poor child, what has happened to you?"

Pet fought the feeling to fall into the woman's arms, to sink into her embrace as she might with Ma or Mrs Kettlepot, "You never answered my first question. Who are you?"

"My name is Loretta Olganna," the woman responded soothingly, "but most people know me as Nurse Olganna."

"Are you a healer?" cried Pet. "Can you help my friend?"

Nurse Olganna nodded. "Let's take her back to my cabin. It's not far and I'll be able to examine her much better there."

Pet followed on foot leading Mucker by the reins and Mucker in turn directed Bounds. Iago hopped alongside Pet occasionally looking up at her. There was something on his mind. He leapt up to Pet's shoulder and whispered in her ear, "Do you think perhaps that we're trusting a stranger too quickly again?"

The toad had a point. Memories of Lilac and how much she took from them continued to dance in Pet's head too, but consideration had to be given to Candice's current predicament.

"She's a nurse. She might be able to help Candice. It's a risk we have to take."

Within a few minutes, they reached Olganna's cabin. It sat in the middle of a clearing circled with wildflowers that showed off every colour of the rainbow and possibly some new ones too. And would you believe it, there were cute fluffy bunnies frolicking in the clearing as well. Everything about this place seemed so peaceful. Who knew such an oasis of calm could exist so close to the Shadowoods?

It took Pet and Olganna working together to get Candice off Bounds without too much jostling. Iago propped the door open as they rushed her inside and placed her on a cot next to the fireplace.

"I might need to touch her," said Nurse Olganna spreading her fingers wide before Pet.

Pet nodded, but kept her eyes on Olganna. Nurse Olganna rested her weathered hand on Candice's stomach to measure her breathing. Then she put two fingers on Candice's wrist to measure her pulse. With each measurement, Pet noticed that Olganna's face became a little bit grimmer.

Bringing the back of her hand up to Candice's forehead to measure her fever, Nurse Olganna brushed a stray hair away from her patient's face. "Now let's take a look at your beautiful face."

Then Nurse Olganna stopped cold.

And then she started to sob.

And sob.

Pet and Iago did not quite know what they should make of this development. Pet stared quizzically at the old nurse. She couldn't be sure, but it looked like Nurse Olganna was smiling.

"Glory be!" Nurse Olganna finally caught her breath. "What are you doing with the Lost Princess?"

For once in her life, Pet did not have an answer.

CHAPTER FORTY-THREE

Probing her hair with insistent fingers, Pet tried to work out the mud and the bits of rubble tangled in it. Her fingers were caked with clay, so she rinsed them in the basin and then went straight back to cleaning her hair. The mirror fogged up again. Pet raised a hand to wipe away the mist and was faced by her own reflection.

So, Candice Butler was the long-lost daughter of King Piotr the Just? How? She wasn't adopted, was she? She did naturally have black hair and oddly enough, blue blood. Nobody had been after Pet. They had been after Candice the entire time. She was the Lost Princess. Not Pet.

Stepping out of the bathroom, Pet found herself in the hearth of Olganna's cabin.

A fire raged in the fireplace, a series of pots suspended over its flaming tongues, bubbling and hissing with strange fluids. Nurse Olganna gave one of the pots a quick stir before turning back to her patient.

Candice was lying, wrapped in blankets, on a small cot beside the fire, her head resting on a large pillow. She looked so beautiful and peaceful, resembling a true sleeping beauty. Perhaps Candice is a princess, Pet mused to herself. She certainly looked the part.

"Finally!" croaked Iago. "What were you doing in there? Writing a novel?"

"Hush now, toad," Olganna intoned. "The girl just needed some time to herself."

"You'd better have left some hot water for me," proclaimed Iago as he hopped towards the washroom.

"Where do you think you're going?" asked Olganna. "My washroom isn't for animals. You go outside and use the brook. It's good enough for the bunnies."

Indignation seized the man-toad, "I will do no such thing. I am Iago von Klein the Third, the Master of…"

"I don't have time for this," Olganna sighed, "I have a sick girl who needs tending to. Wash in the brook or don't wash in the brook. It makes not a whit of difference to me. All I know is that if you use the bathroom, Pet and I will be having frog's legs for dinner tonight."

"Fine," Iago humphed as he hopped towards the front door, taking special care that each hop thwacked loudly against the floorboards.

Olganna chuckled, "Listen to him stomping away like a child in a tantrum. His kind are all the same really. They think they are entitled to anything and everything under the sun."

"All toads are as temperamental as Iago?"

"Not at all. Most toads are nice gentle creatures. I meant noblemen. A boisterous unnecessary lot they are."

A hearty laugh escaped Pet's lips. It felt good. Then her eyes rested on Candice and she stopped. Laughing at a time like this, with her friend in such a condition, felt like betrayal. "How's she doing?" she asked.

"Her Highness's going to be just fine. She'll need plenty of rest though." Olganna dabbed Candice's forehead with a damp cloth. "But in a few days she should be on her feet."

Candice was going to live. There were no words to express the relief Pet felt. "Thank you. You're a great nurse."

"The Petros Bluebloods only hired the best."

"Is that how you knew Candice was the Lost Princess? You cared for her when she was a baby?"

"She was my charge." Olganna looked tenderly at Candice. "My life's purpose was to tend to her every need. I memorized every detail of her face. I never imagined she would grow up to be quite so beautiful."

"Where were you when she disappeared?"

Olganna hung her head, "I was right outside the door. I will never forgive myself for not stopping it." Olganna's mood shifted like a terrible storm. She spat on the floor, "This is all her fault. She masterminded the disappearance of the princess so that she could force the king to give her the throne."

"You mean High Regent Evella?"

"How else can a baby be whisked away from a locked room in the highest tower?" Olganna muttered. "Dark magic must have been used and Evella was the only sorceress in the palace."

Pet went quiet, mulling these accusations around in her mind. It all seemed very improbable, this vast conspiracy tinged with royal intrigue. Olganna snapped, "Don't look at me as if I'm a crazy. This comes from the Grand Vizier Lier. He's perhaps the wisest and noblest man I know. Nobody cares more about the realm than that man."

Pet had to concede that there was something very suspicious going on at the Sapphire Palace. How else could she account for what the Cloaked Man had said? Chances were that that same someone at the palace was also responsible for their run-in with Lilac.

"Someone has been hunting Candice," Pet admitted. She wanted to tell Olganna what happened, but was not sure whether she could finish the story. Pet took a deep breath, glanced at Candice and began, "They've been hunting us since we left Seacrest."

And so it began. Pet recounted every detail of their arduous journey: the fight with Judd, the encounter with the Cloaked Man, the visit to Frontier Keep, the manticore, the mauling of Candice and the death of Mrs Kettlepot. Pet could not stop. However once she was done, Pet did feel better, lighter, and less burdened.

Olganna took a moment to ponder. "It sounds like the handiwork of Evella to me. If Her Highness were to make it to the palace and show she was still alive, Evella would have to hand over the realm to her."

At this moment, Candice coughed lightly. Olganna checked her patient's temperature. Pet was left alone in her thoughts, trying to make sense of what had happened and what was to be done next.

"Someone's coming!" Iago's voice rang out as he hurriedly hopped into the cabin. "A band of armed of men is coming across the plain. They fly the banner of the Sapphire Palace."

"Evella's men," murmured Olganna.

Pet gathered her thoughts, "How long do we have?"

"Not long," Iago informed her, "a few minutes at most."

Olganna looked at Pet in panic, "We can't let them take Her Highness."

"Everybody calm down! I have a plan," announced Pet. It had just sprung into her head. It was wild, but it just might work.

CHAPTER FORTY-FOUR

Prior to first light, Isabob and his men had set out from the Sapphire Palace. Since then they had been zig-zagging across the Hashram Plains. According to the Cloaked Man's report, the Lost Princess was on her way to the Sapphire Palace. By now she should be close. At each homestead, the men questioned the inhabitants and searched the property. So far they had had no luck.

To Isabob's annoyance, the Deadman's Finger loomed closer and closer. He realized that if they could not locate the girl in the Hashram Plains, they would have to continue their search into the Shadowoods. That would not go over well with the men. Hopefully the Princess would be in this last cabin, but Isabob did not hold out much hope. Isabob knew who owned it.

Isabob signaled for his men to stop. "Nurse Olganna. Please come out!"

From within the cabin, a familiar frail voice responded, "Who's that? Why does your voice sound familiar?"

"It's me, Isabob."

Olganna stepped out into the sunlight. Isabob was surprised to find that she did not look much older than last time he had laid eyes on her. This was particularly bizarre considering their last encounter was sixteen years ago. "Guardsman Isabob! It's been so long! Are you here for some tea and biscuits?"

"Unfortunately, I'm here on business," Isabob sighed. "We're looking for a girl. She's about seventeen, from the Southern Province, with hair as dark as night. We have reason to believe she's in the area."

"What could this girl have done that would cause a group of so many guardsmen to come all this way, looking for her?"

It was not the first time Isabob had been asked that question today. "That's on a strict need to know basis, Olganna," he replied. "Have you seen a girl matching the description?"

"Sounds like the girl I found this afternoon."

Isabob could not believe his ears. "You found a girl? Where?"

"Earlier today at the base of Deadman's Finger. She was hurt so I took her in," Olganna remarked. "Looked like some savage beast had taken a few bites out of her."

"I need to see her," Isabob insisted. This had to be her.

Isabob ran into the cabin. As soon as he entered, he saw the girl sleeping by the fire. She matched the description. She looked about seventeen. Her hair was certainly black as night.

"I'm going to have to take her with me. Is that her horse out there?"

Olganna nodded. She gazed at Isabob for a moment without saying anything. Eventually she spoke. "I have something to show you."

She went over to the sleeping girl and unwrapped her bandages. She folded them back, showing an ugly blue stain on the bandages. "She has blue blood. She's one of the Petros Bluebloods. This is the Lost Princess!"

Isabob whispered harshly to Olganna, "You can't tell anybody about this."

"Knowing who she is, do you still plan to deliver her into Evella's clutches?"

"I'm sorry." Isabob tried to be as gentle as possible, while remaining firm. "She has to come with me. I have my orders."

Resigned, Olganna bent down and whispered her farewells to the sleeping girl. Given Olganna's infamously low opinion of the high regent, Isabob would have expected more resistance from the former nurse-maid. Instead, as Isabob swept the girl into his arms, all she did was stand back and plead, "Please be careful with her."

A brainwave suddenly struck Isabob. "Why don't you come with us, Olganna? You can continue to treat her at the palace."

Olganna shook her head, "The palace already has some excellent healers. I should know. I trained them. In any case, I have responsibilities to attend to here."

Isabob thought Olganna would have leapt at the opportunity to spend more time with her former charge. Oh well, it mattered little to him. He had found the Lost Princess and was about to deliver her home. His mission was almost complete.

As she was taken away, feigning unconsciousness, Pet could not help but wonder what exactly she had got herself into.

CHAPTER FORTY-FIVE

Pretending to be unconscious was not as easy as Pet had initially predicted. The guardsmen had roughly bound her to Mucker's back for the journey back to the palace. Isabob had instructed them to be as careful with her as possible, but was there a careful way to strap somebody to a horse?

Wrapping herself in Candice's used bandages and feigning unconsciousness might not have been Pet's most well thought out or hygienic plan ever, but Isabob's surprise arrival had not given her much time. Whoever was behind this had to be confronted and this person was in the Sapphire Palace. So Pet decided to take Candice's place and get a free ride there.

After several thousand more bumps and bangs, Mucker came to a halt. The straps were loosened and rough hands grabbed her. Pet was taken inside. Then she found herself being carried upwards, then up some more. At one point, her arm grazed the cold stone of what Pet assumed to be the passage wall. Eventually she was laid down on a bed. The mattress was so soft that her body literally sank into it. There were more whispers and then the door closed.

Pet opened her eyes and took a peek at her surroundings. The room was clean and simple enough, but hardly befitting her royal expectations. Looking out of the window, Pet could see only a darkening sky. Evening was already fast approaching.

A sound caused Pet to throw herself back down on the bed and again feign sleep. The voice of Isabob spoke. "She's in here."

There was a shuffling of feet and delicate fingers touched Pet's stomach. They reached around her body and unwrapped her bandages. Before Pet knew it, the bandages were off. A feminine voice exclaimed, "They're blue…"

"How are her wounds?" asked Isabob.

"What wounds?"

"She was supposedly attacked by a savage beast."

"There are a few minor scrapes but nothing like that," the woman replied.

So Pet had been in the palace all of five minutes and she was already going to be discovered. The woman concluded, "Olganna's still a good nurse."

Pet breathed a sigh of relief.

"Would you like me to let some blood instead?" asked the woman.

Pet tightened right back up.

"That shouldn't be necessary," Isabob whispered. "I still want those bandages tested. We have to make sure that the blood is legitimate and this isn't another imitator."

Pet could not just sit there pretending to be unconscious forever. Now was just as good a time as any. In a theatrically groggy voice, Pet asked, "Who's there?"

"She's awake," announced the woman. Pet slowly opened her eyes. Standing before her was an older man in a guardsman uniform and a young woman dressed in a shawl. They both looked eager to talk to her.

"Allow me to introduce myself." Isabob bowed down low. "I am First Guardsman Isabob. This is Urseffe. She's one of the high regent's personal handmaidens and the best healer on our staff."

"Where am I?"

"You are in the Sapphire Palace. Your horse is being well-treated in the stables," Isabob informed her. "Do you know why you're here?"

There seemed little point in beating around the bush. "Is it because I am the Lost Princess?"

Isabob and Urseffe exchanged surprised glances. Isabob answered, "Yes. We've gone to a lot of trouble to find you."

"So this is home?" Pet sat up in bed.

"Yes," Urseffe replied. "This is actually the same room you had as a child. We're at the top of the Spire. It's the tallest point of the entire Sapphire Palace. It seemed appropriate to room you here. There will be a guardsman posted outside your r…"

Isabob could not wait any longer, "Your Highness, I need to know. What has happened to you in the last seventeen years?"

He was going to have to wait a little longer, "Do I have to go into that now? I've been journeying for six days without rest. I'm dirty and starving. Certainly these questions can wait till I've washed myself and eaten."

Isabob opened his mouth as if to protest, but Urseffe spoke up first. "Certainly, Your Highness. If you're hungry, the high regent will be dining in a couple of hours. I think she would be pleased to meet you."

"That would be delightful," Pet responded hoping her voice did not give away her fears. Was Pet to confront her archnemesis already? In two short hours? What does one wear to a nemesis confrontation?

"Until then, Your Highness!" Isabob bowed and promptly left the room. As Urseffe went about drawing a bath for Pet, she flung herself back on the bed. She was in the middle of a nest of vipers with no clue what she was actually doing. At least this bed was remarkably soft.

CHAPTER FORTY-SIX

Pulling another twig from Candice's hair, Olganna momentarily considered just yanking it out, but quickly reconsidered. Some hair would most certainly come with the twig and Her Highness would probably not be too appreciative of that. Instead, Olganna extracted each twig individually by delicately untangling it from Candice's blonde locks. Her dark roots were beginning to show. It was disconcerting to Olganna to see what the Princess had done to her hair.

Taking a breather, Olganna walked onto the porch of her cabin and found Iago sprawled out on the step. He was apparently relaxing while Olganna was in there slaving away. "When I said hide her in the woods, I didn't mean bring it all back with her."

"Lest you forget, I am a toad," Iago responded. "Dragging a human around in the woods isn't an easy task for me."

Olganna agreed. It was true that Iago had effectively hidden Candice in the woods. She should not take her anger out on him, when she herself was the guilty one.

"You couldn't have stopped her," Iago mentioned as if reading Olganna's thoughts. "Once Pet puts her mind to something, nothing can stop her."

"An executioner's axe will stop her. This will be her fate when they find out she's not the Lost Princess." Then something moved in the distance, "Someone's coming, Iago. You had better hide Her Highness in the woods again."

Before Iago could move, two figures emerged into the clearing. Fear gripped Olganna's heart. Who were these new visitors? What did they want?

Iago peered at the new arrivals, "That will not be necessary. One of them is an old friend of mine," Then with a mighty croak, he shouted to one of their new visitors, "Hey, Bumpkin! You look good for a dead man!"

"You!" A voice shouted back, "What are you doing here, Pondscum? What have you done with Pet and Candice?"

As he approached, Olganna could see that, despite his large frame, this man was still only a teenager. She asked Iago, "Who is this loud boy?"

"This is the reliable Judd Duncanson," Iago announced, "though I wouldn't have thought he had the intellectual capacity to track us."

Judd did not want to admit that Sentry had done most of the tracking. Regardless, he was preoccupied with something else Iago had said, "What do you mean, I look good for a dead man? Is that some sort of class thing?"

"The Cloaked Man told us he had killed you."

This did not go over well with Judd, "What? Where are Candice and Pet? I have to show them I'm still alive."

Olganna frowned. This boy had just come onto her porch and without any sort of proper greeting, was already demanding things. She sighed, "Please do come in."

The moment Judd's eyes fell on Candice, his jaw fell open. "What happened to her? Tell me, Pondscum, before I bash you."

Iago was in no mood to be pushed around. "Try to recall what happened the last time you uttered a threat in my direction."

As far as Olganna was concerned both Judd and Iago were visitors in her cabin and very rude visitors at that. However, before Olganna could say anything, a booming voice declared, "Enough!"

The authority of the voice stopped both Iago and Judd in their tracks. The voice had an even more startling effect on Olganna. She had never expected to hear it again, but given her recent visitor, she should have suspected this day was coming.

"Your Majesty," Olganna uttered, as she curtsied down to the floor.

Sentry entered the cabin with a majestic stride. "Olganna. It has been a long time."

Iago whispered to Judd, "Why is she curtsying to a common guardsman?"

Judd announced proudly, "That common guardsman is none other than the returned King Piotr."

Sentry turned to Judd, "You knew?"

"There were lots of hints," Judd revealed, "Your extraordinary interest in finding Pet, your unknown past, your dark hair that you shave off and that mysterious ring you flash, which I suspect is the royal signet ring... and I mean, 'Sentry'? What kind of name is 'Sentry'? It had to be fake."

Iago hopped up to Sentry. "Your Majesty, my name is Iago von Klein the Third, the Master of Murky Swamp. I am your loyal servant."

If Sentry heard Iago's words, he gave no indication. Instead he was distracted by the sleeping form of Candice. "My daughter, how is she?"

Judd's eyebrows arched. Candice was Sentry's daughter and not Pet?! He did not see that one coming.

Olganna grabbed one last twig out of Candice's hair and answered, "Resting."

"She will live?" There was such happiness in Sentry's voice.

"To a ripe old age," Olganna smiled, "If she avoids crossing the paths of any more wolves."

"She encountered a wolf?"

Instantly, Olganna regretted saying anything.

"And a manticore and the crazed Cloaked Man," piped in Iago, "It's a miracle she made it this far really."

Olganna put a comforting hand on Sentry's shoulder. Perhaps this was not the most appropriate way to approach royalty, but Olganna's training as a nurse and a healer overrode those sensibilities now. Before her was a man in pain and she sought to confront him, "You could not have predicted this, Your Majesty."

"Perhaps, but she's my daughter and I was not there to protect her."

"You can't change the past," Olganna intoned. "What's important is that she's safe now."

"You speak wisely as ever, Olganna. From now on, I shall ensure she's never in harm's way again. Can she be moved?"

Olganna had to tell the truth, "Yes, but further rest will do her a world of good."

"I fear there's no time for that." Sentry swept Candice into his arms. "We must go."

"Well at least let me gather a few things for you!" With a speed that belied her age, Olganna started darting around her cabin, "Here is some Googleberry salve which will help reduce the swelling. If her temperature spikes, ensure she drinks plenty of water and takes two drops of…"

Sentry took the bag from Olganna, "I remember everything you taught me. She will be fine."

"He did a good job with me," remarked Judd.

"Let me come with you," Olganna pleaded with Sentry, "Just in case."

That was not going to work. Sentry wanted to ride at a blistering pace. A storm was gathering at the Sapphire Palace and when it struck, he did not want Candice to be anywhere near. Olganna would just slow them down, "Olganna. I discharge you of your duties. You have spent your entire life in service to the realm. You deserve a rest."

Judd interrupted him. "Wait! We can't just go. We don't even know what happened to Pet."

Iago was happy to inform him. The mention of Pet's name caused Sentry's brow to tighten. "I have lost all patience with that girl. If it had not been for Pet and her fool's errand, my daughter would be safe in Seacrest."

"That's hardly fair," Judd countered.

"Death has little sense of fairness." Sentry stalked by Judd, exiting the cabin with the unconscious Candice.

Judd followed him out. "What about the realm? It's falling apart at the seams. There's a usurper on the throne. The Magistrates are corrupt. People have had enough!"

"What usurper? I have no clue what you're talking about." Sentry put Candice on top of his steed and swung up behind her. "Never mind. It doesn't matter. My only responsibility is to my daughter."

Judd could not believe what he was about to say to the King, "Fine then. Be a coward. Abandon the realm. I will go and do your job for you. I'm going to save Pet."

"That's fine by me, boy," Sentry declared. And with that, the man who was supposedly King Piotr the Just rode off.

"Well that was certainly unexpected." Iago hopped up. "So what's the plan now, Bumpkin?"

"Plan for what?"

"Your plan to save the lovely Pseudo-Princess Petunia Peasant, of course."

CHAPTER FORTY-SEVEN

Popping bubbles brought a smile to Pet's face. She sighed with pleasure as the warm bath water washed over her. Being a princess was not so bad after all. If only Pet could let herself forget about the dire circumstances that had brought her here.

Her friends had been killed or brutalized on the orders of someone here in the Sapphire Palace, possibly the high regent herself. Then there was the original purpose of this entire trek to consider as well. The Southern Province, her home, were on the edge of economic ruin. Pet had a lot to do.

With renewed determination, Pet emerged from the bath and grabbed a towel. Just as Pet finished dressing, Urseffe asked, "What are you planning to wear, Your Highness?"

Pet looked down at her clothes. "My clothes?"

Urseffe smiled. "Your Highness, you are a princess again. You must dress the part."

With a quick clap of Urseffe's hands, the door flung open and half a dozen people poured into the room. They immediately set to work. The Royal Manicurist filed Pet's nails. The Royal Aesthetician removed any stray hairs. The Royal Perfumer sprayed her with a floral scent. The Royal Make-up Artist applied copious amounts of blush. The Royal Clothier fitted her into a gown.

During the arduous process, Pet developed a new respect for princesses everywhere. The hours of primping and preening, tight corsets and hair-dressing had been conveniently skipped over in the fairy tales. It certainly took a lot longer than her usual routine in Seacrest. Now it took an entire entourage to make her 'presentable.' Was she to endure this before every meal from now on?

It took almost two hours but they eventually left, leaving a beautiful but tired Pet behind. Then Urseffe entered the chamber with a box. "There's just one final touch."

Pet pleaded, "No more. Please. I've had my fill of final touches for the day."

"You haven't seen what's in here yet!" Urseffe opened the box.

Pet's eyes grew large and round. She had heard them mentioned, but did not think they actually existed. They seemed just too decadent and impractical really to exist. Pet lifted the glass slippers out of the box. "I don't believe it."

Without instruction, Urseffe bent down and helped Pet put on the glass slippers. Pet gingerly rose to her feet and took tiny steps around. The slippers might have been glass, but they certainly felt sturdy.

Pet took a final look at herself in the mirror. There she stood in her black-haired, blue-gowned and glass-slippered glory. Not too shabby. Not too shabby at all. Still Candice could have pulled it off with less effort. That is, if she was not at this moment fighting for her life. Pet took another glance at the mirror and saw only ridiculous pageantry.

Her frown did not go unnoticed. "Pardon my brashness, Your Highness, but why are you sad? You're home again."

"It doesn't feel right," Pet admitted. "What if I let everybody down?"

"Well, I wouldn't worry too much about that," Urseffe smiled. "The realm has been without a princess for sixteen years. Most have forgotten what it's like to have one. As I see it, you can make up the rules as you go along."

There was a gentle knock on the door. "That's probably the guardsman to escort us down to the banquet hall. Should I tell him you need a few more minutes?"

Pet gazed at herself once more in the mirror. "No. I'm ready. Let the intrigue begin."

CHAPTER FORTY-EIGHT

Precarious steps were needed to get down the many steps of the Spire. Glass slippers were not easy. Urseffe followed Pet, ensuring that she did not trip over her gown. After the descent, the guardsman led them through many a twisting and turning hallway. Pet was unable to get her bearings in this labyrinth of a palace. She was about to make some pithy comment, when she noticed Urseffe scowling.

Urseffe brought her lips to Pet's ear. "This is not the way to the banquet hall."

"Guardsman," Pet asked, "where are you taking us?"

"Somebody would like to meet you," the guardsman informed her.

They were soon standing in front of a large door which the guardsman promptly opened. "Please enter, Your Highness."

Pet took a few steps through the door. She was a little intrigued as to the identity of whoever had called this meeting. At this point, Pet realized that she was entering the room by herself. Answering the question before Pet could ask it, Urseffe said, "Some things are not meant for common ears." The guardsman then closed the door.

Suddenly alone, Pet inspected her surroundings. It was a large ornamental study with books covering every wall and column. Even though she enjoyed a good book, Pet felt turned off by the sheer quantity of them. No single person could ever read this many books.

"Welcome, Your Highness!" A man with a long beard stepped out from behind a pillar and bowed dramatically. "Allow me to introduce myself. I am the Grand Vizier Lier."

"Why did you summon me here? Could this not have waited till after dinner?"

Lier took a seat behind his desk. "It is dinner that I hoped to discuss with you."

Recalling that Olganna had mentioned this man and his wisdom, Pet decided she should at least listen to what he had to say. She sat down but was clear to point out, "You have five minutes."

Lier smiled, "I wanted to preface any conversation by telling you that I remain a loyal servant to your father and by extension yourself. Unfortunately, not everyone in the Sapphire Palace feels the same way."

"Are you talking about the high regent?"

"Yes," whispered Lier, "and her agents."

"You mean Isabob?"

"That's why I had to sneak you away when he wasn't looking," Lier replied. "I needed to let you know that it's not safe for you here. Your presence is a threat to the high regent's authority. She went to a lot of trouble to get rid of you the first time. She won't be too happy to see you back."

This was it. This was finally it. Pet was finally going to get some answers. "Evella was the one who took me away?"

"Yes. She used her dark magic so that the winds would pick you up and spirit you out of the window."

"How do you know this?"

"There is no other possible way that you could have been taken."

That answer did not totally convince Pet, but it would do for now. "Why did she do it?" she asked him.

"To increase her influence over King Piotr," Lier explained. "After the death of your mother, you were his only reason for living and ruling. By banishing you, she sought to control your father. He tried to continue ruling without you, but his heart simply wasn't in it anymore. So he abdicated the throne and went searching for you. However, before he left, Evella made sure he installed her as high regent in his absence."

Pet tried to understand. If Evella was the one who banished the Lost Princess, did this mean that Evella had sent the Cloaked Man and Lilac after her? Why now? What had changed? What Pet really needed was some time to just sit and sort all this out. Unfortunately, that was not happening any time soon.

"I know this is very sudden, but we don't have much time," Lier intoned. "We need to discuss our plan."

"Our plan for what?"

"There's no delicate way to put this," Lier paused dramatically, his eyes burrowing into Pet. "You need to claim your legitimate throne and overthrow the high regent."

Pet could not believe what she was hearing. Masquerading as a princess was one thing, but masterminding a coup was quite another! "Is that all?"

"Your Highness, I fear you don't fully fathom the danger you're in. Evella was willing to use blackmail and magic to rise to power. I fear the extremes that she will go to, to retain it."

"I am fully aware of the danger we face." It was now Pet's turn to let her eyes burrow into Lier. "Two of my friends have already lost their lives."

"My apologies, Your Highness." Lier bowed his head. "I hope I didn't insult you."

Pet sighed. The stakes had been irrevocably raised. They were discussing overthrowing the high regent of the realm. "You're right. We need a plan."

CHAPTER FORTY-NINE

Preoccupied with her thoughts, Pet wordlessly followed Urseffe and the guardsman towards the banquet hall. This time there was no worrying about glass slippers, the route they took, or anything else for that matter. Instead she kept on repeating the conversation she had had with Lier over and over in her mind.

The guardsman brought them to a halt outside two massive oak doors. Urseffe told Pet, "Behind these doors is the banquet hall. Are you ready, Your Highness?"

"Not in the slightest," Pet confessed. Urseffe nodded to the guardsman who flung open the large doors.

Before Pet could process the huge proportions of the banquet hall or the vast number of people, she first had to come to terms with the noise. There were hundreds of conversations going on at once, jumbling together to make a tremendous roar. Pet gulped and gingerly took her first step in.

And then it all stopped.

One could have heard a pin drop in that hall. Pet noticed that every face was looking at her with the same peculiar look, as if they did not know what to make of her. There was a tremendous number of people packed into that hall. This was only meant to be a spot of supper before bed, wasn't it?

Pet smiled awkwardly at the people as Urseffe escorted her through the crowd to the head table at the end of the hall. As Pet approached the table, she felt a measure of relief. The people sitting at the head table were examining her just as much, but at least there were fewer of them.

One patron examined Pet closer than most. It felt like her dark eyes were boring directly into Pet's very soul. Pet did not even need to see the throne she occupied to know who this woman was. The sense of authority that emanated from her was identification enough. This was the High Regent Evella and she was about to speak.

"Welcome, daughter of the realm!" Evella rose and all attention was immediately on her. Her voice was both crisp and tender at the same time. "The First Guardsman informs me that you are the returned Lost Princess. Would you please be so kind as to join us for dinner?"

Pet replied, "Yes I would. Thank you."

Evella gestured to the empty throne next to her. "Please sit next to me."

Was it really a good idea to sit next to her evil sorceress nemesis? Evella could turn her into a toad or worse. However Pet was never one to run and hide. She could do this. All she had to do was sit next to the high regent and eat dinner. That was all. Then Pet's eyes wandered to the seat on her left. Then she really did want to run and hide.

Dashing stood up from his chair and smiled warmly at Pet. His lips were just as delectable as ever as they cooed, "Your Highness."

This was unfair. Despite all the attacks and intrigue, Pet had spent a significant amount of time thinking about what she would say if she ever saw Dashing again. She had composed a sonnet about her appreciation of his symmetrical beauty and the depths of her passion for him. Unfortunately, said monologue vanished from her memory. Pet struggled to come up with something of the cuff, but all she could come out with was, "Hi."

As Dashing pulled back Pet's throne for her, he whispered in her ear, "There is something I must tell you. We arrested the Cloaked Man who attacked you and his boy."

"Thank you," breathed Pet. Knowing that the Cloaked Man was now behind bars was encouraging. She was a little surprised to hear about a boy, but before she could ask further she got distracted by the realization that Urseffe was no longer beside her.

Pet scanned the table trying to figure out where she had gone. She spotted Urseffe at the back of the hall with the other attendants. Pet was sitting between her arch enemy and her potential love interest. It was a curious sensation, feeling so alone in such a crowded room.

At least the throne was comfortable. It was made of solid wood with a golden trimming and lined in plush velvet. "That throne was the queen's," Evella told her. Brushing the mahogany with her fingertips, Pet briefly imagined how regal Queen Polly must have looked sitting in the throne.

"I see that you're sitting on my father's throne," Pet observed. It was particularly difficult for her to say 'my father' and think of King Piotr and not Pa Peasant.

"It's customary for the reigning regent to occupy the High Throne," replied Evella. Pet was a bit disappointed that her challenging words did not seem to faze Evella in the slightest.

Pet noticed that Lier was only now taking a seat. He scowled ever so slightly as he saw Evella and Pet conversing. Pet could not overcome the temptation to rattle Evella just a little. After all, what was she going to do in front of a hall full of witnesses? Pet whispered in Evella's ear, "Why did you send the Cloaked Man and the Big Bad after me?"

A confused look crossed Evella face. "I don't have a clue what you're talking about, dear."

Playing dumb was not going to work with Pet. "I know how you banished me and then usurped the throne."

Evella's eyes darted around the table to ensure no-one else heard what she was saying. "I'm afraid this is hardly an appropriate time to discuss such matters. We have a hall full of hungry people before us who would like to start their dinner. I will send for you after dinner and we will speak frankly then. I will say this, though. I would not take everything that is told to you at face value." She then gestured to one of the attendants, "Please serve the first course."

In a synchronized dance, the attendants presented the first course across the hall. Dishes were set down and lids removed to reveal tempting bowls of soup. Pet had feared that all this intrigue might have some diminishing effect on her appetite. It did not. Pet eagerly picked up her spoon and was about to dive in when she noticed that everyone was looking at her.

"I believe they want you to say something," murmured Dashing.

Pet took a moment to compose the words in her head. She then called out in as clear a voice she could muster. "Thank you for this warm welcome. Now let us enjoy a long overdue meal together."

And with that, everyone began to eat. Pet took special care to slowly spoon her soup. If she was to finish her meal too quickly, Evella or Dashing or anyone of the other patrons of the table might be inclined to ask her something and she was in no mood to answer any more questions.

Only one thing was on her mind, her upcoming meeting with Evella. What was she going to say? Maybe Evella was going to have Pet killed. This could very well be her last meal ever. Pet sighed. At least it was delicious soup.

CHAPTER FIFTY

"Put her to death!" The boss's orders rang clearly in Isabob's head. Given his many years in the service, he thought he had heard it all. He had been wrong.

"She is illegitimate. She does not belong. She could throw everything into chaos. She must be disposed of, Isabob. You must do this. The fate of the realm relies on it."

There had been more explanations and justifications on the matter, but Isabob did not need them. He wanted to do this. He wanted to do it for everything she had caused him to lose. This was about getting even. This was about justice. Of course, it would also be treason.

As Isabob approached the kitchen, Urseffe was just leaving, holding a large jug, "Urseffe, where are you going with that?"

"I'm just taking this upstairs," responded Urseffe.

Isabob smiled briefly. Urseffe was such a beautiful girl. Death was always more readily accepted when served by a pretty face. "I need to perform a test on that."

"Really?" Urseffe was surprised. In all her years of service in the palace, the testing of food and beverage was usually performed in the kitchen.

"No need to worry. This is just a random test. Please turn around."

Urseffe complied. One did not argue with the First Guardsman.

Isabob took the vial of Morpheus Root extract out of his pocket. He quickly unscrewed the cap and poured a generous measure into the jug, but not all of it. He wanted to keep a little extra for later. Replacing the vial back in his pocket, Isabob took a loud sniff of the jug for Urseffe's benefit.

"Everything looks good," Isabob declared. "Please continue on your way."

"Thank you, First Guardsman." Urseffe gave no indication of just how odd she found Isabob's behaviour to be.

Once Urseffe left, Isabob dashed back to his office. He closed the door and sat behind his desk. A small part of Isabob desperately wanted to watch her take the juice and ingest the poison. He would find it quite consoling to watch her drift into her endless sleep. He envied her peaceful passing. Too few people died with dignity anymore.

Now it was time for Isabob to fulfill his duty. He removed the vial of Morpheus Root extract from his pocket and admired it in the light. There was only a little left, but it would be enough. Isabob unscrewed the cap.

Though Isabob was not specifically asked to do this next part, he knew that it had to be done. One last piece of business had to be attended to first. Isabob grabbed a random piece of paper from the piles on his desk. He flipped it over and haphazardly wrote his final message to the world.

That was it. There were no loose ends left, no lingering clues. He had thought of everything. The trail would lead to an end with him. Just the way it should.

Isabob brought the vial up to his lips. With a swift knock back of his head, the essence was soon within him. A yawn rose up deep inside Isabob. He smiled and closed his eyes.

CHAPTER FIFTY-ONE

Patience had never been Pet's strong suit. What was taking that woman so long? Evella had said she would send someone to get Pet after dinner so they could discuss matters. Where was her summons? Had she forgotten?

It had only been five minutes, but Pet feared that if she sat down her nerves would overtake her completely. Maybe at that moment the high regent was making plans to have the Royal Guard come and arrest her. Pet gulped and brought her ear to the door. Nothing.

Fine. If the high regent was not going to come to Pet then Pet would go to the high regent. Unfortunately Urseffe had not returned to show her the way so Pet asked the guardsman outside her door to take her to Evella's chambers.

Soon they were outside the chambers. Pet did not need her guide to announce this. It was obvious by the size of the ornate doors and the two guardsmen stationed outside.

"Your Highness," the guardsman on duty said, "What may we do for you?"

"I'm here to see the high regent. We had arranged to meet after dinner."

The two guardsmen on duty looked at each other, "The high regent didn't leave word of that with us."

"Is she in there?" asked Pet. "Can I just go in and chat with her?"

"She gave strict instructions not to be disturbed. Very strict instructions."

"Alright then," grumbled Pet. "But when she does emerge, please inform the high regent that I was here to see her and that I would like to speak to her as soon as possible."

Upon arriving back to her chambers, Pet took a sip of the pomegranate juice that Urseffe had brought up. It tasted good and had a calming effect on Pet.

She promptly went over to the bed and lay down. Pet closed her eyes. She took in a few more deep breaths and tried to relax. She did not have to try very long. Before Pet knew it, she was fast asleep.

CHAPTER FIFTY-TWO

Prolonged purrs escaped Candice's lips as the sunlight warmed her cheek. This was it. She was going to have to get up now. At least she had had a pleasant dream about a strong and gentle man who took her around town to buys lots of salt water toffee candy.

Candice's eyes cracked open. The canvas undulated up and down, just like the ocean in Seacrest. There must be a breeze outside causing it to move in such a fashion.

Wait a second...

Candice sat bolt upright. She was in a tent, but she and Pet had not brought any tents with them. Whose tent was this and what was Candice doing sleeping in it?

Her mind raced backwards and tried to remember. She remembered escaping the manticore with Lilac. Then Lilac turned into some horrible monster. Then there was pain... lots of pain.

"Pet? Mrs Kettlepot? Are you two outside?" called Candice as she stumbled to her feet. There was no immediate response, but she did hear twigs crunching. There was definitely somebody outside. "Who's there?"

"You should be resting," returned a gruff but familiar voice.

The flap of the tent was pulled back and a large figure filled the entrance.

"Sentry?! What are you doing here?"

At least Candice assumed it was Sentry. The broad strokes of the man before her resembled Sentry, but there was something missing in the details. His face looked more tired and haggard than usual. His purple cape was torn and stained. He lacked his usual bearing. He no longer looked like a guardsman, more like a man on the edge of desperation.

"I came to ensure you were safe," responded Sentry.

"Are the others alright? Did that monster get them?"

"Relax. Apply this to your wounds." Sentry handed Candice a steaming bowl of poultice, "Pet took care of the wolf. I just wish she had taken better care of you."

Candice noticed that Sentry had let his hair grow. A fine brush of black hair sat on top of his head. If someone had such a full head of hair, why would they shave it all off?

"So Pet is okay? Where is she?"

"When I caught up with you, you were hurt. Pet wanted to abandon you, so I volunteered to get you to safety."

Candice's lips fell numb. Her eyes grew large and glossy. It was not Sentry's intent to cause Candice any pain, but she needed to forget about Pet and her fool's errand. Sure it was a lie, but it was for the best. Candice would be safe now. Still this rationalization did nothing to dissolve that betrayed look on Candice's face. Perhaps Sentry could say something to make her feel better. Unfortunately, Sentry could not find the words. After so many, what could he possibly say?

Sentry sucked in a calming breath. He was a guardsman. He was supposed to be brave and decisive. This hesitation was not in his character. He should just tell her and be done with it, "Candice. I've got something to tell you. I'm..."

"A liar!" cried Candice as she swiftly threw the bowl of poultice into Sentry's face.

Not expecting the blow, Sentry keeled over as Candice's hand darted for the sword attached to his belt. However, Sentry had been a good guardsman for many years. Over this time, he had developed quite fast reflexes. Candice's fingertips barely brushed the sword's hilt before his hand had a very strong grip on her wrist.

"Pet would never abandon me!" Candice screamed.

"Why do you say that? You know full well she left Judd behind."

"That was different."

"This is all Pet's fault," growled Sentry. "If she had listened to me and stayed in Seacrest, I could have protected both of you, but no... She had to do things her way and look where it got you. You almost died, Candice!"

"Let me go!" Candice brought her free hand around and smacked Sentry hard in the face.

Sentry shook off the slap. "Fine, I'll tell you the truth...."

Their eyes locked. This was it. He was going to reveal all to her. She would understand then.

"I'm your father."

Again Candice smacked Sentry hard. That was certainly not the reaction he had been expecting. Sentry decided to try a different tack.

"I'm your king."

Another slap.

"Will you please stop slapping me?"

"You need to stop lying to me, Sentry! Tell me what really happened to Pet."

Her eyes were so bold and without fear. Strangely, Sentry could not have been more proud of his daughter. He lowered his head and began explaining the best he could. He explained how he had found Judd, encountered the Cloaked Man and caught up with them at Olganna's cabin. He explained that by the time he had arrived, Pet had already been taken by the guardsmen back to the Sapphire Palace.

"What about Mrs Kettlepot? What happened to her?"

There was never an easy way to impart news like this, "From what I gathered, she sacrificed herself to stop the wolf that attacked you."

A single tear escaped Candice's eye. "Why did you lie to me?"

"I didn't want you to worry about them. I wanted you to be happy with me."

Candice examined the guardsman. Sentry had always been a source of security, consistently emanating feelings of incredible solace. That had now evaporated. Why had he claimed to be her father? She had a father. He knew she had a father. Why did he claim he was the king? He certainly did not look anything like King Piotr the Just. She had seen the portraits.

"You don't believe me, do you? You don't think I'm the king. You don't think I'm your father. I'll prove it to you." Sentry grabbed a dagger from his belt. He brought the edge up to his arm...

"Stop!" cried Candice, "There's no need to cut yourself. I believe you."

Once the dagger was sheathed, Candice intoned, "I understand and I appreciate your efforts to deliver me from danger, but you know that I can never truly be happy unless I know Pet is safe too. She is my sister. We must go to the Sapphire Palace to get her."

"Going there would be perilous and I refuse to expose you to more danger."

Candice face remained stoic, "You misunderstand. I will go to save her with or without you. I just think that it would be safer with you."

"You have no idea about the forces conspiring against you." The guardsman began wiping the poultice off his face. "I'm sorry, I know you want to help your friend, but I can't let you go."

"How exactly do you intend to stop me? Will you keep me tied up for the rest of my life? You had better because I would flee at the first opportunity."

Sentry could see that Candice had inherited her mother's stubbornness, "Fine. You've made your point. I will take you to Pet."

"Thank you." Candice's face remained tense and straight, but inside she smiled.

This was not the way Sentry had intended this conversation to go. He had expected tears of joy and a warm father-daughter hug. Instead she refused to recognize him as her father and insisted that he return her to the same dangerous circumstances he had delivered her from. He left the tent, "Be ready to leave in twenty minutes. I want to get this over with as soon as possible."

CHAPTER FIFTY-THREE

Purple hues painted the early morning sky. Taking a sip of his coffee, Dashing continued on his way to the First Guardsman's Office. The meeting was scheduled for dawn and he did not want to be late. The door to the office was closed so Dashing knocked. There was no response.

Had he got the time right? Again he knocked on the door. Again no response.

Dashing opened the door. "First Guardsman, are you in here?"

There in the centre of the room was First Guardsman Isabob, his face flat on his desk. The poor guy must be exhausted. The arrival of the Lost Princess probably meant a lot of additional paperwork for him. With a gentle shake, Dashing tried to rouse the First Guardsman. "Come on, Isabob. We have a meeting now."

No luck.

Dashing's voice turned stern. "Isabob, it's time to wake up now."

Still no response. The time for subtlety was over. Dashing firmly shook Isabob and shouted, "Wake up Isabob! Wake up!"

Then Dashing's eyes spied the open vial on the desk. No. He wouldn't have. Why would he? Dashing did not want to entertain the thought any further but he could not ignore the vial. He brought the vial up to his nose and gingerly sniffed it. The familiar scent made Dashing reel back. Morpheus Root!

One question came to Dashing's mind immediately. Had Isabob been poisoned by someone else or had Isabob poisoned himself?

Frantically, Dashing searched through the papers on Isabob's desk. Then Dashing noticed something under Isabob's head. Dashing mumbled an apology as he pried up Isabob's head and pulled the note free. The text read:

I'm sorry for what I did to her.

Dashing's guardsman training kicked in. He picked up the note and compared it to the handwriting on one of Isabob's reports. The writing styles matched. All signs indicated that the most prominent guardsman in the realm had just poisoned himself. Why? Dashing repeated the text of the note over in his mind.

I'm so sorry for what I did to her.

Who was 'her'?

Suddenly, Dashing's blood ran cold.

No.

He wouldn't have... Not after they had just found her. Would he?

Dashing darted for the door. His gut instinct told him that the princess was in mortal danger.

CHAPTER FIFTY-FOUR

Padlocked or not, it would have made little difference. Dashing's panicked strength was such that the doors would have given way regardless. He stormed into the dark bedchamber of the Spire and spied a solitary figure laying there in the gloom.

"Princess! Your Highness! Are you awake?" Dashing whispered. With no immediate response, he increased the volume of his voice, "Pet! Wake up!"

"What's going on here?" asked a sleepy voice behind Dashing.

Dashing spun around with his hand on the hilt of his sword. It was Urseffe.

"Thank the realm," Dashing declared. Urseffe's ability with potions and pharmacy was second only to that of her teacher, Nurse Olganna. If anybody could help, it was her, "I believe that the princess has been poisoned."

Urseffe darted over to Pet's side, "Poisoned? Do you know what with?"

"Morpheus Root."

Urseffe sucked her teeth in dismay, "Morpheus Root can induce an all-consuming slumber. Victims cannot wake by themselves. They just sleep and sleep and sleep till they die of starvation."

"Can't we just wake her up?" Dashing could feel a panic growing inside him.

"It wouldn't work. There's only one way of bringing someone safely out of Morpheus Sleep. All other methods ultimately fail."

"So what is this method?"

Urseffe chuckled, "It doesn't make much sense. At least there's no scientific explanation for how it works…"

"Just tell me what the cure is," Dashing interrupted.

"A kiss," Urseffe gulped, "but unlike other spells, not just any kiss will do. The power of the Morpheus Root is ancient and powerful. Only a kiss of true love can break its hold. It must be a kiss so fierce and burning that it can re-ignite the victim's very soul."

"Oh," was all Dashing could manage to say. A moment ago he was willing to fight the fiercest monster or travel to the farthest lands to find the cure for Pet's condition, but now his cheeks just burned crimson. A kiss of true soul-igniting love was a tall order. Sure he liked Pet plenty, but was it true love?

"Do you think you can kiss the princess in such a fashion?"

Now was not the time for second-guessing himself. "I think so."

Standing over her sleeping form, Dashing regarded Pet. She was such a beautiful and fierce creature. He gently moistened his own lips with the tip of the tongue. Wordlessly, he descended his lips towards Pet's.

Just as their lips were about to brush, a small breath escaped Pet's mouth and tickled his lips. Dashing smirked. Maybe he did love this girl and his kiss was going to prove it.

Pet's eyes flew open. Wait, what was going on? Dashing had not even kissed her yet. Then Pet's fist came crashing into the side of his face.

"By the realm!" screamed Pet at the stumbling form of Dashing, "What's going on here? Are you trying to take advantage of me?"

Stunned, Dashing brought his hand up to cradle his inflamed cheek.

Pet raised her fist again, "You had better explain yourself, Dashing!"

"Your Highness," Urseffe interjected, "We thought you were poisoned. Dashing was only trying to help you."

"What? How?"

Rubbing his cheek, Dashing did his best to explain, "First Guardsman Isabob put some Morpheus Root in your drink."

All colour suddenly drained from Urseffe's face.

"Isa… bob..." stuttered Urseffe, "Is the poi… poisoner?"

Dashing turned his silver eyes onto Urseffe, "What do you know?"

Tears were welling up in Urseffe's eyes, "He said he was only testing the jug. I didn't realize..."

"Who did you deliver the jug to Urseffe?" Dashing gripped the handmaiden.

"The high regent!" gasped Urseffe, "I'm sorry..."

Urseffe's apology fell on deaf ears, because Dashing was already gone.

CHAPTER FIFTY-FIVE

Presences of a certain nature were required in the high regent's bed chamber. A guardsman arrived to escort Pet there. She was the last one to arrive. Evella lay asleep in bed with Lier and Dashing standing beside her.

"Urseffe confirms it," Dashing informed the others. "The high regent was poisoned with Morpheus Root."

Lier shook his head, "This is dreadful."

"Has anyone tried kissing her?" asked Pet.

"I don't know of anyone in the palace who feels that way about her," replied Dashing.

Lier nodded in agreement, "Do we know who did this?"

"First Guardsman Isabob." Dashing took out the evidence. "He left this note about being sorry about what he did to her. I suppose the 'her' refers to the high regent."

"Really?" exclaimed Pet, "The First Guardsman poisoned the high regent?"

"There's something else." Dashing frowned. "I didn't put it together till just now. A Junior Guardsman was reported as coming down with some sort of sleeping sickness a few days ago. I checked what duty he had and found out he was responsible for monitoring the Big Bad."

Pet was having a hard time keeping everything straight. "You're saying Isabob had the Junior Guardsman release the Big Bad and then poisoned him and the high regent?"

Lier sighed. "Neither of you would remember this, but Isabob was one of the guardsmen assigned to watch over the princess the night she disappeared. He took the disappearance of the princess particularly hard. He saw it as a personal failure on his part and a blemish on his character he could never remove. Now that Your Highness is back, perhaps he felt the only way he could ensure your safety was if Evella was removed from the picture."

Pet's mind was all a fluster. She had met her nemesis only a few hours ago and was gearing up for a fight. Then this happened. Her nemesis just fell asleep. Pet did not even have to lift a finger. It felt so anti-climactic.

"Sounds like a plausible explanation," nodded Dashing, "I'll conduct an investigation and see what further evidence we uncover."

A scowl flashed across Lier's face. "Yes, an investigation should be performed, but not by you. Dashing, as the highest ranking guardsman on the premises, you will temporarily assume the duties of First Guardsman till further notice. That will keep you busy enough. I will arrange for someone to conduct the investigation in your stead."

Dashing simply nodded at the unexpected promotion.

"No-one must know that the high regent has been poisoned," Lier continued. "Dashing, I need you to convince Urseffe of the importance of being as discreet as possible about this matter. I will inform the others that Evella has come down with a particularly debilitating sickness."

Pet was not so sure. "Why can't we just be honest about this?"

"The palace cannot afford to appear weak." Lier's eyes narrowed. "The realm has just lost its leader. This is a very delicate time. The succession must be planned very carefully."

"There is one other thing," Dashing interjected. "I have just received reports about a growing peasant movement marching towards the palace. They appear to be armed."

"This can't be happening at a worse time," moaned Lier. "How many are there? How far away are they?"

"We don't have confirmation of their numbers, but they are still a day's march away. We can have three battalions here by the time they arrive."

All of this came as a bit of a surprise to Pet. Several people she had met on her journey had expressed some dissatisfaction with the current government, but Pet had never got the sense that there was any organized opposition in the works. They must have found some strong individual to lead them. She wondered who it was. "What do they want?"

Dashing shrugged his shoulders. "I don't know."

"Don't you think we should find out before we go in with swords swinging?" asked Pet. "This could simply be a protest rather than an invasion."

"They are armed," Dashing reminded her.

"With what?"

"Pitchforks and hoes, for the most part."

"These pitchforks wouldn't be very effective against the swords and arrows of the Royal Guard, would they?"

"I suppose not," Dashing mumbled.

"So before we cut down a group of farmers, we should at least find out what they want."

"I will go to meet them myself," declared Dashing as he turned and left the room.

Once he was gone, Lier turned to Pet. "You are very much your father's daughter."

"Thank you." Pet started feeling like a fraud again.

"Now we must discuss how we're going to get you ready for your role as leader."

Pet gasped. It was one thing to deceive everyone in order to protect Candice and get Tax Law 106 repealed, but could she really bring herself fraudulently to assume the throne?

"I can't rule," Pet protested. "What about you? Can't you lead?"

Lier smiled a sad smile, "I'm a commoner. I have no claim to the throne."

"There must be someone else, then."

"There is no-one else. There is only you," Lier declared, "It is true that you are inexperienced in matters of state, but you are also smart, quick to learn and adaptable. You seem to seek what is fair and have just shown you think before committing yourself to action. These are the essential characteristics of a good ruler. Of course, I would be assisting you by lending you my knowledge and experience in order to make any decisions."

Pet gulped. She did not like where this was going.

"You love the realm and its people. So set aside your insecurities and assume the throne, secure in the knowledge that it will be best for the realm." At this point, Lier's eyes darkened. "For if you don't, there will doubtlessly be a war of succession. People will die and the realm will be torn asunder. The wolves are already at the gate. We have to have a strong and decisive transition as soon as possible."

Pet recalled the Great Unrest and how it had permanently scarred the Songtrees, "And you're sure there's no other way?"

Lier replied in the sternest tone Pet had ever heard, "There are no other options. This needs to be done."

"I need to think about this." Pet could not believe what was being asked of her. All she knew was that she had to get out of there.

"Don't take too long deciding, Your Highness. The fate of the realm rests on your shoulders."

CHAPTER FIFTY-SIX

Piqued ire boiled Dashing's blood. No matter how fast his horse galloped, he continued to slam his ankles into its hide to spur it on ever faster. His anger had nothing to do with the treason of the First Guardsman or the group of armed farmers marching on the palace. It all had to do with that girl. That frustrating, beautiful girl. Pet.

Dashing knew he was a catch. He was good looking and well groomed. His job kept him in top physical condition. He was only two years out of high school and had already reached the highest rank of guardsman. He could have any girl he wanted. Any girl except one.

What was it about her? It wasn't that Pet was secretly the Lost Princess. He liked her the moment they first set eyes on each other. Dashing could not imagine a girl who could possibly rival Pet in terms of pure and unadulterated passion. She was just so alive.

Unfortunately, Dashing had screwed it all up with that stupid almost-kiss. He had tried to do the right thing and now Pet thought him some sort of creep. Perhaps there was a way to make it up to her….

This train of thought came to an abrupt end when Dashing spied the trademark orange hues in the sky. There was a fire ahead. Where there was fire, there were people. He signaled to his fellow guardsmen to slow down. Dashing had brought only two other guardsmen with him on this trip. This was after all, supposed to be a diplomatic mission. Dashing turned back to his fellow riders and issued orders. "We will approach the encampment openly. I will address their leader and ask him his intentions. You are to keep your weapons sheathed unless I expressly order you otherwise. They may try to provoke you. You must not respond."

When Dashing came to the crest of the hill, he was surprised indeed. Where he had been expecting a single bonfire, there were many. Dozens, perhaps. This gathering was much larger than initial reports had suggested. There must have been at least a thousand people there. This had the potential to be a bigger threat than initially suspected.

By the time Dashing and his men reached the encampment, a large group of men wielding pitchforks had gathered to greet them.

Dashing brought his horse to a halt, "I am Dashing. I come as an envoy of the high regent. I request an audience with your leader."

"Dashing!" A cry came out from the crowd. The gathered men parted to reveal a familiar face. "What do you want?"

This was not good. In Dashing's previous experiences, imprisoning people was not a great way to get in someone's good graces. "Trusty, what are you doing out of prison?"

"Your guardsmen released me for good behaviour," the boy responded. "And by the way, the name's Judd."

His story seemed highly unlikely. Dashing made a mental note to find out at a later date exactly how this Judd ended his imprisonment early and what had happened to Mr 'Azor.' "Well then, Judd, I was hoping to discuss something with you in private."

Judd scowled. "There's nothing to discuss. The facts are simple. You took her, Dashing, and I want her back."

"I don't know what you're talking about."

"I'm talking about Pet and if you don't give her back, we're going to take her back."

Dashing could hardly believe his ears, "Her Highness is certainly not a captive! Why just last night we had a feast in her honor."

"You people just take and take and take, and you expect us just to sit back and smile. You will say anything to get your way and have us go home, won't you? We won't be falling for your lies, guardsman." Dashing could not quite figure out if Judd was addressing him or the crowd.

"Her Highness came willingly to the palace and has given no indication that she wants to leave."

Judd followed with a cry of, "More lies!"

Wordlessly, Dashing jumped off his horse and strode purposely towards Judd. "Twice now you have accused me of dishonesty. I pride myself on being honest in all my interactions. Can you say the same?"

Suddenly, Judd's fist crashed into Dashing's face. He was getting punched an awful lot today.

Behind him, Dashing could hear the familiar scraping of steel against scabbard. He shouted at his men, "Hold. Your orders still stand."

Dashing stood up and tried to muster as much dignity as he could. Judd was standing back, breathing hard, with violence still in his eyes. Dashing brushed a piece of dirt off his sleeve, "That was a cheap blow, Judd."

"You deserve worse. You took Pet prisoner!"

With the most reasonable tone he could muster, Dashing said, "I don't know how I can convince you she's not a prisoner. She stays at the Sapphire Palace of her own free will."

"Then we will march on the palace, she can come out and tell us as much herself," Judd shouted.

"Let me assure you that the Princess is in good hands. The return of the Lost Princess is a reason for celebration, not insurrection." Dashing approached his horse and swung up into the saddle. "But let that also be a warning. We lost the Princess once. We don't intend to lose her again. Accordingly any march on the Sapphire Palace will be regarded as an act of aggression and will be dealt with accordingly."

With that Dashing turned his horse around and signaled his men to follow. Judd silently watched Dashing and his men leave. The hooves of their steeds beat mercilessly on the Hashram Plains as they galloped away, echoing into the morning air.

CHAPTER FIFTY-SEVEN

Pinching herself for the fourth time once again confirmed Pet's suspicion. She was not dreaming. This was actually happening. She was going to become queen.

There was still something nagging Pet. It was what Evella had said at the banquet. She had warned Pet not to believe everything she heard and that was exactly what Pet was doing.

Pet drummed her fingers. If she was ever going to sleep easy again, she was going to have to be certain that Evella was actually guilty. Pet needed some cold evidence, but where could she find it?

"Did Evella have a study or office or anything like that?"

"Do you mean her inner sanctum, Your Highness?" inquired Urseffe.

"Exactly!" A jolt of excitement rode up Pet's body, "I need you to take me there."

Soon, Pet and Urseffe were approaching an ominous, ebony door. Two solemn guardsmen watched the door in silence. Upon seeing Pet approach, they quickly opened the door for her. Apparently as the highest ranking royal, she was allowed access anywhere she pleased. Royalty had its privileges.

Everything in the sanctum was covered in dust. The floors looked like they had not been swept in years. The books on the shelves were caked in the dust. The only place that was not as covered with dust was the desk in the centre, presumably because that was where Evella had done most of her work.

Urseffe grimaced at the dingy conditions of the sanctum. This was not how a room in the Sapphire Palace should appear, "Evella didn't let anybody enter, not even the cleaning staff. I can have someone come to clean this room if you'd like."

"No thank you. They might disturb something."

"Is there anything in particular that I can help you look for?"

Now that was the million gold piece question wasn't it? What exactly was Pet hoping to find down here?

"I'll know it when I see it."

"Perhaps I may be of assistance, Your Highness," a voice called out from the gloom.

"Lier!" The presence of the Grand Vizier irked Pet. "What are you doing here?"

The Grand Vizier smiled. "I suspect, the same thing as you."

Pet stalked over to his side. "Found anything?"

"Not yet." Lier gestured with his eyes towards Urseffe. "But what we do find might not be appropriate for all ears."

Pet looked over at Urseffe. If there was anyone Pet had come to trust in the entire palace, it was her. However, Urseffe did not deserve to get caught up in all this intrigue, "Urseffe, you're dismissed."

The moment Urseffe was gone, Pet asked, "Where should we start?"

"Look around," Lier responded. "Notice anything unusual?"

The large wooden desk seemed the obvious place to start. Pet flipped through all the sheets and scrolls at a reckless pace. She disregarded drafts of signed treaties, old press releases and proposed laws. This went on till Pet came to one odd piece of clean paper.

The parchment caught Pet's eye because its colour was slightly different from the rest. It was an order from the Royal Treasury for five thousand gold pieces. Though the name of recipient was not familiar to Pet, the amount gave her pause.

"The Cloaked Man!" shouted Pet. "This is the money order for the Cloaked Man for tracking us down and capturing us."

Lier inspected the sheet, "Are you sure?"

"Look at the date. This order was issued just days before we encountered the Cloaked Man and the amount of five thousand gold pieces is the same amount he was promised. This has to be it." Pet peered at the fine print, "There's no signature on this document. There's a seal, but no signature."

"For treasury transactions, the Royal Seal is sufficient certification," Lier informed her. "But the high regent must have approved of this transaction. The high regent is the only one issued with a Royal Seal."

"I guess that's proof enough then," Pet mumbled. "Evella hired the Cloaked Man to kidnap…."

Something else on the table caught Pet's eye. Beneath the money order there was another piece of paper. Pet picked up the sheet of paper and let her eyes roll over the text. With each word she read, the heavier her breathing got.

"What are you looking at?" inquired Lier.

Pet was too angry to speak. She took a few calming breaths and handed the sheet to Lier. As he read it over, she explained, "It's a prison release order for the Big Bad. It's also stamped with the Royal Seal."

This was it. The proof was in Pet's hands. Evella was not only responsible for the death of Judd, but also the death of Mrs Kettlepot and the attempted murder of Candice. She was the one who was responsible for all that needless bloodshed and grief.

"Eternal sleep is too good for her." Pet's voice trembled with rage. "That witch has caused so much pain to so many. She deserves worse."

Pet's legs went wobbly so she slumped down in Evella's chair. Staring at all the papers in front of her, Pet realized that this was where Evella had done it. This was where that witch had sealed the orders which had in turn sealed the fates of her friends. Disgust coursed through Pet's blood.

With a mighty cry, Pet rose to her feet and swept all the contents of the desk onto the floor. She contemplated turning over the desk, but what good would come of that? Evella was never going to wake up. She was already defeated.

Lier surveyed the chaos Pet had just wrought. "Feeling better?"

Pet opened her mouth to respond, but something else grabbed her attention instead. There was an odd soft glow coming from the mirror on the wall. "Lier, there's something strange about that mirror."

"Never mind that, Your Highness."

Undaunted, Pet approached the mirror and saw her own face in its surface, bathed in a strange light. Pet turned to Lier and said, "This mirror… It's generating light rather than reflecting it. It's a Magic Mirror, right?"

"Right," responded Pet's reflection.

The real Pet let out a little eek and jumped back. Once she collected her wits, Pet decided to attempt a dialogue with the mirror, "Um... Hello me."

"Hello, you," the reflection responded.

The entire notion of having a conversation with one's reflection was entirely alien to Pet. Still, she tried to be cordial, "So you must be Evella's Magic Mirror."

The Reflection did not respond.

Pet turned to Lier. "Why isn't it answering back?"

"Magic Mirrors are very picky about what kind of questions they answer," explained Lier. "They prefer questions to be phrased in rhyming verse."

"Oh, you mean like this?" asked Pet.

Magic Mirror Magic Mirror,
Is Evella Your Primary Peer-er?

Silently, Pet thanked Mrs Kettlepot. It appears she had been right after all. Singing did have its uses. Not only was it useful for soothing savage beasts, but it was also useful in communicating with enchanted furniture.

Lier made a bit of a face, "Not bad for a beginner, but '*Peer-er?*' That's not a real word is it? The Language of Mirrors requires a bit more nuance than that."

"I liked it. Her verse had pizzazz," the reflection interjected, "Yes, Evella does look into me a lot but so do a few other people."

This could be it. A Magic Mirror knows all and there were quite a few things that Pet still needed to know. But where to start? Well, the beginning was as good a place as any,

Years Ago the Princess Was Taken.
Was This A Plot of Evella's Makin'?

The Reflection glanced over at Lier, "Evella had some help coming up with the plan, but yes she did summon the powerful wind that carried the princess away."

So it was her. Evella was the one who had Candice kidnapped all those years ago, but there was still one thing bothering Pet, "Why? I don't understand! Why did Evella send her to Seacrest?"

Lier gripped Pet's arm, "That's enough, Your Highness."

Pet shook off Lier's grasp, "And if Evella was the one to send Candice away, why send the Cloaked Man and the Big Bad to bring her back? Why would she do such horrible things? It just doesn't make sense. Please, you must tell me."

The Reflection looked at Pet with abject disgust, "Gross. Humans sound so boorish when they don't rhyme. I would eat glass rather than listen to another minute of this. 'Bye!" The Reflection promptly disappeared from view.

"What happened?" cried Pet, "Where did she go?"

"Don't worry," chuckled Lier, "That's why I tried to stop you. Magic Mirrors are very fussy. You can annoy them by asking too many questions at once. Mastering the Language of Mirrors requires a lot of patience. It took me sixteen years to get the hang of it myself. Maybe you can try again in a few years."

Pet frowned.

"I'm not sure why you're unhappy," Lier commented. "We discovered ample evidence that Evella was the one behind your recent troubles."

Lier was right. Evella did it. Questioning her motives served little purpose. "I'm just frustrated that I didn't get a chance to avenge my friends, to punish Evella, myself, for everything she did."

Lier paused for a moment and then ventured, "Perhaps you can avenge your friends another way. Evella went to a lot of trouble to ensure that you never took the throne so that she could rule in perpetuity. Perhaps your best revenge is to take the throne, become the Princess you are meant to be, and rule kindly and justly."

"He isn't my father."

"Excuse me?" Lier asked, despite having heard perfectly well what Pet had said.

"King Piotr is not my father," Pet confessed, "and I'm not the Lost Princess."

CHAPTER FIFTY-EIGHT

P assing another minute in such uncomfortable silence was going to be torture, but Pet dared not say a word. Pet glanced in Lier's direction. He was standing quite calmly, resting a finger against his upper lip.

"I should have known," Lier intoned. "You never did strike me as particularly regal."

"What?" Pet protested, "I'm very regal."

"If you're not the Lost Princess, then who are you?"

It felt refreshing to be honest again, "I'm Petunia Peasant of Seacrest, the foundling daughter of Ma and Pa Peasant."

His voice remained terse and stoic. "And why did you decide to masquerade as the Lost Princess?"

"It wasn't a choice," Pet explained. "It was a necessity. I did it to protect a friend."

"But you had blue blood."

"The blood on the bandage was from my friend. The real Lost Princess."

"So you know where the real Princess is."

"Not any more. Far away from here, I hope."

"Perhaps this is for the best," Lier mumbled.

Once again, Lier descended into deep thought. Pet gazed at that finger tap against his lip and tried to figure out what he was thinking. "Are you going to have me arrested?"

"I can't do that," Lier answered. "The realm still needs a ruler."

"You still want me to be queen?" Pet could not believe what she was hearing.

Lier's eyes narrowed. "Your revelation does little to change the challenges we currently face. With Evella gone and the present civil unrest, the realm still needs a decisive ruler."

A sinking feeling descended over Pet. "You want me to continue to lie to everybody?"

"Why should this girl be forced to rule because of some accident of birth? She hasn't undergone any training. We have no idea whether she would be any good at it. The realm needs a queen who is both willing and able. The realm needs someone who will gladly accept the responsibility to rule with grace and wisdom. The realm needs a Queen like you, Petunia."

Pet grimaced, but Lier did make a convincing point. The realm had to come first.

"Fine. I'll do it. I'll be your fake princess."

CHAPTER FIFTY-NINE

Peasants and guardsmen alike were whirling in activity as Dashing returned to the Sapphire Palace. He came upon Grand Vizier Lier in the corridor. Large bags sagged underneath Lier's eyes. It looked like he had not seen a wink of sleep since Evella's poisoning had been discovered.

"Tell me, Grand Vizier," inquired Dashing, "Where is Her Highness?"

"Her Highness has agreed to take on the mantle of queen," explained Lier. "She has retired to bed so that she will be well rested for the coronation tomorrow."

The news dismayed Dashing. The last time he had woken up the princess, it had not gone well, "I must tell her of my findings. You should come. Turns out someone from Seacrest is leading the revolutionary movement."

"I should remind you that the princess will not become queen until tomorrow," remarked Lier. "Accordingly she does not have any official capacity here at the palace yet. In the meanwhile, the responsibilities of head of state fall to me. Technically any reports that are to be made should be made to me."

"I am sorry. That was silly of me. It won't happen again." Dashing's speech stumbled. His intention had not been to insult the Grand Vizier.

Lier smiled, "Don't be too hard on yourself, Dashing. These are unprecedented times. I just think the princess would be better off not being disturbed from her beauty sleep. Now tell me about this friend of hers."

Dashing recounted the encounter with Judd and his group of revolutionaries. He also included a brief description of his previous encounter with Judd and that rogue guardsman back in Frontier Keep. He concluded his report with his own personal thoughts on the character of Judd. "His actions and behaviour do not strike me as that of a rational man. I suspect he might be taken with our princess."

"Our princess has quite a captivating effect on certain men," mused Lier. The young guardsman could not stop his cheeks from burning crimson. If Lier noticed this, he did not let it show, "And what is their current position?"

"The group continues to march on the palace," Dashing reported. "They could be here by tomorrow afternoon."

Lier paused for a moment with his finger resting against his lips. "I want you to take three battalions and ensure that these men never reach the palace. Your orders are simple. Find them. Stop them. Use whatever means necessary."

Dashing's eyebrows arched. Lier noticed this and asked, "Is there a problem? You won't need more guardsmen will you? We do need a few battalions on site for the coronation tomorrow. Anyway, as Her Highness so correctly noted, their pitchforks and hoes should pose no challenge to your swords."

"It's not that," stumbled Dashing. "I thought Her Highness was hoping we could resolve this situation without the shedding of blood."

The Grand Vizier's voice descended into a low whisper. "This is not the time for sentimentality, First Guardsman. We need the people to know that the palace always remains strong."

The guardsman within Dashing had to agree with what Lier was saying. The order and stability of the realm were paramount.

Lier added, "I want to keep the princess out of this until after the coronation. I'm not sure her perspective can be trusted when it comes to one of her own countrymen. This won't be a problem will it? I am aware that you and Her Highness have a particular relationship."

"No problem, Grand Vizier." Dashing turned to leave. "Now if you will excuse me. I will go gather the men. We will depart in the morning."

As Dashing made his away over to the barracks, a crushed feeling came over him. He could not quite understand why. He was a guardsman, following orders which had been issued by the acting head of state, all in the name of defending the realm.

Then why did he feel such a traitor?

CHAPTER SIXTY

Powder-blue walls glistened at Candice and Sentry as they crossed the Hashram Plains. Candice had expected the walls of the Sapphire Palace to be a touch darker, but in the morning light the city glistened brightly.

"The blue colour comes from the sapphires encrusted in the city walls," explained Sentry. "Sapphire is the signature stone of the Petros Bluebloods."

Candice glanced at her companion. Over the course of their journey, he had tended to speak more and more of his illusions of being both the missing King Piotr and her father. Such behaviour greatly worried her, but Pet was still a prisoner and that had to take priority. As soon as Pet was safe and delivered from danger, Candice swore she would get Sentry the help he so desperately needed.

A loud trampling sound roared from the West. Candice looked up to see the drawbridge of the palace lowered and a massive group of armed men charge out on horseback. There was something vaguely familiar about their leader.

"Where do you think they're going?"

"I can't imagine they're going very far," Sentry observed. "They don't seem to be carrying much in the way of supplies. Perhaps they are going to quell that gathering we passed earlier."

Her mind flew back to the large group they had passed the previous day. They had not seemed particularly happy, shouting angry chants and regularly spearing the air with their pitchforks as they marched. Sentry had given them a wide berth. At the time, Candice had wondered why those people were so upset.

"With all this activity, it should be easy to slip into the palace unnoticed," Candice mused.

Sentry smiled, "This is the Sapphire Palace, the seat of governance and commerce for the entire realm. One doesn't just slip in, as one would for the Mariners' Day Dance at Old Foggy's Barn."

"Can't we just say that we're there to pay our respects to the high regent?" Candice glanced over at the unshaven Sentry, "Then again maybe that isn't such a good idea."

"We'll just take the back door." Sentry directed the horse on a path away from the main gate and towards the rear of the Sapphire Palace.

Candice was incredulous, "The palace is the most secure location in the realm, but its back door is left wide open?"

"Not exactly."

On the east side of the Sapphire Palace, the green pastures of the Hashram Plains turned into a sea of rocks and pebbles. Candice and Sentry dismounted and tied up Sentry's horse to a nearby tree. Candice watched Sentry carefully as he scrambled down and then followed him.

A few minutes of scrambling down the slope brought Candice and Sentry to the fabled back door of the palace.

"A sewer?! This is your secret back entrance…"

"If it's too odorous…," began Sentry.

Candice inspected the crisscross of bars covering the hole. She gingerly tapped at the bars, "So do you bend steel with your bare hands too? Because I'm not skinny enough to fit between these bars."

"Just give me a moment." Sentry ran his hands along the wall beside the sewer grate, "Here it is."

Sentry found the stone he was looking for and pushed it. A shuddering noise erupted around the sewer mouth. Candice stepped back and marveled as the bars over the mouth slowly began to slide away. Sentry had really delivered. He was granting her access to the Sapphire Palace and through the secret back door no less. There was definitely more to him than initially met the eye. She was still far away from being convinced that Sentry was King Piotr the Just, but she had to admit that there was something about him.

The last of the bars slid away. Candice took her first step into the dank depths of the sewer tunnel. Suddenly, a voice rang out from deep within, "Stop where you are!"

A guardsman emerged from the shadows with his spear aimed squarely at Candice's chest.

"Stan, is that you?" Sentry asked.

"How do you know my name? Identify yourself."

Sentry removed his left gauntlet to reveal his gold signet ring with the dazzling sapphire, "I'm dismayed that you don't remember me, loyal guardsman."

"I remember that ring. I kissed it at my guardsman convocation." Stan dropped to one knee, "Your Majesty! You've returned!"

Candice's mouth dropped open. If this guardsman was right, then Sentry was indeed the missing King Piotr. What was the missing King Piotr doing in Seacrest for all those years posing as a regional guardsman? If Sentry was right about being King Piotr, what else was he right about?

Could he, despite all reason, actually be her father?

CHAPTER SIXTY-ONE

Primping to the degree that was expected of a Princess had quickly become quite draining. The first time Pet had undergone this preparation, it had been sort of fun and novel. However, only two days later, it bordered on tediousness.

As she fixed the final strand of stray hair, Urseffe asked, "Excuse me for speaking out of turn, Your Highness, but I have a question for you."

"Oh please, I quite prefer it when people speak out of turn," Pet replied, "I've made quite a career out of it myself."

"You don't seem happy."

Pet looked up at Urseffe. "Why should I be happy?"

"You're about to become queen!" gasped Urseffe. "If that's not an occasion for celebration, I don't know what is."

"So you would like to become queen?"

Urseffe blushed. "It isn't my place even to dream about being a queen."

"Why is becoming queen such a big deal?"

"What do you mean, 'why'?" Urseffe asked in surprise, "Every girl dreams of being royalty; the romance, the glamour, the princes, the attention. I know becoming queen isn't happiness in and of itself, but I'd imagine it would give you the means of finding true happiness that much easier."

Pet smiled at herself in the mirror. Try as she might, she could not quite muster an entirely sincere smile. There was still one thing bothering her...

A knock on the door pulled Urseffe's attention away. Urseffe answered the door and was greeted by the old face of Grand Vizier Lier. Dispensing with any pleasantries, Lier asked, "How's she doing?"

"She's fine," Urseffe responded.

Lier was in a rush, organizing all the last-minute details for the coronation. He pushed a piece of paper into Urseffe's hand. "This is the menu for the post-coronation banquet. Review it with her and ensure that she can eat everything on it. I don't want our new Queen suffering from an allergy at her own coronation banquet."

Urseffe closed the door and found Pet staring at her.

"What did he want?"

Urseffe waved the document. "He wanted me to review the menu with you."

Pet's eyes narrowed, "Let me see that."

Urseffe passed the menu to her. Pet's eyes went down to the big wax seal on the bottom of the paper. "What is this?"

"It's the Royal Seal. It means that the Grand Vizier has reviewed and approved the information on this document."

Running her finger over the dried wax, Pet asked, "And Lier has always had a Royal Seal?"

"Just him and the high regent."

Pet frowned. Lier had specifically told her that the high regent was the only one who had a Royal Seal. That was now revealed to be a lie. The seal had secured the case against Evella as being the one responsible for releasing the Cloaked Man and the Big Bad. Pet groaned in frustration. Again she was being confronted by questions that she did not have the answers to…

But there was someone who did have all the answers.

Pet shot up from her seat. "I need to return to Evella's sanctum!"

"The coronation begins in less than an hour." Urseffe watched her words bounce off Pet unheard. "Fine! I'll alert Lier that we might be a bit late."

"No." Pet's tone turned stern. "Lier is not to know. I'll go by myself."

Pet stood up and tried to take a few steps, but tripped over the train of her dress. Urseffe observed, "Looks like you might require my assistance to get to the inner sanctum, Your Highness."

The two of them made their way through the corridor as silently as a woman with a five-metre train, followed by an attendant, could. Luckily the halls of the private quarters were virtually empty as the staff and guardsmen attended to the preparation for the coronation. As they approached Evella's sanctum, Urseffe poked her head around the corner and reported a single guardsman on post there.

Not in the mood to be delayed in any way, Pet walked straight up to the guardsman, "Let me in!"

The guardsman hesitated. "Grand Vizier Lier instructed that no-one, except himself, be granted access to the sanctum."

Last time, Pet had walked straight in. Perhaps on that occasion, Lier had wanted her in the sanctum.

Pet could not believe that she was actually going to say what she was about to say. Unfortunately, desperate times called for desperate measures. "Do you know who I am?"

A few minutes ago, this poor guardsman was minding his own business, but now, all of a sudden, he was trapped between a rock and a hard princess. "I understand, Your Highness, but my orders were quite explicit on the matter. Perhaps if you spoke to the Grand Vizier..."

Pet interjected, "I understand that I am not quite yet the queen and as a result you don't yet answer to me, but in less than an hour, I will be crowned. You need to ask yourself if this is really the first impression you want to make with your new queen?"

Within seconds, Pet and Urseffe had been granted access to Evella's sanctum.

Urseffe remained acutely aware that the coronation was set to begin soon. "So what are we here for, Your Highness?"

Pet pointed at the wall, "This."

The Magic Mirror hung on the wall, humming ever so slightly with light and incantation. Pet strode up and chose her words carefully.

Mirror, Mirror hanging right there,
Tell me the whole truth of this sordid affair.

CHAPTER SIXTY-TWO

Piloted by Stan, the last of the Petros Bluebloods made their way through the crowded corridors of the palace.

"You were once part of my personal guard," Sentry addressed Stan in a low whisper. "Why were you guarding the sewer entrance?"

"Not everyone was as forgiving as you about our failure to protect the princess." Stan looked at Candice with curious eyes. "Once you left, the gossip and innuendo spread. Isabob and I were punished by our fellow guardsmen for our failure by being given the very worst of details."

A confused look appeared on Sentry's face, "But didn't Isabob become First Guardsman?"

"It is not my place to speak ill of my former partner," Stan gulped. "But I think it would be fair to say that he might have made some compromises to get that position."

"I understand," Sentry nodded, "I will make this up to you somehow."

Excitement coursed through Stan's entire body. "It would do me a great honour to announce your return, Your Majesty."

"I appreciate your loyalty, but discretion is the highest priority right now."

Stan's shoulders sagged. Noticing this, Candice decided to spark up conversation with him. "Is it always this crazy here?"

"This is all because of the coronation," Stan informed her. "It is supposed to start in a few minutes. You didn't know?"

"Whose coronation?"

"The Lost Princess is to assume the throne, since the high regent has fallen ill." Stan then brought his hand up to his mouth and whispered, "Just between you and me, they say the high regent was poisoned."

"Pet's certainly been busy," mused Sentry. "She's been here only a matter of days and she's already got herself the top spot."

Candice's eyes blazed darkly at Sentry, "There will be a perfectly good explanation for all this."

Stan escorted them past queues of peasants waiting for admittance to the Grand Hall and soon enough they were inside. The Grand Hall was bursting at the seams. People were everywhere. Stan cleared a path for Sentry and Candice. Sentry rested his hand on Stan's shoulder. "This is far enough. I don't want any undue attention."

With that Stan departed leaving Sentry and Candice adrift in a sea of people. Candice darted her eyes around the chamber and muttered, "Where is that girl?"

Movement on the podium at the top of the hall caught Candice's attention. An old man, draped in fine robes, flanked by several guardsmen, stepped out. Soon after, a blare of trumpets filled the room and the main doors swung open, revealing Pet.

"All rise for Her Highness," cried the herald. Candice dutifully stood up. She could not believe how beautiful Pet looked in that gown. Everything was so perfect; the embroidery of her dress, the dazzle of her jewelry, the curl of her hair. Everything was so perfectly princess-like. Everything, that was, except her eyes.

"That should be you up there, instead of her," muttered Sentry. "What game is she playing at?"

"Relax. She knows what she's doing."

"We came here under the assumption that Pet needed to be delivered from danger. It seems that she's delivered herself quite nicely. Let's get out of here!"

Candice gripped Sentry's arm before he could make the slightest move. "Something's up. We're staying."

Pet reached the podium and took the ornamental throne. Her gaze rested evenly on the crowd.

Grand Vizier Lier stood up and began to speak.

The coronation had begun.

CHAPTER SIXTY-THREE

Proclaiming in a loud voice, Lier addressed the gathered assembly, "This day is truly the dawn of a new golden age. A wondrous hope has returned to our realm. The Lost Princess has returned!"

Huge applause thundered through the Grand Hall. Pet flashed a royal smile. Candice clapped along as Sentry scowled. Once the applause had subsided, Lier continued, "Her Highness's return could not have come at a better time. As most of you know, the High Regent Evella has been struck down by disease and is unable to perform her royal duties. So that the realm is not left leaderless, the princess has decided to embrace her royal heritage and become the queen of the realm."

Lier turned to Pet. "Your Highness, please approach the altar."

Pet rose from the throne and approached the altar. Simultaneously, a page approached Lier with a pillow holding the crown. Pet knelt before Lier at the altar.

Lier held the crown over Pet's head, "Your Highness, do you accept this crown and promise to rule kindly, wisely and honorably as queen of the realm?"

"No. I do not."

A wave of gasps echoed through the Grand Hall.

Lier's face alone was worth the hours that Pet had spent getting ready for this pageant. He spluttered, "For realm's sake, why not?"

Pushing the crown away, Pet rose up from the altar. She turned to address the crowd, "Because it would be dishonest. These people should know that I am not the Lost Princess returned."

Numb with shock, the crowd remained hushed. Lier promptly snatched back the crown and shouted, "Guardsmen! Seize this imposter!"

The guardsmen had been just as caught up in the drama and it took a moment to snap into action. That moment was all Pet needed to address the crowd in a calm tone, "But I know where the Lost Princess is and why she hasn't revealed herself yet. If the people will allow me, I will reveal all."

The colour vanished from Lier's face, "Stop her!"

Despite the fact that Pet was standing there quite calmly, the guardsmen circled her like some ferocious animal. They seemed unsure what to make of her.

Pet took a quick breath. Everything had led to this point. She would have expected herself to be terrified or nervous, but she was not. She was calm. She was the eye of the storm.

"What are you waiting for?" Lier screeched, "Get her!"

Realizing her time on the podium was limited, Pet opened her mouth and spoke in a loud clear voice, "It all started sixteen years…"

Unfortunately the remainder of Pet's sentence was drowned out by boos from the crowd. Some had come a long way for a once-in-a-lifetime coronation, but now it was not happening. In this cacophony of noise, it was difficult to make out any one sentence, but one struck out like crystal. "Throw that lying girl in prison like she deserves!"

Pet's lips trembled. She had expected that the people would be on her side. She tried again, but her words were once again lost in the angry wave of noise from the audience.

In the audience, Candice turned to Sentry, "If she doesn't get a chance to speak, the guardsmen will take her away. We have to do something!"

"Yes," Sentry grunted, "We have to leave."

Sentry gripped Candice's arm roughly and pulled her back through the crowd towards the exit. Candice looked back at Pet. A guardsman had now roughly grabbed Pet's arm as she continued to shout out to the deaf ears of the audience.

There must be some way Candice could help Pet, but what could she do?

Of course.

Candice turned to Sentry, "Father! Stop!"

Sentry stopped cold. He loosed his grip and turned back to look at his daughter with loving eyes. She had finally accepted him as her father. At that exact moment, Candice slipped out of his grasp and fled into the crowd towards the podium.

"Let her speak!" cried Candice in the loudest voice she could muster.

Perhaps there was a lull in the booing or perhaps it was a testimony to the conviction behind Candice's cry, but in that instant everybody in the Grand Hall paused. Just to make sure, Candice repeated her cry, "Let the girl speak!"

"That's true. I want to hear what she has to say," said an elderly woman behind Candice. She then called out in a raspy voice, "Let her speak!"

Perhaps the elderly woman's voice did not reach all the way to the podium, but it certainly caught the attention of a large bald man a few metres up. This man then repeated, in a much louder voice, "Let her speak!"

A few minutes later, another voiced echoed, "Let her speak!" Then there was another voice and another and another. Soon the entire audience chanted, "Let her speak!"

It was music to Candice's ears.

"Let her speak!"

"Let her speak!"

Lier barked some order or other, but they were drowned out by the chants of the people. The guardsman released his grip on Pet's arm and cleared a way so she could address the hall. The people had spoken. They wanted to hear what Pet had to say.

Pet stood forwards and put up her hand. The chants of "Let her speak!" came to a close and she proceeded to do just that.

CHAPTER SIXTY-FOUR

Prefacing her speech with an introduction and an apology, Pet began, "My name is Pet Peasant and I'm sorry for my part in this charade, but once you hear what I have to say, I think you'll agree that such deception was necessary to flush out the true culprit responsible for both old and recent troubles.

"As many of you doubtlessly remember, many years ago, the realm was ruled by King Piotr the Just and his wife Queen Polly. On the same day that they were blessed with a beautiful daughter, tragedy struck, for the fair queen died in child birth."

Candice glanced behind her at Sentry and saw his head hung low. Her heart went out to him.

"Unfortunately, despite the king's fair and gentle rule, there were still those with greed and sinister intentions in their heart. One man in particular decided to take advantage of the king's grief. One day while standing over his infant daughter's crib, the king noticed a note pinned to her bedclothes. The anonymous note demanded greater power and authority in the palace or else the treasured princess would be harmed."

The Magic Mirror had been most helpful in filling in this part of the story.

"The king dared not tarnish the reputation of the court by rewarding such base tactics. At the same time, there was no ignoring the fact that this villain had got close enough to the princess to pin a note to her bedclothes despite all her security. What could he do? As much as he wanted to watch over the princess every moment of every day, his royal duties could not permit that."

The audience listened with rapt attention. The broad strokes of the story were generally well known, but the details like the villainous note were new to them.

"At first the king tried locking the princess away under lock and key in the spire, but that proved no use. The villain was still able to leave threatening notes in her cot. At a loss for what to do, the king turned to his loyal court sorceress, Evella."

At the mention of Evella's name, one character in the audience let out a loud hiss. This was greeted by very cross looks from those around him.

"Under the king's instructions, Evella cast a powerful spell which caused the winds to pluck the princess out of the spire, away from the palace and take her to a place called Seacrest where she could be raised by loving parents in safety. Knowing his daughter was safe, King Piotr tried to continue ruling fairly. However, he grew increasingly sad and despondent. He simply missed his daughter too much. So one night, the king rode away to join his daughter in exile. Before he left, he entrusted rule of the realm to the capable hands of his most trusted ally, Evella."

Lier grimaced.

"Evella ruled the best she could. However, the anonymous villain, upset that his blackmail attempt had failed, worked against her behind the scenes. With his double-edged tongue, he succeeded in poisoning both the House of Magistrates and the general public against Evella with rumours of usurpation and dark witchcraft."

Pet paused to regard the audience and saw some guilty faces. She sympathized with them. She had been just as willing to jump to the same conclusions about Evella. If she had been just a little more careful, she would have noticed the frame-up earlier. Neither the money-order nor the prisoner-release had originated in Evella's sanctum. They were both clear of dust while the rest of the papers were caked in it. In addition, the paper grade of these documents didn't match anything else in the sanctum. Somebody had planted them there to convince Pet of Evella's guilt.

"Evella sacrificed so much. Popularity. Happiness. Romance. Family. All in order to battle day after day against the villain's nefarious machinations."

Sentry's eyes brimmed with tears.

"But that was not enough for the villain. He wanted the princess for himself, but try as he might, he couldn't find her using conventional means. Only Evella knew where she was gone – well, Evella and her Magic Mirror... It took our villain sixteen years to master the Language of Mirrors." Pet turned to address Lier directly, "And I've got to say, this Language of Mirrors isn't really all that cryptic. All you have to do is the same structure that nursery rhymes and lullabies employ. You really ought to try to sing more, it provides some unexpected benefits."

Her aside over, Pet returned to the matter at hand. "So our villain used the Magic Mirror to find out where the princess was. Once he found out her location, the villain sent an assassin and a wolf to bring him the Lost Princess. If the villain could get his hands on the Lost Princess, he reasoned that he would be able to use her to cement his control over the realm."

Pet took in a steadying breath. This was the difficult part to recount. "These agents of the villain did not succeed in capturing the princess, but they did succeed in terribly wounding her and killing her friends. I should know. I was there. It was then that I decided to take the princess's place, so that she could have an opportunity to heal. I came to the palace disguised as her in order to root out the identity of this villain. Once I arrived, the villain promptly poisoned Evella with Morpheus Root and tried to have me crowned as quickly as possible. I guess he believed that once I was made queen, he would be able to control the realm through me."

Pet glanced behind her. "Sorry to disappoint you, Grand Vizier Lier, but I am no man's puppet."

Candice smiled. Pet had done it. She had figured it all out.

Pointing straight at the culprit, Pet declared in a loud voice, "Grand Vizier Lier, I charge you with attempted regicide and high treason against the realm."

The hall was still. No-one dared speak. To his credit, Lier did not appear the slightest bit fazed. He spoke calmly, "That's quite a fanciful yarn, little girl. But you're a self-admitted liar. Why should we even begin to believe you? This is ridiculous."

Pet instructed the guardsmen, "Arrest this man!"

The guardsmen advanced on Lier, but his laugh gave them pause. "You never became queen. You're not even the real princess. You're just a common liar. You don't have the authority to have me arrested."

"That's true," boomed a voice from the audience, "But I do."

The entire hall turned around to find Sentry casting off his cloak and standing tall. He had his gauntlet removed and was holding his signet ring high.

CHAPTER SIXTY-FIVE

Piotr had returned. However, not everyone immediately recognized the King for who he was. Some recognized him because of the familiar engraving on his ring. Others recognized his jet black hair. Many wondered who this joker with the bling was, but as more and more people bowed and curtsied before Piotr, they eventually followed suit. The words, "My liege," echoed through the hall like a wave, emanating outwards from King Piotr the Just. Even Pet curtsied for the first time in her life.

Only one person remained standing in the Grand Hall. Lier could not believe this turn of events. All his carefully laid plans, years in the making, were falling apart before his very eyes. He turned his wrathful gaze to Pet. That satisfied smile on her face irked him the most.

In a single swift movement, he reached down to the belt of one of the bowing guardsmen. Lier's hand grasped the sword's hilt as he kicked the hapless guardsman over. The sword slipped free of the scabbard as he lunged at Pet.

"You little trollop," Lier cried, "I was going to usher in a golden age for the realm, but you've ruined everything!"

Pet leapt to her feet and hopped aside with surprising nimbleness, given the length of her coronation gown. The other guardsmen at the altar reacted simultaneously, unsheathing their own swords, desperately trying to block Lier before he could reach Pet. Unfortunately Lier was too close.

Luckily, Pet was not unprepared. As Lier swung his sword towards her, Pet pulled away the side of her gown revealing her sheathed sword strapped to her thigh. She unsheathed the blade and clashed it against Lier's sword, crying out, "Stop! I don't want to fight you, Lier! I just want to talk."

Lier struggled, but try as he might, he couldn't unlock his blade from Pet's. The guards circled the pair, unsure what to do.

"You weren't there when Queen Polly died," Lier explained. "The king was consumed with grief for his dead wife and concern for his remaining daughter. The welfare of his kingdom came in a distant third. The realm deserved better, so I stepped in and did what needed to be done."

Pet looked into Lier's eyes. "Go on!"

"No-one was supposed to get hurt. The king was just supposed simply to abdicate the throne and let someone else take over for the good of the realm."

"And that someone was meant to be you?"

"I was the best qualified, but the king went with Evella. He chose a sorceress over me!"

"I believe you did what you did because at first you thought you could rule the realm better than King Piotr," responded Pet. "You could justify your actions because at the end of the day, you thought that you were helping the realm. But let me tell you this. You weren't. You were not a good vizier. You were not a loyal servant to the realm. You, Lier, are a traitor to everything you ever stood for."

Lier's eyes grew large and lost. They darted around the Grand Hall. His grip loosened as he felt his legs give way from under him. His sword clattered loudly on the floor and his body followed soon after, crumpling into a heap. "What have I done?"

The guardsmen pulled Lier away. Pet let out a gasp of relief and sheathed her sword.

Before Pet could grab her breath, she suddenly found herself in a hug. It was Candice. She had pushed her way through the crowd and now had her arms wrapped around her best friend. Pet's best friend squealed, "You did it! You did it!"

Pet promptly corrected Candice. "We did it. Together."

Candice glanced down and could not believe her eyes. "Wait! Are those glass slippers? They really make those?"

As King Piotr made his way through the crowd, the gathered audience parted to let him pass. Despite having been away so long, he still had that royal presence. Pet remarked, "So that's your dad?"

"I guess so," Candice hesitated, "but I don't understand it yet. Why didn't anyone ever tell me I was adopted?"

By now King Piotr had reached the altar. He reached down and picked up Lier's dropped sword. With blade in hand, King Piotr walked calmly up to Lier and raised it high. Pet could not help but gasp. King Piotr the Just intended to execute Lier right there and then. Pet was about to shout something when somebody beat her to it.

"Stop that right now!" called out Candice.

King Piotr turned around to address his daughter, "This foul cretin has soured the very soul of the realm. He deserves this fate."

Candice disagreed, "You need to think clearly. It's not about what he deserves. It's about what you deserve."

"I deserved the chance to be a good father to you," King Piotr declared, "But this creature's actions didn't allow that and caused us to be separated for years. If it weren't for him, I could have been a real father to you, rather than the hollow one I am now."

"You are King Piotr the Just," responded Candice. "You have always believed that everyone had the right to a fair trial and the right to be judged by a jury of their peers. I think you still believe that. Do you deserve to have this cretin ruin all that? You're better than that. You're better than him."

Lowering his sword, King Piotr called to his guardsmen, "Take the Grand Vizier away. Just looking at him makes me sick."

It occurred to Pet that someone was missing, "Where's Dashing?"

"Stop!" Pet shouted at the guardsmen taking Lier away. Pet gripped Lier's crumpled form. "Where's Dashing?"

Lier refused to meet her gaze, "I sent him and a battalion of guardsmen to quell that farmer rebellion."

"You did what?!" cried Pet.

Somewhere out there a battle was about to begin. Who knew where this single battle could lead? Could the realm be facing another civil war? There had to be something she could do to stop this.

Candice walked up to King Piotr and asked "So what now?"

King Piotr responded, "This seems to be Pet's show. You should ask her."

Unfortunately, Pet was already gone.

CHAPTER SIXTY-SIX

Prepared guardsmen stood in a position just a few miles across the Hashram Plains. The banner of the Sapphire Palace flapped in the gentle breeze. Their armour and weaponry glistened in the sunshine. Judd could not help but sigh as he looked up at the clear blue sky. It seemed a shame to spend such a beautiful day engaging in battle.

"There seem to be quite a few of them," croaked Iago as he pressed his eye against the lens of his telescope, "and they appear quite well armed."

Judd looked over his shoulder at his fellow countrymen. When Judd, Iago and Olganna had visited the neighboring villages and spread the word that they were gathering an army to oppose the high regent, they had expected only a few local firebrands to show up. They certainly did not expect the thousands they ended up with. The many gathered farmers now looked back at their leader. They could all see the guardsmen too. Some looked nervous. Others bewildered. Most remained determined.

Below him, Bounds gently neighed. Poor Bounds. Judd had been reunited with his trusty steed at Olganna's cabin, but their reunion was probably going to be a short one. Judd planned to ride Bounds into battle against the Royal Guard. Chances were that neither of them would emerge alive.

"You need to talk to them," croaked Iago. "You need to inspire them."

How could Judd inspire them when he couldn't even inspire himself? He gulped back, "Do we really have to go through with this?"

"Are you willing just to go home and abandon Pet?"

Judd retorted, "Of course not."

"Then you know what has to be done."

After sucking in one final breath, Judd addressed his men. "We gathered together because we all believe in a common cause. We resent the abuses of the current government and see a need for change. For years, the Sapphire Place has ignored our pleas for reform. Each and every one of us has lost something to the palace. I lost a girl. They just took her. Just like the high regent took your jobs, your farms and your money. I need you all to remember what the palace took away from you."

The entire crowd had become a silent chorus of nodding heads. Iago smiled. Judd was doing it! He was successfully rallying an army. All these people needed was for someone to stand up and take the lead. They would have followed anyone who dared speak out against the Sapphire Palace. Perhaps even a talking toad?

Cursing his missed opportunity, Iago glanced over and saw Olganna weeping. He hopped over. "Whatever is the matter?"

"I can't believe I'm party to this," sniffed Olganna. "These people are going to die."

Not everyone had the stomach for war. Iago understood this, "Perhaps you shouldn't be here. You've done your part."

"That's the point." Olganna glared at Iago with tear-tinged eyes. "I am a healer, Iago and I helped gather an army! My life's work has been dedicated to curing injuries and saving lives. Now I'm sending them off to hurt others or get hurt themselves. I'm a hypocrite."

"They all knew the risks when they signed up."

Olganna was far from convinced, "Most of them are only boys."

"They are standing up for what they believe in," Iago retorted. "In my book, that makes them men."

"Is this what Mrs Kettlepot would have wanted?"

Ire coursed through Iago's body. "You didn't know her!"

"Yes, but you've spoken about her a lot," Olganna continued unabated. "It doesn't sound like she would have approved."

"The high regent had her killed!"

"And this is how you're serving her memory? With war?"

An image flashed in Iago's mind of the battlefield after the battle, scattered with the bodies of young men... boys. The soil would be stained with their blood and the eyes… There would be many dead eyes looking out on nothing.

Curses!

Olganna was right. Mrs Kettlepot would not have approved. Suddenly, Iago knew with cast-iron certainty that he needed to stop this.

A few metres away, Judd was still addressing the gathered farmers. "I need you to remember the things you lost. I need you to remember how it felt to lose it. I need you to feel the anger you felt when you found out it was the palace that took it away. I need you to feel the betrayal of how she, who was charged with governing the realm, saw fit instead to ransack it. We are here because we want to tell the high regent that we won't let her take anything else from us."

Iago hopped over to Judd's position. Judd looked down at the approaching toad and smiled, "We're going to do it. We're going to stop them."

There was such enthusiasm in Judd's face, that Iago momentarily dreaded saying what he had to say next. "No we're not. We can't go through with this."

"What are you saying? Of course, we are. There's no turning back now."

Iago tried to use the same logic that had been so effective on him. "What would Pet think of all this?"

"All I know is that Pet is in danger and I am going to rescue her." His army was primed and ready to go. Judd did not have any time to continue a conversation with Iago. "I have to go, Iago."

The fisherman-turned-general raised his sword high and spurred his horse on.

"Wait," Iago shouted, but to little avail. Judd was already gone.

Iago returned to Olganna's side. Tears flowed freely down her face. There was nothing that could be said or done. They could do nothing but watch in complete horror as two armies engaged in battle.

CHAPTER SIXTY-SEVEN

"**P**reposterous!" the look-out blurted out. "They really are charging."

Dashing frowned. He had joined the Royal Guard to defend the realm from dragons, ogres and invading manticore armies. He certainly did not join the Guard to cut up farmers.

Dashing turned to the men behind them. Though the revolutionaries outnumbered them three-to-two, the weapons and armour of the guardsmen were far superior. This was going to be easy, possibly too easy. Dashing saw the same look of unease from several of his fellow guardsmen. It served as cold comfort for Dashing. He was not alone in his doubts.

All the battalions had all been briefed and they all knew their mission. They were to quell this revolution by any means necessary.

This was not about glory.

This was business.

Still Dashing felt compelled to say something, "Let's keep the bloodshed to a minimum, gentlemen."

With that he turned and led the charge against the peasants. There were no rallying cries, just the thundering of hooves as the guardsmen rode into grim battle.

CHAPTER SIXTY-EIGHT

Pretty as they were, glass slippers were not designed for running. Accordingly, Pet kicked them off somewhere just outside the Grand Hall. Then with a mighty yank, Pet tore off the train of her dress. The gown was bad enough, but she couldn't afford the time to clamber out of it quite yet. Time was of the essence.

Pet soon reached her destination. She barged into the stable and demanded, "Where's my horse?"

"Your Highness?" questioned the startled stable-hand. The news that she was not actually the Lost Princess had not reached him yet and it was not in Pet's current interests to correct him.

"My horse! Where is my horse?"

Now a little scared, the stable-hand pointed to a stall in the corner. There in all his mangy glory was Mucker. She promptly flew open the stall door and cooed, "Hello, my neglected friend. I am so glad to see you."

"Would you like me to prepare a saddle for Your Highness?" stuttered the stable-hand.

"No time!" Pet grabbed Mucker's side. With a strong shove and a good jump, she swung herself onto the horse's back.

This horrified the stable-hand, "Princesses can't ride bareback!"

"Lucky for me, I'm not a princess," Pet winked. With a mighty neigh, Mucker galloped out of the stable.

"There she is!" "What's she doing?" and "All that dirt on such a pretty dress!" were some of the comments Pet half-heard as she directed Mucker towards the main gate. Expecting a mass exodus after the coronation, the main gate was wide open and the draw-bridge had already been let down. Pet took advantage of this to make a speedy exit from the palace.

Pet barked at the guard on duty, "Which direction did Dashing go in?"

"Due West, toward the Hashram Plains," responded the guard as Mucker darted through the gates.

"Giddy up!" Pet slapped her heels into Mucker's flanks and, with that, they were off. The sudden acceleration pushed back her hair and Pet found she had to hold even tighter to Mucker's mane to stop herself falling off. The scenery flew by as Pet shouted, "Go Mucker!"

Pet instantly regretted all the times she had called Mucker lazy or useless. In this incredible burst of speed, he had proved he was neither. The horse was just choosey about his moments. At this speed, they were sure to catch up with Dashing and his men in no time. She just might still have a chance of stopping this battle.

All of a sudden a speck appeared on the horizon. Pet squinted.

These were Dashing's men! But where were they going? And what was that?

After galloping a little further, Pet saw the entire scene unfolded before her. To her dismay, Dashing and his men were charging. Their lances were held ready for striking. Beyond the guardsmen, Pet could make out the opposition. They appeared to be ordinary folk, some on horseback, most on foot. Against all reason, they appeared to be charging head on towards the guardsmen. Did they all want to die?

There were barely minutes before the two armies clashed. She directed Mucker along the east side of the guardsman battalion. She considered asking Mucker to go faster, but there was no need. The horse seemed to read the urgency of the situation and somehow galloped even faster than before. Pet brought her body close to Mucker's heaving frame as the wind whistled passed her ears.

Some of the guardsmen noticed Pet's arrival. They slowed down a little and shouted at her to go away. A battle was no place for a girl. Pet ignored them and kept riding by.

Their path brought Pet and Mucker immediately between the two advancing fronts. Pet could not quite believe how fast Mucker was going, nor could she quite believe what she was seeing. At the head of their respective armies were Dashing and Judd.

Judd?!

Judd was alive! So he hadn't been killed by the Cloaked Man? It had all been a mistake, a joyous mistake. Tears welled up in Pet's eyes.

Judd was alive!

But possibly not for much longer! Pet urged Mucker onward between the two converging armies. By now, more and more guardsmen and peasants were aware of Pet's presence. She made quite a sight. The girl in a coronation gown riding the fastest horse in the realm, charging head on into the middle of battle. Unfortunately, the only two who really mattered remained oblivious to her approach.

"Judd! Dashing! For the love of the realm, stop this!" Pet screamed, but to no avail. As she got even nearer, Pet tried again, "Judd! Dashing!"

The silly boys still failed to notice her presence. She was getting so close now. In a few more gallops she would be able to touch them. Fine, Pet thought to herself, we'll just have to do this the hard way.

Judd lifted his pitchfork high in the air.

Dashing prepared to strike with his sword.

Pet raised both her hands high and leapt off Mucker.

It is no easy feat leaping from one charging horse into two others. Even so, perhaps due to her sheer determination, Pet was able to accomplish it. As she arched through the air, mid-leap, Judd and Dashing suddenly became aware of her presence, but it was too late. Her left hand grasped Judd's as her right hand grabbed Dashing's. With desperate strength, she managed to halt their strides. The momentum behind her leap pushed both boys off their horses as their steeds clashed together.

The three bodies crashed into the Hashram Plains with a thunderous wallop.

Both sides drew up short as they tried to figure out what had just happened. Had some maiden really just ridden into the middle of a battlefield and taken out both generals?

Pet was the first to regain her senses and pushed herself to her feet. She saw the farmers and guardsmen regarding her with incredulous eyes. It suddenly occurred to her that they were not fighting. They had just stopped there, looking at her.

It had worked. It had really worked. She had stopped the battle!

"Pet? Is that you?" asked Judd's broken voice.

Simultaneously, Dashing mumbled, "Your Highness, what are you doing here?"

Wordlessly, Pet went over and gave Judd a hug. She let her head rest on his chest. Judd was still breathing hard from all the exertion and Pet liked the way the heaving of his chest lifted her head. It was all further proof that Judd Duncanson was indeed still among the living. "You're alive, Judd! You're alive! How is it you're alive?"

Dashing picked himself off the ground and scowled slightly at the attention Pet was lavishing on this rebel.

Then Pet's joyous tone soured. "You silly boy! You come back to life and the first thing you want to do is kill yourself in battle?"

"I just wanted to save you," mumbled Judd.

Not to be outdone, Dashing interjected, "I just wanted to preserve your honour."

Judd turned on Dashing, "What are you talking about? I was doing this in Pet's honour. Not you."

"If either of you had stopped for a moment and thought about what you were doing, you would have realized that resolving a conflict with needless violence is against everything I stand for."

Pet then looked at the lines of men on each side of her and addressed them as well. "Was violence the only way you could think of to resolve this? Did you guys consider any sort of dialogue? Any negotiations?"

Heads hung low on both sides. Pet took this as license to continue, "Did you even think of the consequences? What if you had been killed? How would your families feel? Would they take pride in your death or wish you were still with them? Answer me!"

Nobody, neither farmer nor guardsman, dared speak a word.

"Fine, then. I officially declare that this battle is over."

Pet had nothing else to say. She simply turned her head, gazing at each of the almost-combatants with the most withering and condemning of stares. Slowly, one by one, the men dropped their weapons.

"I'm sorry," murmured Judd.

"Me too," mumbled Dashing.

And that was how the Battle of the Hashram Plains never quite happened.

CHAPTER SIXTY-NINE

Pronouncements were made by the guardsman on duty. The girl who claimed to be the Lost Princess was returning and she was not alone.

"I think I see them," exclaimed Candice as she peered into the horizon.

As Pet got closer, the sight of her became more and more impressive. Sitting regally on top of Mucker, she was leading a large motley collection of farmers and guardsmen. Despite the stained gown and her mangy steed, she looked every part a true leader.

"Pet," called King Piotr as she entered earshot, "It appears that you have brought some company back with you."

Pet got right down to business, "These men are here to engage in peace talks. Apparently they forgot all about the diplomatic process. I was hoping we could host them at the palace."

"Please enter. The Sapphire Palace used to be known as a place of dialogue and diplomacy. It is high time that we restore that reputation," King Piotr boomed in a loud kingly voice. As an afterthought he added, "Finding enough beds might be a challenge, though."

And so they all entered the palace. The courtyard was soon bustling with guardsmen and farmers alike as Pet quickly dismounted Mucker. Various people tried calling to her, but Pet pretended not to hear. However, there was one person who was not going to let Pet get away that easily.

"Pet!" Judd grabbed Pet gently by the arm. "Do you think you will ever be able to forgive me?"

She flashed a sad smile. "I was going to ask you the same thing. I left you tied up in the forest. Friends don't do that to each other."

Across the courtyard, Dashing saw Pet and Judd conversing. He quickly looked away and with a 'humph' attended to other duties.

"There's something I've been meaning to tell you and it can't wait," Judd added. Pet's heart skipped a beat. Such a clumsy prelude meant only one thing. He was going to say something important, "Pet, I think I l…"

"Don't say it," Pet interrupted, "Please don't. You have demonstrated yourself to be an incredibly loyal, forgiving and dedicated friend. There isn't anything in the world more valuable than that. Don't ruin that with those three silly words."

Pet simply did not love Judd Duncanson. Well, not in a romantic sense at least. She would always love him as a brother.

Judd glumly nodded, "So you don't think I should tell Candice that I love her?"

Candice?

Candice Butler?

Judd had loved Candice all this time? Pet found herself unjustly filled with anger. Why Candice? Why not her? It did not make any sense. Why go to the extremes he had gone to, to rescue Pet, if he was in love with Candice the whole time?

Silly Pet! The answer was obvious. In fact, Pet had just articulated it a few moments earlier. Judd was an incredibly loyal, forgiving and dedicated friend. If Judd would gather an army and (wrong-headedly) wage war for a friend, Pet wondered what extremes he would go to for the woman he loved.

"No, that's not what I meant." Pet quickly scrambled to find the right words. "I meant that you shouldn't just say it. You should show it. Actions speak louder than words. Now if you excuse me, I've got to get out this gown."

"Thank you, Pet," Judd said as he watched her walk away. "You're a great friend."

Pet waved the compliment away as she entered the palace. If she was such a great friend, she would not be feeling quite so… disappointed.

Judd's mind was a-flutter. How on Earth was he going to show Candice that he loved her? He needed time to think about this and come up with some ideas. Unfortunately, fate had other ideas.

"Judd!" cried Candice as she darted out of the crowd, "I'm so happy to see that you're alright!"

As Candice gripped Judd in a warm hug, he lowered his head and rested his cheek against her dark hair. He no longer had to worry about what he was going to say. The words came easily to him, "Thank the realm! You look so much better! I was so worried about you. What are you doing here?"

"I came back to help," answered Candice.

Judd lifted her head and looked deep into Candice's eyes, "You are so beautiful, Candice Butler."

Candice smiled broadly, "You're not so bad yourself, Judd Duncanson."

No further words were exchanged. The two of them just looked at each other and smiled. Unfortunately the moment was not to last.

"Excuse me, sir," one of the farmers interrupted Judd, "There are some details concerning the lodgings which required your attention."

"Go!" Candice cooed. "I should be checking on Pet anyway."

"She went up to her room to change," Judd informed her, as he went to attend to his duties. Candice watched him leave and was impressed by the way he wore his new responsibilities so effortlessly. He had truly become a man.

Candice left the courtyard and eventually made it to the top of the spire. She found Pet sitting on her bed with her back to her.

"Pet?" Candice asked, "Is everything all right?"

Pet's head darted up. She wiped her cheeks and smiled broadly, "Everything's fine. Why wouldn't it be? We just won, didn't we?"

Candice was not convinced, "What's wrong?"

"Nothing," Pet broke eye contact, "Everything."

Sliding onto the bed next to her, Candice put an arm over Pet's shoulders.

"I know I ought to be happy." Pet tried to fight back the tears. "I know we won. Everything's going to be okay now, but the moment I rode into the palace and got off Mucker, I was all ready to whoop and cheer, when it hit me, like a punch to the belly."

Candice stroked her hair, "You've been through so much over the last few days and even if you don't want to admit it, they took a toll on you. But you were Pet Peasant, the leader. You always had a job to do. So rather than feel the pain or the fear or the whatever, you just swallowed it up and buried it deep inside. I guess now that the job is done, your body won't let you keep those feelings buried any longer."

"How can I stop it?"

"You don't stop it," Candice told her. "You just let it all out."

Pet nodded meekly. Candice made sense. Pet sucked in a deep breath and prepared to cry. She tensed her body and waited for the feelings to swell to the surface. There was only one problem. They were not coming.

Instead Pet decided to ask Candice a question that had been on her mind, "Why didn't you tell me you were the Lost Princess? I would have kept your secret."

"I didn't know."

"You had blue blood," Pet noted. "You can't tell me that for seventeen years you never once got cut or scraped."

"Once when I was six, I tore up my knee badly," Candice conceded. "My parents took me to Sentry. He treated me and then told me that my blood was blue because of a lack of antioxidants or something. He told me that if I wanted to make a full recovery, I needed to lay off the physical activities and never tell anyone I had blue blood."

Pet's eyebrows arched skeptically, "That doesn't make any sense. How would not telling anyone help in your recovery?"

"I don't know. I was six," Candice protested. "I certainly didn't know that my blue blood meant I was secretly royalty. I thought that being blue-blooded was just an expression..."

Candice had more to say on the subject but one look over at Pet made her realize that now was not the time.

The discussion of blue blood had reminded Pet of when she had found Candice in the cave, ravaged and clinging to life. The accompanying torrent of tears and anguish that suddenly swelled up inside of Pet took her by surprise. Tears, sobs and cries all surged out of her body at once. It was not a pretty sight, but Candice stayed strong, holding her best friend and cooing gently in her ear.

CHAPTER SEVENTY

Parchment scrolls lay scattered everywhere. King Piotr was sorting through the mess as Pet entered the sanctum. "You wanted to see me, Sentry?" Pet said before correcting herself, "I mean... Your Majesty."

King Piotr the Just was looking a lot better these days. He resembled those portraits of himself a bit more now. His beard had been trimmed. He had traded in his tattered purple cape for a fur-lined sapphire-blue one.

"Please come in," the king called. "I'm just finishing."

King Piotr stood above the oaken desk in Evella's sanctum. He was saying something to Stan about some security measure or other. Stan nodded tersely, "Right away, Your Majesty."

As Stan exited the sanctum, Pet asked, "What happened to Dashing? I thought he was the First Guardsman."

"Dashing is very talented," explained King Piotr, "but he simply doesn't have enough experience for the position. Stan does."

"I understand Pet's dismay," Evella interjected as she stepped into the room. "Guardsman Stan unfortunately lacks Dashing's good looks."

"Who? Dashing? I hadn't noticed." Then Pet noticed that she was speaking to a woman who was supposed to be in a coma, "Evella! You're awake! What happened?"

Evella glanced over to King Piotr, "His Majesty managed to stir me from my enchanted slumber."

"That's great! But wait... I thought only a kiss of true love would break the enchantment." It took a few more moments for the full gravity of the situation to dawn on Pet, "You two love each other? I had no idea!"

"Nor did I at first," King Piotr blushed, "but it was you who made me realize the true depth of my gratitude and love for Evella."

"What did I do?"

"At the coronation, you spoke about how much Evella had contributed to the realm and how she had fought bravely alone against Lier's machinations. It reminded me what an amazing woman she is." King Piotr put his arm around Evella's waist. "I really let her down. When I left all those years ago, the only thing I could think of was my daughter. I didn't give a single thought to the massive strain I had put her under. I have a lot to make up for."

Evella smiled briefly at the King before turning to Pet. "However, this is not why we called you here. Please sit down. Excuse the mess. In my absence someone got in here and made a total mess of things."

"Sorry about that." Pet was not quite sure if she was apologizing for ransacking the sanctum or casually accusing her of treason over dinner.

"Please don't apologize. Quite frankly, I'm sick of hearing it," Evella said, "It seems these days that everyone is apologizing to everyone else about something or other. I think now that we're all on the same page, we should take this as opportunity to start over and forget the sins of the past."

Relief washed over Pet. This conversation could have been a lot more awkward. Evella tapped a piece of parchment in front of her. "However, that isn't why I called you here. The Princess gave this to me and I wanted to talk to you about it."

Pet's eyes grew large in recognition of what was before her. It was the brief on Tax Law 106 that she had given to Candice. Though it had been only a matter of days, it seemed a very long time ago that Pet had written it. "Um... about that..."

"It's good. Very good in fact," Evella commented. "You're right. I don't think the House of Magistrates considered the full ramifications of these changes when they passed this bill. I wanted to let you know that I've repealed Tax Law 106 pending review. It does require some retooling."

And that was it. Pet's quest to repeal Tax Law 106 was successful. She had won. Pet was a bit surprised that she did not feel more excited. "Wait, can you still do that?"

"I've decided not to take back the throne," King Piotr told her. "Instead I plan to return to Seacrest with Candice so that we can get to know each other better. Accordingly Evella will stay on as the high regent temporarily."

"But you love each other. What about that?"

"Not that it's any of your business," Evella scolded lightly. "His Majesty and I will continue to see each other long distance."

King Piotr wanted to get this meeting back on track, "Petunia, have you given any thought to what you're going to be doing now?"

"The prosecutors want me to give evidence against Lier in his trial. There's that. I guess I'll go back to Seacrest in the meanwhile and figure things out."

"What if I had a different proposal for you?" asked Evella with a mischievous glint in her eye.

Pet was intrigued, "I'm listening."

"Piotr and I have been discussing changing the realm's form of government," Evella explained. "Why should any future leaders of this realm come from only one blood line?"

The initial pitch sounded good to Pet's ears, but something quickly occurred to her. "Wait a second! Candice would make a perfectly good queen when her time comes."

"But do you think she really wants to rule?" King Piotr asked. "Candice is a very talented botanist. Flowers give her fulfillment, not adjudicating on tax issues."

Pet nodded in agreement as she remembered how Candice had once mentioned that she had no interest in ruling. "How will you find someone to rule the realm instead?"

"Through an election," Evella announced and then promptly launched into an explanation of her vision for the future of the realm. The positions of king or queen and prince or princess would be decided through a ballot. Those interested in ruling would put themselves forward as nominations, campaign among the people and then the people would decide who they wanted to rule them.

"There are still many details to work out, but the possibilities are endless. Perhaps in two years' time, we can have elections for the House of Magistrates rather than have the positions appointed."

After Evella concluded, Pet's eyes grew large. What Evella was proposing was revolutionary. It would change the shape of politics in the realm forever.

"Which brings me to this." Evella leaned forward in her chair. "Pet will you run as my running mate in the election?"

"You must be joking."

"Not at all," Evella responded. "You have a good public-speaking style. You have an excellent grasp of the current state of politics in the realm. You now have a public reputation as somewhat of a firebrand revolutionary, willing to shake things up where necessary. Also coming from the Southern Province, you'll be able to help secure their vote. Most importantly, you would have no problem telling me if you thought I was wrong about something."

"You're serious!" Pet was in utter and complete shock. "But I'm too young."

"Your age will be a factor," King Piotr acknowledged. "But I think we can spin it as a good thing. Your youth means you're fresh, eager, idealistic and hungry. What more could you want in a leader? So what do you say?"

Pet mulled it over a bit in her mind. "I'm sorry. I wish I could, but I can't."

"Why ever not?"

Pet sighed. She really did not want to go into her current crisis of conscience, but these two did deserve an honest answer. "I used to live my life with this one central tenet: violence is never the answer. Discussion, compromise and negotiation should be the tools used to resolve conflicts, never violence."

Evella smiled, "And that's a very noble sentiment."

"But I didn't survive the encounter with the Cloaked Man or the Big Bad using discussion, compromise and negotiation," Pet countered. "I survived through the use of violence."

King Piotr was not following, "But those people attacked you, Pet. You were just trying to defend yourself."

"I know," Pet conceded, "and I don't think I did anything wrong *per se*, but I also didn't live up to my ideals. I'm just very confused. Is violence okay in certain situations? Who chooses these situations?"

Pet needed to slow down. Words were just pouring out. A calming breath later, Pet continued, "That's why I can't accept your offer. How could I expect people to choose me to stand up for them, when I don't really know what I stand for?"

"The world does not cater well to absolutes, Pet," answered Evella. "Pacifism is a noble ideal, but it isn't the answer to every situation. If your child was being attacked and the only way to save your child was to use violence, what would be the right thing to do?"

"I don't know," Pet answered frankly. "I'd have to think about it."

"That's why I think you'd be the best person for the Vice-Monarch position," Evella continued. "I don't want anyone who follows any dogma slavishly. I need someone who will think about each situation individually and weigh it on its own merits."

Then Evella asked again, "So Pet, with that mind, I want you to reconsider. Will you or will you not be my running mate?"

"I'm in."

CHAPTER SEVENTY-ONE

"**P**ersonal assistants aren't often recognized as heroes of the realm, but Mrs Kettlepot was no ordinary personal assistant. Unfortunately, most people didn't recognize her innate heroism. They looked at her and saw a chatty old woman, or a widow, or a secretary. They didn't see the important work she did with veterans from the Great Unrest or the important administrative function she performed within the local provincial government. I have to admit that at first I was one of those people, but then I was blessed with the opportunity to get to know her."

Pet dabbed her eyes. She was determined not to cry. Mrs Kettlepot deserved a proper eulogy. "Under circumstances so dire and dangerous that lesser people would have fled, Mrs Kettlepot stood firm. With nothing but her wits and wisdom, she overcame a devious assassin, a rampaging manticore and a blood-thirsty wolf. Unfortunately, her final victory came at the ultimate cost."

Pet had planned to say more, but she was finding it increasingly hard to fight the tears back.

"So here's to Mrs Kettlepot. A true hero of the realm," and with that Pet pulled on the rope which unveiled the statue behind her.

Here in the beautiful morning light in the Sculpture Garden, Pet admired the statue of Mrs Kettlepot. It was not a perfect likeness by any stretch of the imagination; still, one important feature was totally correct, her brave smile.

All in all, Pet's first public address as the newly-elected Princess of the realm had gone quite well. As she stepped off the podium, Pet was greeted by Candice, "That was good. You did Mrs Kettlepot justice."

"Thank you," Pet replied, but her mind was elsewhere. There were some key visitors expected and Pet was looking over the audience to see if she could see them...

And there they were...

Pet grabbed Candice's hand and they dashed through the crowds to greet their visitors with complementary cries of, "Mum! Dad!"

"Pet!" squealed Ma Peasant, "I'm so glad to see you."

It felt like an eternity since Pet and Candice had seen their parents. Managing the electoral campaign meant that they had had to stay on at the Sapphire Palace longer than initially expected. They had sent letters home assuring their parents of their safety and had received letters in turn, but nothing quite compared with seeing them in person.

Forcing back unexpected tears, Pet murmured into her father's embrace, "You were right about Mucker. He was magnificent."

"From everything we've heard," Pa Peasant responded through misty eyes, "So were you."

Ma Peasant's cheeks were stained with joyful tears, "You did it! You did your great thing and to think I tried to stop you from going on this trip..."

Candice, however, was not greeted with large hugs or wet kisses. Instead her parents were strangely standoffish. Mr Butler kept his arm around his wife and murmured hesitantly to Candice, "I'm glad to see you are safe, Your Highness."

"Your Highness?!" repeated Candice in shock.

Mr Butler gulped, "Should I have said, 'Your Highness?' I was never any good at this kind of protocol."

Candice was about to say that she was technically no longer princess of the realm, but that was not what was important now. "You don't have to address me by any title. I'm your daughter."

"You'll always have a special place in my heart," Mr Butler hesitated, "But your father is Piotr now."

"He's not my fath...Well, I guess he is," Candice sighed. "We don't know where we stand in each other's lives. He loves me terribly, I can see that, but I don't know how I feel about him. I don't even know if I could or should love him."

For such a usually gentle woman, Mrs Butler's stern words took Candice by surprise. "Candice Butler, the man is your father. He gave up a lot just to be near you, to protect you as you grew up. It must have been torture, so desperately wanting to be a bigger part of your life, but denying himself, because he thought it was best for you."

"The King didn't sing me lullabies when I couldn't fall asleep, or chop my vegetables just the way I like it." Candice glanced over at Mr Butler. "My real father did all that. I don't need another one."

Mr Butler smiled broadly, "Candice, don't shut him out. This isn't his fault. You have the most love in your heart of anybody I know and I bet you even have enough love to love another father."

"I guess," murmured Candice. She was not quite convinced yet, but at least with her father's blessing, she would not feel like she was betraying him.

Whatever reserve Mr Butler was grasping onto suddenly melted. He grabbed his daughter and pulled her into a big embrace. "We missed you horribly, princess."

"I missed you too, Daddy." Candice sank into the great embrace; but one question remained. "By the way, were you ever going to tell me that I was adopted?"

Luckily for the Butler parents, the dinner bell rang at that moment.

A banquet was being held in Mrs Kettlepot's honour and accordingly the audience began to move over to the banquet hall. Pet did not go at first, she wanted to spend a little bit more time gazing up at the statue and remembering her friend.

Suddenly Pet realized she was not entirely alone, "I haven't seen you in a while."

Iago croaked, "I thought it best to lie low for a while. I thought you wouldn't be too happy with my part in that attempted coup."

"So how have you been doing?"

"It still hurts," Iago admitted, "I'm surprised by that. It's been months and still every day I wake up expecting to see her and I get disappointed when I realize she isn't there and crushed when I realize she never will be again."

Pet's heart could not help but go out to Iago. "It'll get easier."

Iago did not answer.

"You know, Evella's more than happy to remove that enchantment on you," Pet noted. "She's long since forgiven you for your little transgression. I think she's even a little embarrassed by the way she treated you."

The man-toad swayed his head from side to side, "No. I'm not ready yet."

In an effort to change the topic, Pet asked nonchalantly, "So did you vote in the election?"

"Yes," Iago admitted.

Pet wondered just what the voting restrictions were that allowed a talking toad to vote. She made a mental note to follow up on that point later.

"But not for you."

Pet smirked. Some things never changed.

"Your tax changes are interesting. They do a lot to protect the local agricultural and fishery industries, but do little to attract foreign investment..." There was of course more. Iago launched into a long and winding summary of everything that he perceived as being faulty in modern society. Apparently there was deterioration in the morals of our youth, a lack of focus on family values and too much market regulation.

A small part of Pet wanted to argue each and every point with him, but she opted not to. She simply did not feel up to it at that moment. Instead she suggested, "You should run for Magistrate. A dissenting well-informed voice should always be heard."

"Forget magistrate!" Iago turned to hop away. "Next election, I'm running for king!"

As Iago hopped away, Pet could not help but wonder if this was the beginning of the opposition.

THE PRINCESS SAYS 'BYE

Pet could not believe it. The dreaded day had finally come. Candice was going back to Seacrest and Pet was going to be left all alone in the Sapphire Palace. Well, that was not technically true. There would still be Evella, Stan, Dashing, Urseffe and all the other staff and guardsmen who worked there, but as far as Pet was concerned, without Candice she might as well have been alone.

"There you are," shouted Candice on seeing her, "I thought we were going to miss you."

"I wouldn't miss this for the world."

Candice looked at Pet with a quizzical expression, "What's wrong?"

The game was up. "I don't want you to go."

"Ohhh Pet," Candice took Pet into a large hug, "I know, but I have to."

As Pet embraced Candice, she glanced up across the courtyard. There were Evella and Piotr saying their good-byes to each other. They whispered in each other's ears, smiling broadly and held hands. They seemed happy. Maybe goodbyes did not have to be such a bad thing. After all, it was not going to be forever.

Pet whispered, "Goodbye, Candice Butler."

"Goodbye, Petunia Peasant," murmured Candice Butler in response.

Pet patted Judd on the shoulder and said, "I don't want to hear about you starting any more coups."

Judd half smiled at Pet, "Don't reckon I'll have any time for that with the fishing season upon us."

The travelers mounted their steeds. It did not escape Pet's notice that Judd seemed particularly attentive as he helped Candice up on her horse.

Piotr looked down at Evella and Pet, "We leave the realm in your capable hands. Do the Petros Bluebloods proud."

"We will," smiled Evella. "We will."

And then they left, Pet ran up to the wall to watch them leave. She lifted her arm high in the air to wave to them. They continued to ride further and further away across the Hashram Plains. Soon they were only small specks on the horizon.

Pet Peasant, girl of Seacrest was gone. Now there was only Princess Petunia, Vice-Monarch of the realm. A few months ago, she was writing letters to the editor on government policy and now she was making government policy.

"Your Highness? Are you all right?"

She did not even have to look around to know who it was. "I'm fine, Dashing. I just suddenly feel a little lonely."

"I'm a bit jealous actually," Dashing told her. "I've never ever had a friend like that. In all my years of focusing on becoming a guardsman, I never much saw the need for friendship, but after seeing what you and Candice did together, how you are with each other, I think I might have missed out on something important."

"Maybe it's for the best," sniffed Pet. "At least you'll avoid this pain I'm in."

Dashing looked at Pet with sceptical eyes. "Are you telling me that you would really give up all your years of friendship with Candice just to avoid this momentary feeling of loss?"

The sudden slap of perspective set Pet right. "No. You're right. I wouldn't give up those memories for anything."

"There you are!" Dashing said comfortingly, with a smile. "You know, perhaps I can be your friend," he suggested.

"What did you say?"

"Well you're going to need a new friend and I've never really had a friend," he explained. "Maybe we can be friends with each other."

Dashing looked at Pet with his spell-binding silver eyes. She briefly wondered what was going on in that well-proportioned head of his at that moment.

"I'd like that," answered Pet. She could not help but smile broadly.

They both sat on the wall of the Sapphire Palace looking out on the Hashram Plains. It was a beautiful day. As good a day as any to start a new life. Here she was, Petunia Peasant with a new home, a new job and a new friend (and potentially something more), wondering what adventures her next passage would bring....

We are interested to know how you enjoyed reading
The Perilous Passage of Princess Petunia Peasant.

Write to our email address, giving us a few sentences
which you are willing for us to publish,
describing your response to this book.
If your comments are chosen to be included
in our E-Newsletter or website,
we will select another title published by Proverse
and send you a complimentary copy.
Please include your name, email address
and mailing address when you write to us,
and state whether or not we may cut or edit your comments
for publication.
We will use your initials to attribute your comments.

THE PUBLISHERS

Proverse Hong Kong (PVHK) is based in Hong Kong with long-term and strengthening regional and international connections.

We have published novels, novellas, non-fiction (including autobiography and biography, history, memoirs, sport, travel narratives), single-author poetry collections, children's, young teens, educational and academic books. Other interests include diaries and academic works in the humanities, social sciences, cultural studies, linguistics and education. Some Proverse books have accompanying audio texts. Some are translated into Chinese.

We welcome authors who have a story to tell, wisdom, perceptions or information to convey, a person they want to memorialize, a neglect they want to remedy, a record they want to correct, a strong interest that they want to share, skills they want to teach, and who consciously seek to make a contribution to society in an informative, interesting and well-written way. Proverse works with texts by non-native-speaker writers of English as well as by native English-speaking writers.

The name, "Proverse", combines the words "prose" and "verse" and is pronounced accordingly.

THE INTERNATIONAL PROVERSE PRIZE

The Proverse Prize, an annual international competition for an unpublished single-author book-length work of fiction, non-fiction, or poetry, the original work of the entrant, submitted in English (translations are welcomed) was established in January 2008. It is open to all who are at least eighteen on the date they sign the entry form and without restriction of nationality, residence or citizenship.

The objectives of the prize are: to encourage excellence and / or excellence and usefulness in publishable written work in the English Language, which can, in varying degrees, "delight and instruct". Entries are invited from anywhere in the world.

The Proverse Prize

1) Publication by Proverse Hong Kong, with
2) Cash prize of HKD10,000 (HKD7.80 = approx. USD1.00)

Extent of the Manuscript: within the range of what is usual for the genre of the work submitted. However, it is advisable that novellas be in the range, 30,000 to 45,000 words; other fiction (e.g. novels, short-story collections) and non-fiction (e.g. autobiographies, biographies, diaries, letters, memoirs, essay collections, etc.) should be in the range, 75,000 to 100,000 words. Poetry collections should be in the range, 5,000 to 25,000 words. Other word-counts and mixed-genre submissions are not ruled out.

PROVERSE PRIZE WINNERS WHOSE BOOKS HAVE ALREADY BEEN PUBLISHED BY PROVERSE HONG KONG:
Laura Solomon, Rebecca Jane Tomasis, Gillian Jones, David Diskin, Peter Gregoire, Sophronia Liu, Birgit Linder, James McCarthy.

PROVERSE PRIZE WINNERS WHOSE BOOKS WILL BE PUBLISHED BY PROVERSE HONG KONG IN NOVEMBER 2015:
Philip Chatting, Celia Claase.

Annual Entry Dates
(subject to confirmation and/or change)

Receipt of Entry Fees / Entry Forms	14 April - 31 May
Receipt of entered manuscripts	1 May - 30 June

More information, updated from time to time, is available on the Proverse website: proversepublishing.com

NOVELS, SHORT STORY COLLECTIONS AND OTHER FICTION
Published by Proverse Hong Kong

Those who enjoyed **The Perilous Passage of Princess Petunia Peasant** by **Victor Edward Apps** may also enjoy the following (all titles in English unless otherwise stated):

A Misted Mirror, by Gillian Jones. 2011.
A Painted Moment, by Jennifer Ching. 2010.
An Imitation of Life, by Laura Solomon. 2013.
Article 109, by Peter Gregoire. 2012.
Bao Bao's Odyssey: from Mao's Shanghai to Capitalist Hong Kong, by Paul Ting. 2012.
Bright Lights and White Nights, by Andrew Carter. 2015.
cemetery miss you, by Jason S Polley. 2011.
Cop Show Heaven, by Lawrence Gray. 2015.
Death has a Thousand Doors, by Patricia Grey. 2011.
Hilary and David, by Laura Solomon. 2011.
Instant Messages, by Laura Solomon. 2010.
Man's Last Song, by James Tam. 2013.
Mila the Magician, by Zhang Jian 章簡. 2013. (English / Chinese bilingual)
Mishpacha – Family, by Rebecca Tomasis. 2010.
Odds and Sods, by Lawrence Gray. 2013.
Paranoia (the Walk and Talk with Angela), by Caleb Kavon. 2012.
Red Bird Summer, by Jan Pearson. 2014.
Revenge from Beyond, by Dennis Wong. 2011.
The Day They Came, by Gérard Louis Breissan. 2012.
The Devil You know, by Peter Gregoire. 2014.
The Monkey in Me: Confusion, Love and Hope under a Chinese Sky, by Caleb Kavon. 2009.
The Monkey in Me, by Caleb Kavon. Translated by Chapman Chen. 2010. E-book. 2010. (Chinese)
The Reluctant Terrorist: in Search of the Jizo, by Caleb Kavon. 2011.

The Shingle Bar Sea Monster and Other Stories, by Laura Solomon. 2012.

The Village in the Mountains, by David Diskin. 2012.

Tiger Autumn, by Jan Pearson. 2015.

Tightrope! A Bohemian Tale, by Olga Walló. Translated from Czech by Johanna Pokorny, Veronika Revická & others. 2010.

Tightrope! A Bohemian Tale, by Olga Walló. Translated by Chapman Chen. 2011. (Chinese)

University Days, by Laura Solomon. 2014.

Vera Magpie, by Laura Solomon. 2013.

OTHER GENRES

We also publish in other genres, including autobiography, biography, children's illustrated books, educational books, Hong Kong educational and legal history, memoirs, poetry, teenage / young adult books, and travel. Other genres may be added.

FIND OUT MORE ABOUT OUR AUTHORS AND BOOKS

Visit our website <http://www.proversepublishing.com>
Visit our distributor's website <www.chineseupress.com>

Follow us on Twitter
Follow news and conversation: twitter.com/Proversebooks>
OR
Copy and paste the following to your browser window and follow the instructions:
https://twitter.com/#!/ProverseBooks

Request our free E-Newsletter
Send your request to info@proversepublishing.com.

Availability
Most books are available in Hong Kong and world-wide
from our Hong Kong based Distributor,
The Chinese University Press of Hong Kong,
The Chinese University of Hong Kong, Shatin, NT,
Hong Kong SAR, China.
Email: cup-bus@cuhk.edu.hk
Website: <www.chineseupress.com>.

All titles are available from Proverse Hong Kong
and the Proverse Hong Kong UK-based Distributor.

We have stock-holding retailers in Hong Kong,
Singapore (Select Books),
Canada (Elizabeth Campbell Books),
Principality of Andorra (Llibreria la Puça and La Llibrera).

Orders can be made from bookshops in the UK and elsewhere.

Ebooks
Most of our titles are available also as Ebooks.